J. Robert Whittle's sensitive, easy-going style earns passionate support from multi-generational audience …

"I fell in love with Lizzie ... (she) makes you young and adventurous again."
James Cumes, former Ambassador/High Commissioner; author of *Haverleigh*

"... a hidden gem ... Lizzie is a fun, memorable and enchanting character."
Gustav BenJava, author of *Nikki*

"... has the firepower of a Dickens ... invokes the impish merriment of an Oscar Wilde." Prof. Roger Sandilands, Strathclyde Univ., Scotland

"We need more Lizzies and Quons in this world." J.A.
"Like *Pippi Longstocking* for adults ... thoroughly enjoyed." A.C.
"*Lizzie* was the most intriguing, rich book I've ever read." K.B.
"My 7 year old nephew (and others) thoroughly enjoyed ... (the plot has) many history, philosophy & ethical issues that we can learn from." P.H.

"... read many novels of England, *Lizzie* ranks up among the top." S.M.
"Couldn't put it down. Inspiring." M.A.
"Delightful ... a great story ... enjoying relationships of characters." D.F.
"Lizzie and Quon are a terrific pair." G.M.

"... truly inspirational ... a gift to younger generation" C.P.
"... a must read for all young readers, an enjoyable read for everyone." A.B.
"... an unforgettable character...lots of spunk and drive." N.L.
"Lovely story! Hardly wait to read more & more & more..." U.A.

And from younger readers . . .
"At my young age I don't really like old books' but this book is something else, I love it!" Tara, 14 years
"Excellent novel ... well developed characters...intriguing plot. I think people of all ages would enjoy it." Sarah, 14 years
"A great book. Once you start to read it you can't stop." Tarra, 10 years
"A wonderful book. Thank you for writing it." Christina, 11 years
"*Lizzie* is a blast! Our whole family loved it." Andrew, 14 years

By J. Robert Whittle

The Lizzie Series

Lizzie: Lethal Innocence
Lizzie's Secret Angels
Streets of Hope
Lizzie's Legacy

* * *

Victoria Chronicles

Bound by Loyalty
Loyalty's Reward

* * *

By J. Robert Whittle and
Joyce Sandilands

Moonbeam Series

Leprechaun Magic

Lizzie:
Lethal Innocence

Book One
'The Lizzie Series'

To Manju & Nitin
Happy reading

J. Robert Whittle

Publisher's note: This book is a work of fiction. Names, characters, places and incidents either are the product of the author's imagination or are used fictionally, any resemblance to actual persons living or dead, events, or locales is entirely coincidental.

First Printing 1999
Second Printing 2001
Third Printing 2004

Whitlands Publishing Ltd.
4444 Tremblay Drive, Victoria, BC
Canada V8N 4W5 250-477-0192
website: www.whitlands.com
email: info@whitlands.com

Cover design by Desktop Publishing Ltd.
Cover art by Auguste Renoir;
Back cover photo by Terry Seney

Canadian Cataloguing in Publication Data

Whittle, J. Robert (John Robert), 1933-
Lizzie

ISBN 0-9685061-3-5

I. Title.
PS8595.H4985L59 2000 C813'.54 C00-911235-9
PR9199.3.W458L59 2000

Printed and bound in Canada by
Friesen's, Altona, MB

To my wife, Joyce, for her energy,
her unfailing encouragement, and
for being my partner in everything.

Acknowledgements

The author's grateful thanks to:

Dorothy Carlson, Jack Law, and the countless friends and family members who offered helpful critique and boundless encouragement, especially on my earlier manuscripts, which enabled Lizzie to be born; Jo Miles for her special assistance and encouragement; Rona Murray and Michael O'Hagan for their invaluable encouragement and professional expertise; Marilyn Gravel for her friendship and helpful suggestions; Deborah Wright of Precision Proofreading of Victoria, for her patience, time and expertise without whose encouragement this manuscript would still be sitting in a drawer; Jim Bisakowski of Desktop Publishing Ltd. of Victoria for his valuable assistance and wonderful cover design; to my wife, Joyce, my mentor and trusted editor; and lastly, to my broken leg without which absolutely none of this would have happened.

Many, many thanks to the Vancouver Islanders and thousands of visitors from Canada, the USA, and 40+ countries who have purchased our books supporting Joyce and I at summer markets and year-round shows on Vancouver Island and in greater Victoria, BC; customers who patronized supportive BC and Alberta bookstores; and those who have found us on the internet. You have all assisted in making this new literary career a totally enjoyable experience for both of us. In 2002, you also made "Lizzie" a Canadian Bestseller, despite our limited distribution, and we are so grateful.

2004: As our third printing of "Lizzie" goes to press, Joyce and I want to again thank our loyal readers and, particularly those who asked for our books to be more available in stores, even in other countries. During early 2004, North American distribution will begin first in the USA and then Canada. Our books are also available internationally through our website and others. Check our website or contact us for further information and announcements.

J. Robert Whittle
robert@jrobertwhittle.com
www.jrobertwhittle.com
www.whitlands.com

Key to Dialect

Common Words

'ere – here
'em – them
bin – been
luv – love
sumthin – something
ta – to
tamorra – tomorrow
yer – you are, you're
ye've – you have

Irish Words

begorra – for goodness sake
boyo – my boy
daft – silly
hoy – I
loyk – like

Yorkshire Words

av't – have not
darsn't – dare not
ee – oh
ee bye gum – oh dear me
elow doy – hello love
'elp – help
inta't – into it
luv – love
on't – on it
'ome – home
sumet – something
tha'd – you would, you had
wor – were
yersen – yourself

Scottish Words*

ach/ach aye (ah-k-eye) – yes/oh yes
ag'in – again
ah – I
am'a – am I
arouwn - around
dinnae – do not
heed – head
lassie – a young girl
ma – my
nae – as a suffix, produces negative
no/noo – not
tae – to, too
tek – take
weel – well
ye – you

*multiple r's (ie. yerr) = rolling of r's

Main Characters (in order of appearance)

Lizzie Short – London street waif of about 9 years of age
Joe Todd – old Londoner and ex-mariner
Abe Kratze – London tailor and teacher
Quon Lee – Chinese boy of about 8 or 9 years
Bill Johnson – baker from Yorkshire, relative of Martha
Missus Johnson – Bill Johnson's wife
Ben Thorn – 1st Mate on government excise ship, *Falcon*
One-Eyed Jack – 2nd Mate on government excise ship, *Falcon*
Tom Burns – butcher-owner of slaughterhouse
Captain Davis – captain of government excise ship, *Falcon*
Minister – prominent local churchman
Lefty – one-legged ex-mariner and messenger
Ada Mason – bookkeeper, former teacher and mother of Willie
Mick O'Rourke – Irish building foreman, an ex-mariner
Martha Johnson – Joe's housekeeper/cook from Yorkshire
Tom Day – lame ex-sailor and delivery boy
Billy – homeless lad, Tom Day's helper
Jemima Nicholas – Mick's aunt, a Welshwoman
Nathan Goldman – Jewish businessman, cousin to Abe Kratze
Charley Mason – ex-marine engineer, Ada's brother-in-law
Angus McClain – brewery manager
Patrick Sandilands – rag merchant from Aberdeen, Scotland
Dr. Burges – local dentist
Capt. Long John Stroud – evil ship captain in Minister's employ
Walter Drake – young lad, aka Fish, Capt. Stroud's cabin boy
Bessie Drake – Walter's mother
Jeb Dark – local gypsy leader
Grey and Green Grim – sailor twins

Lizzie:
Lethal Innocence

Part 1

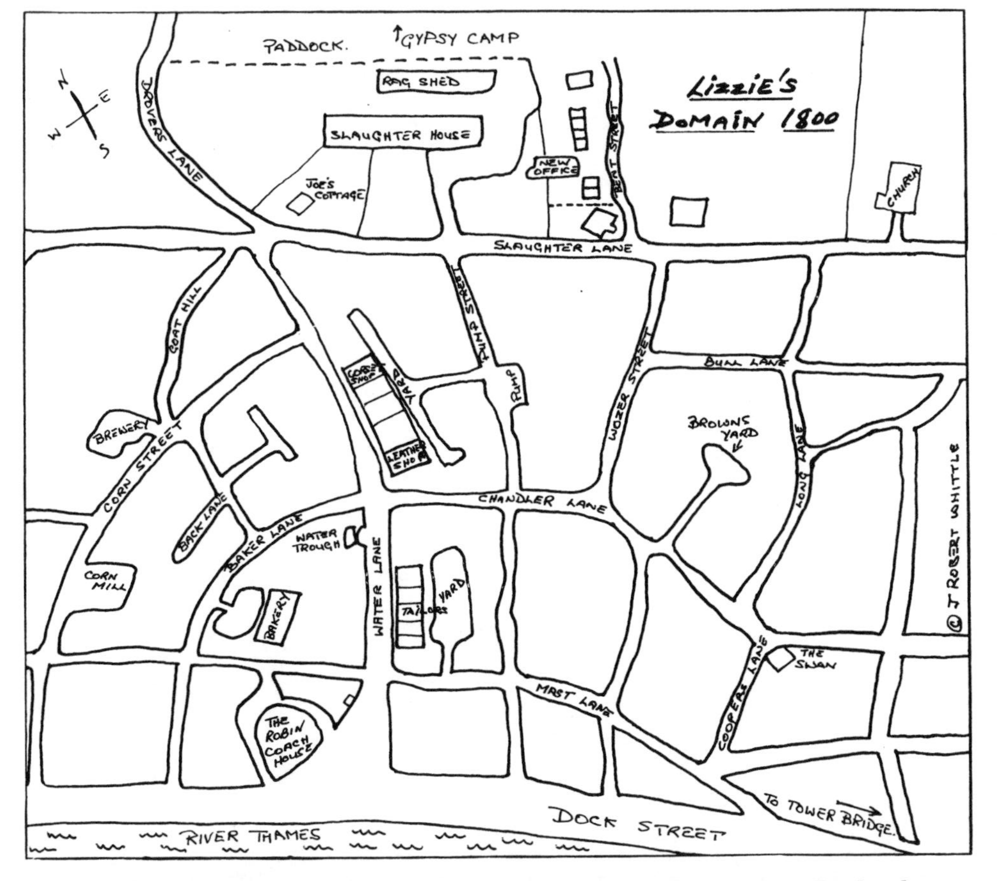

Map of 'Lizzie's Domain' a fictional area in 1800s London, England

Chapter 1

Lizzie Short ran down the lane as fast as her young legs would carry her, slowing only long enough to round the corner at Baker Lane. The fear of being caught and its consequences terrified her—stealing food was the only way a street urchin could survive.

However, this time she and her cohorts, Will, Kate, and the Smith boys, had been much too reckless—stealing those cakes from the window sill at *The Robin*, with all those people about, could very well have gotten them into more trouble than they had bargained for.

Lizzie had never known her father—a soldier who had been killed while serving in the army before she came into this world. Stories her mother told her were often embellished—especially if she had been drinking that foul tasting liquid she liked so much—but she had often told Lizzie, she was far better off not having known him.

Fending for herself at nine years-of-age on the streets near London's dockland was difficult for one so young, but Lizzie was a wily, cunning little thief with a winsome smile and a merry twinkle in her bright blue eyes. Her beautiful auburn hair hung in disarray over slim shoulders covered by an ill-fitting grubby, grey dress, which had not been washed in weeks—her tatty, black coat had been recently torn when she collided with a workman on the docks.

This seemingly frail child, however, was far from ordinary. She was accustomed to life on the street and brighter than most. Some of the older children of the streets tried to copy Lizzie's enterprising tricks, but most were caught for their efforts.

Then one day, life as she knew it, almost ended. It was mid-morning and she and her friends were making their usual rounds picking pockets and pinching what food they could find, when she almost got caught. She barely escaped by hiding under the skirt of a dressmaker's model that stood in a shop doorway.

Sadly, her companions were not so lucky. They were soon caught by the eager hands of the law and apprehended. Willie Dent kicked and screamed like the devil himself were holding him; Kate Moor cried as if her heart was being broken—forcing a lawman to pick her up bodily; and the two younger ones sobbed their hearts out, calling Lizzie's name as they were being dragged off . . . but she knew she could do nothing to help them.

She only saw them one more time—the day she sneaked into the court and witnessed their sentence for deportation to the Colonies of the New World. No one seemed to care what happened to those poor little lost souls . . . except Lizzie and now it was too late.

Tears streamed down her face as she trudged back to the garret where she and her mother lived in total poverty. As her weary bare feet landed on the top step and she reached out for the door latch, she heard the voice of a man, a guest of her mother no doubt—it was a common practice.

Standing there in the last rays of sunshine, her thin elbows resting on the rickety top rail, she made the decision to leave. There was nothing inside she either needed or wanted . . . so turning her back on the only home she had ever known, she slowly descended the stairs, for the very last time.

By the time her feet landed on the cobblestones of the back lane, she had a plan and the drunken sailor lying in a doorway was the first stepping stone to her newfound independence. Deftly, she searched through his pockets and relieved him of his money purse. Her young, experienced hands worked both quickly and gently, and caused him not the slightest discomfort.

All the rest of that day and into the evening, Lizzie walked the streets, begging for only as much food as she dared. Nighttime came and she carefully searched her familiar locations until she found a place to sleep.

And so her bed that night was a handsome cab left by the owner until morning in a stable yard. Soft, comfortable leather seats made a resting-place of pure luxury for her young body. Her old and dirty coat was her blanket, her folded arms her pillow, and it was not long before sleep overtook the worn-out child.

The clip clop of horses' hooves rattling on the cobblestones awoke her as dawn broke. Quickly, she slipped away unobserved into the fresh morning air of dockland. With her tummy rumbling from hunger, Lizzie Short started her first full day of freedom by heading straight to the big coaching house, *The Robin*, on the corner of Dock Street and Water Lane. It was a popular place for travellers to get a last meal before boarding their ships for a long sea voyage to a far-off land.

Slipping off her ragged coat and hiding it behind the stable block, she quickly walked over to the wash trough, washed her hands and face, and with a little giggle, made her way over to the kitchen entrance.

Behind the back door hung the aprons belonging to the serving girls. Making sure she wasn't being followed, Lizzie unhooked an apron from a nail and closed the door again, without even going inside—this was a trick she had pulled off many times before. Putting it on and smoothing out the wrinkles, she cautiously entered the front door and snatched up the first tray she found left unattended. Now it simply took strong nerves to walk into the kitchen and load up the tray with food.

In a few minutes, she was walking out into the public area with a full tray and a jaunty air of self-confidence.

Suddenly, a large hand fell on her small shoulder and a rough voice asked, "Who the hell are you?"

Quick as a flash, Lizzie smiled her sweetest smile back at the man, giving her answer in her most innocent voice.

"New girl, sir."

The hand fell away and out she walked into the yard, passing between the many travellers, stable hands and coachmen. Hiding behind the stables, the girl ate hurriedly at first. Her blue eyes were shining brightly as she turned over in her mind the plan for the rest of the day. Stuffing the surplus food from breakfast into a bag and hiding it under her coat in a corner of the stable, she returned the apron to the nail and laid the tray on the first table inside the door.

As she turned to leave, four girls almost knocked her over, as they ran screaming and laughing into the coach stop, bumping into everything in their urgency to get to a table and food. A big, well-dressed man followed them—a scowl on his face and an air of importance in his manner.

Lizzie watched in envy at the carefree antics of these well-to-do young ladies and momentarily considered if she would be as silly if she had a private coach to ride in and fancy clothes to wear.

Out in the yard, the private coach that had just brought the girls was being unloaded—trunks from the rear carrier, bags and more bags were being thrown from the top rack, and a stable lad was unhitching the matched pair of beautiful Cleveland Bays.

Watching the action with interest, Lizzie noticed the dark blue coat lying on the ground—no doubt dropped by one of the girls. In a flash, she scooped it up as she hurried across the yard.

She returned quickly to the stable to collect her own coat with her bag of food tucked inside, but not needing her tatty coat anymore, she threw it to one side and was soon out in the back lane and on her way.

What a wonderful start to the day she was having. Thoughts danced merrily through her young mind as she walked beside the river and watched the tall ships pass gracefully on the great river she had heard the adults call the Thames. Dockland was waking to a new day.

I need a place of my own, she mused, her eyebrows puckering in deep thought, but where? With all her friends gone, no relatives she knew of—this was certainly going to be a problem she needed to solve—and very soon.

As she walked through the streets of dockland, she saw many things she hadn't noticed before. She became surprisingly aware of the many small shops that lined the streets and lanes—clothing shops and blacksmiths, hat shops and food shops—and with each passing day, she acquired a new interest in the people she saw.

One day, she noticed an old man with walking sticks crossing the road just ahead of her. At the same time, she saw a carriage driven at full gallop and in a wildly irresponsible manner careening toward him.

She tried to cry out a warning but the words stuck in her throat as she stood paralysed with horror as the carriage came closer. Then it was too late, as it collided with the old man sending him and his walking sticks flying in all directions.

Instinct forced Lizzie to run to his assistance, tears escaping her eyes as she saw how badly he was hurt. Cradling the old head in her thin arms, blood trickling from his battered face, she held him gently and his eyes slowly opened.

Bravely, he tried to smile as he haltingly mumbled, "Take . . . me home . . . please."

His eyes began to close, but Lizzie shook him gently and demanded, "Ware is home, mister?"

Slowly, he tried to open them again, but the effort seemed too great.

"Ten . . .," he mumbled, swallowing hard and struggling for the words. "Ten . . . Slaughter . . . Lane," he whispered, but his head flopped limply to one side, eyes shut once more.

A lad pushing a two-wheeled cart stopped to take a look.

"Looks dun for, ta me," he said, in a serious tone.

Lizzie looked up with her tear-stained face and clutched the lad's arm.

"Load him on yer barra an tec us home . . . an ah'll give yer a penny," she said urgently, ignoring his comment.

The lad nodded eagerly.

It took their combined strength and a great deal of effort, to load the man onto the transport. Lizzie threw her new blue coat over him for warmth and off they went, the lad pulling and the girl pushing,

Fifteen minutes later, they turned into Slaughter Lane. After struggling up the hill from the river, locating number '10' was easy, being the first cottage at the top of the lane. Finding a key in the man's coat pocket was no problem to Lizzie's quick fingers. Helped by the lad, she half-carried, half-pulled the old man inside and laid him on the rug in front of the fireplace.

"Ah want me penny!" the lad demanded, sticking out his grimy hand.

Lizzie paid him from the purse she had stolen from the sailor, and the happy lad left in a hurry.

Closing the door behind him, she glanced around the seemingly little house. It was neat, tidy, clean, and much larger than originally appeared.

The fire was laid with dry grass, wood shavings, and sticks, all ready to light. She located some matches on the side-pan water boiler; striking a light and applying it to the dry grass, it took hold immediately. Moving over to the tiny window, she had no difficulty opening it to let some air in, but closed it quickly to stop the draft.

Finding a pillow and blankets in a rear bedroom, she proceeded to make the old fellow comfortable. Dipping her fingers into the water boiler to test the heat, and finding it barely warm, she looked around for more fuel for the fire and found it neatly stacked just outside the back door.

As she turned to carry the wood inside, her nose detected a foul smell. Not being able to identify the stench, she hurried inside, slamming the door to keep it out.

Stoking up the fire, Lizzie glanced down at the frail, sad-looking man who had become her patient. His eyes were open and he now watched her intently, a slight trace of a smile on the bloody, battered face.

Gently stroking his brow, she smiled back at him. She looked around for an earthenware bowl and a cloth, so she could clean up his face. Finding both on a shelf, she filled the bowl with warm water and proceeded to gently wipe off the dried blood and dirt. Soon she was humming a little tune as her wet cloth did its work.

Stopping to review the result, she murmured, "That's better, old lad."

With the cloth rung out and placed over the big brass fender to dry, it was time to get rid of the water. She picked up the bowl and moved toward the door, but hearing his weak voice in the background, caused her to hesitate.

"Put it . . . on me garden . . . lass," the voice haltingly instructed.

Without looking back, she nodded, disappearing outside.

As Lizzie turned the corner, she could see a huge, well-tended vegetable garden at the side of the cottage. The little green sprouts were several inches high on some of the plants, while others were just beginning to show their heads out of the soil.

Lizzie had never seen a garden close up and she was fascinated by it, but she also became aware of that smell again. It was putrid and made her tiny nose wrinkle up in revulsion. Quickly, she deposited the water on the plants and returned at a run to escape the obnoxious stench.

Slamming the door behind her and then putting the bowl back in its place, she decided to have a closer look at her patient.

She dropped on her knees by the side of the old man and asked, "Now, wot's yer name, old lad, and are yer hungry? An who's ta be lookin after yer . . . what's that awful stink out there?"

The old man painfully waved his hand for her to stop.

"'Am Joe Todd," he said, very quietly, "tenant of this house. Yes, 'am hungry and thirsty . . . an that smell is from the city slaughterhouse." Painfully, he tried to sit up and would not have made it if Lizzie hadn't jumped to his assistance. "That last question you asked, little lady . . .?" Joe hoarsely whispered, tears welling in his eyes from pain, " . . . will you stay an take care of me—ah'll gladly pay yer."

Lizzie knelt down beside him, slipping a tiny arm around his bowed shoulders.

"Couldn't leave yer like this na, could ah?" she said, with a rueful smile. Then she arose to find him something to drink—remembering her bag of food, she found some bread and a piece of cheese just large enough to give them each a small meal until she could check out this man's pantry. If she were going to make this her new home for awhile, she would need to familiarize herself with this kitchen very soon.

As the weeks passed, old Joe grew stronger and healthier, thanks to Lizzie's care, and their friendship grew closer. At the beginning, finding a way to feed them both had been a challenging problem for the nine-year-old girl. She had to resort to some very cheeky and dishonest tricks that she had learned a long time ago from the older children on the streets.

Joe Todd watched her with a fascinated interest, marvelling at the resourcefulness of one so young. Due to his inability to work, it was often necessary for her to find food for them—he never needed to worry where the next meal would come from. She rarely grumbled at the workload and never lost her winsome smile.

He taught her about plants and gardens and she coaxed the little shoots along until, much to her delight, they became healthy plants. She was a pretty child of average height but thin boned, and her auburn hair now hung softy about her face. She learned how to wash and care for it by filling the big washtub with water in front of the hearth, with its warm and inviting flames. He remembered how dirty and unkempt she had looked when she first arrived, but under his tutelage, she was now a much different looking little girl.

Not having been a father, Joe didn't understand the new feelings he was now experiencing, but he recognized that he had become strangely protective of his new, young friend. He found he was hardly able to bear her being away from him. He wanted her to stay forever, but how could he ask, surely she had a family somewhere who needed her.

Hobbling out to the garden on the new crutches he had fashioned from two broom handles, Joe began to question the girl about her family and her life. Finally, one day, Lizzie put down her hoe and walked over to the old man, a fire now burning in those laughing eyes.

"If yer wants me ta go, say so!" she demanded, with hands on her hips.

"No, no, ah wants yer ta stay forever, luv," Joe said softly, barely finding the courage to tell her. "But won't somebody be lookin for yer?" he questioned, his face masked by the sadness he felt.

Lizzie laughed aloud and her little body rocked back and forth in feigned mirth.

"You silly old thing," she declared, the gentle tone creeping back into her voice. Then with a merry giggle, she continued, "Do yer think I've looked after yer for all this time an then would just up an walk away? 'Am stayin an that's the end ov that."

Before he could find the words to answer, she took his arm and guided him over to his bench against the house wall. Reaching into his waistcoat pocket, she withdrew his pipe, scraped the burnt tobacco with a sharp twig, and tapped out the old residue.

Curious now, Joe handed the tobacco pouch over to her. Quickly and expertly, she refilled it and handed the pouch back. Studying the burned old clay pipe for a moment, Lizzie smiled and handed it back to him.

"Stuff that in yer face, an stop talkin so daft, I've work ta do."

Joe struck a match and applied it to the tobacco in the pipe well; tears began to roll down his face in relief at what he had just heard. Now puffing away contentedly, he again watched her with interest.

Suddenly, with a twinkle in her eye, she asked, "How would yer like a big juicy steak for supper tonight?"

Puzzled, he could only nod. The girl sliced the head off a big hard cabbage, picked it up and ran like the wind toward the slaughterhouse. Soon she was back with a huge steak and a large roast under her arm. Blood dripped out of the cloth she was carrying them in, causing a dark dotted line to mark the path as she returned.

"Gawd lass, tha'r a better bargainer than me . . . ah'd a bin lucky ta get a little steak!" Joe volunteered as the meat dropped on the bare table.

"Nothin to it, me old pal," Lizzie bragged, bringing their own homegrown onions and potatoes out of the wooden storage box.

It didn't take long before she had dinner cooking. The cast-iron pans were balanced around the roaring fire . . . when to Joe's surprise, off came her black apron and she headed once again for the door, stopping only long enough to wag her finger and warn him to keep his eye on the cooking.

Fifteen minutes later, she re-appeared carrying bread, tarts and a sweet loaf of fruit bread.

"How the h . . . ?" the old man started to say, but the girl stopped him dead as she put her finger to her lips in a silent warning to ask no questions. Joe shook his old head in amazement, but said nothing.

They both ate heartily—it was the most luxurious meal they'd had in a long time and each morsel was savoured. Finishing off, they each had a slice of fruit bread and a big mug of Joe's home-brewed ale, while the old man puffed contentedly on his clay pipe.

One night after a long day of working in the garden, they sat by the fire enjoying its warmth and each other's company.

"How did yer get bad legs in the first place?" Lizzie asked, watching intently for some reaction.

Joe sighed, drawing in deeply from the smoking pipe; his head slowly leaned backwards as smoke trickled out from between his open lips. His eyes were fixed on the blue wisps that floated up to the ceiling.

"Aye lass, it were a long time ago," the old man whispered, his mind obviously looking painfully back in time. He swallowed hard, sat up straight, and declared, "But ah'll tell yer, little one, so sit quiet and listen."

"I was a sailor aboard the mighty fighting ship *H.M.S. Serapis* in 1779. Aye, it were in September around the 23rd, me thinks." He stopped to take another puff, have a sip of his ale and carried on. "I were a gunner's mate on deck two, an right proud of it . . . Charley Price were my gun master," his voice trailed off, as memories flooded back.

Lizzie sat patiently waiting for Joe to continue.

"Died did Charley, poor bugger, blown in half like a rag doll." A single tear rolled down his face. "It were that John Paul Jones who did it. Blew us all ta hell." There was an excited note creeping into his voice, as he told the story for the first time in many years.

"We should have won easy, but that damned madman lashed the ships together, an just wouldn't stop fightin." He paused again, looking at his young friend with a gentle smile. "Both me blasted legs were broke, an ah couldn't move an inch, but when all fightin were done, them colonials were right kind ta us sailors, patched us up an made sure we would survive before they took off in the *Serapis*."

"Yer mean they pinched yer ship?" Lizzie squeaked excitedly, banging her small hand on the chair arm and leaning closer to Joe.

"Aye, that they did, lass," he answered, smiling at her reaction.

"What happened next?" the youngster asked, her eyes shining with anticipation.

"Well, that wer the end of my sailin days, girl. They gave me a little pension an cut me adrift, yer might say," he said, his face turning sad again.

"Holy hell," the child exclaimed in wonderment, "but don't yer worry none, mister, cos am takin care of yer from here on."

Lizzie rose slowly from her chair and stood behind Joe's chair. She put her arm around the old man's shoulders and gave him a gentle squeeze, gently rocking him to and fro.

Chapter 2

Time passed quickly and the bond between this older man and his young charge grew deeper as they developed a profound respect for each other. Joe persuaded his old friend, Abe Kratze, the tailor, into teaching the girl to read and write in exchange for a supply of fish, which he begged from one of his old navy mates, now a fisherman.

Lizzie showed an amazing aptitude for learning and, on many an occasion, she startled solemn-faced old Abe into a broken-toothed grin, by the quickness of her mind.

In the evenings, she rubbed Joe's aching legs with a mixture of herbs and grease given to her by a Chinese boy, who lived in a barrel down on the riverside.

The long-since torn muscles on the old man's legs grew stronger until he was finally able to take his first faltering steps without a stick to support him. As he stood there looking over their garden, Lizzie squealed with delight at their achievement. Gently, but affectionately, holding the man's knurled old hand, she led him to his bench. Here, over many months, he had spent countless hours watching her at her work or shouting advice to her about certain plants and how to look after them.

He hadn't been much help to her this growing season, but just knowing that he was now feeling better encouraged him to look forward to next year's garden and the thrill of planting his own crop of flowers and vegetables once again.

All too soon, they were into autumn—pleasant sunny days were becoming fewer and far between—preparations for winter had begun in earnest. There were the last of the vegetables to pick and store in the cellar and wood to acquire and stack. Old Joe was doing remarkably well, now walking regularly without even a stick, thanks to Lizzie's administrations.

Lizzie had regularly demonstrated how she could ferret out any opportunity and had been delivering bread and cakes for the local baker for some weeks now. They had given her the use of a handcart, which came in handy for carrying logs home.

A chubby little Chinese boy, who lived on the dock in a large barrel, had become a very special friend and often helped her push the cart home. Of course, she made sure he was never hungry, giving him bread from her delivery route and occasionally taking him home for a meal. His name was Quon Lee and he soon worshipped the ground Lizzie walked on, although she really wasn't much older than he was.

Everything was going so well that Joe was often heard to say, "Ah think I've died an gone ta heaven!"

Lizzie would laugh her merry tinkling laughter and the whole house would have a warm friendly glow about it. His greatest delight was when she read to him by the firelight as he rocked gently in his tattered old chair.

It was in October that first winter that Quon Lee disappeared for the first time. She searched the streets and back alleys without finding a trace of him. Nobody had any idea what had happened to the boy. Then, three days later, he suddenly turned up again—sitting on his barrel as if nothing had happened—grinning from ear to ear, as he watched Lizzie approach.

The grin quickly faded when the girl lit into him with probably the first tongue lashing he had ever received. She realized she was being a bit hard on the lad when she noticed the tears trickling down his face. She finished by wagging her small finger under his tiny nose . . . and delivered a warning that he had better not do that again.

However, in mid-November when the icy fingers of winter were beginning to be felt around dockland, Quon Lee declared he had to go away again for a week. Lizzie stopped the baker's cart, rested it on its legs and walked around it to face her friend. The Chinese boy stretched his aching back and grinned at her.

"Now what yer up to?" she demanded, glowering at her friend while she stamped her feet to get them warm.

"We talk later Wizzy, me velly much damn cold."

Lizzie giggled as she always did when Quon Lee talked in his comical interpretation of the English language.

"It had better be good me lad or yer in big trouble!"

No more on the subject was said all afternoon, as they struggled through the streets pulling and pushing the heavy contraption. The last two deliveries were to ships tied up at the docks.

As the last loaf went up the gangplank and the ship's mate paid the bill, he looked straight at Quon Lee and said, "Remember lad, midnight two days from now."

Lizzie looked at her friend in surprise as he stood there nodding his head vigorously at the sailor. Stowing the money safely away in her money belt, she grabbed the shafts, yelled for her helper to push, and they were off at a trot back to the bakery.

Bill Johnson, the baker, heard them coming—the sound of ironclad wheels rattling over the cobblestones of the lane gave him warning and he had the big doors to the back yard already open when they arrived.

Setting the cart down, they dashed into the ever-warm bake house with its huge wood-fired ovens still glowing with heat from the day's baking . . . and the wonderful smell of freshly made bread tickling at their nostrils.

"Sit an get warm—c'mon and warm thee knees," Bill ordered in his kindly way. He was a big man, almost as far around as he was tall. He walked with a kind of wobble that went quite well with his happy exterior and ever-ready, friendly smile.

They were Yorkshire folk, the baker and his wife, hardworking honest people, with a friendly attitude toward life. Missus Johnson was the bookkeeper. Finances were her first thought as she held out her hand for their moneybag. She counted out the money and chuckled.

"Girlie, yer a wonder wi' brass, never a penny piece short, as usual."

Then she was on her feet getting warm drinks and a hunk of fruit loaf for each of the youngsters. She and her husband had long since begun taking a special interest in this young girl and her little friend. They had soon realized that Lizzie was much older than her years—she had an eye for business many an adult only dreamed of having.

Lizzie pulled herself to her feet ten minutes later, and wiping the crumbs from around her mouth, asked, "Can ah have me pay now, cos I have ta get home an see ta Joe."

Missus Johnson quickly obliged and pointed to the sackcloth bag. "Don't forget to take yer bag lovey, an come back again tomorrow."

Each taking a handle of the bag, the youngsters set off at a run, talking and laughing as they went racing around corners at full speed. Passers-by smiled at the odd pair, bundled up in their layers of clothing to keep out the cold. They were a common sight and now well known and liked by all the local people.

Pulling to a halt at Joe Todd's garden gate, Quon Lee muttered, "Me home go, Wizzy."

A quick, small hand grabbed him by the collar.

"Not yet you ain't, me lad," Lizzie declared fiercely, pulling him toward the door which opened as they arrived.

"Na wot's up?" Joe asked as they shot past him into the house, Lizzie in the lead.

"Shut that door," the girl ordered as she rounded on her Chinese pal, dropping the bag of goodies from the bakery on the floor.

The old man stood and watched, a slow smile creeping across his face as Lizzie, hands on hips glowered at the cowering Quon Lee.

"Come on lad, let's av it," she demanded, no longer able to control herself.

Quon apparently had nothing to say, so it was Joe who broke the silence.

"Coats off, yer supper's ready," he said, as he reached out and helped remove the boy's tatty old coat and scarf.

Lizzie slipped hers off and hung it on a nail behind the door before sitting down at the table. She began tapping her fingers impatiently on the tabletop—a sign Joe and Quon Lee had learned to read which meant she was getting angry or impatient . . . and an angry Lizzie was something they preferred to avoid.

Quon Lee sat opposite her, his eyes downcast and his little legs swinging nervously under the table.

"Yer might as well get started, cos yer going ta tell me before ya go," Lizzie snapped, glaring across the plate of food Joe had just put in front of her.

Joe dared not interfere in the drama unfolding in front of him—he knew better.

"This no damn velly good," the Chinese boy exclaimed, looking up. "Dem kill me easy if dey find out I tell."

The girl looked him over carefully.

"Ah . . . an I will if yer don't, so come on, out with it. 'Am waiting!"

Joe looked from one to the other, but could make no sense of anything.

"Don't . . .," was the only word he got out before Lizzie held up her hand and stopped him.

Quon still looked ill at ease but he realized the girl was right and so he finally began to tell his story.

"Dey bring barrels at night. I'm spy out for dem," he said, fiddling with his food nervously.

"An what's in the barrels, lad?" the girl insisted.

"Flench stuff, dlink, big men come get with horse cart."

The girl sat back in her chair, sighed, and at last began eating; her eyes screwed up in deep thought as she chewed each mouthful.

"Can I say somethin now?" Joe asked grinning.

"Yes," Lizzie answered, squinting up at him.

"It's probably brandy from France, an they are avoidin the duty men."

The girl thought for a while before inquiring, "Is there money in it, Joe?"

"Big money," he reported, "but lots of danger. What have yer got in mind?"

Lizzie didn't answer straight away—the meal proceeded in silence and they were almost finished before she looked up again.

"I think we will do a bit of snoopin around before we decide what our next move is, Joe," she said, through pursed lips. "Quon will keep us informed so we can watch what goes on. It's two nights away yet."

She finished talking then suddenly the Chinese boy let out a groan.

"Now what's yer problem?" she asked looking at the boy who just rolled his eyes and shook his head.

Jumping up, he grabbed his coat from behind the door and muttered, "Me gone, Wizzy. Me gone." He opened the door and disappeared into the night.

Two nights later, Joe and Lizzie were concealed on the roof of a building opposite the dock. A light flashed three times out on the Thames, then complete darkness. Twenty minutes passed before they heard a horse and cart approaching. Below them lanterns were lit and held aloft, and they could just make out the shadow of a boat drawing alongside the dock—barrels were being unloaded, men groaned under the strain and muffled voices were heard.

"That be Ben Thorn an his mate, One-Eyed Jack," Joe gasped.

Lizzie reached out and touched the old man's hand.

"Who are they, Joe?"

"Why bless me soul, they sailed wi' me."

"Are they bad or good, tell me quick."

The old man turned to face her.

"Hard as old hell, but good men, both."

Indicating it was time to leave, Lizzie led the way back to the rickety stairs. Quon Lee was waiting for them below.

"So did yer find out where they took it?" Lizzie asked.

"Sure did," the Chinese boy replied, lending a hand to help support Joe. Cautiously, the three of them made their way back home to Joe's cottage.

Later in the evening, they all relaxed in front of the big blazing fire. Joe sat in his armchair, his pipe glowing red as he puffed away happily. The youngsters sat cross-legged on the floor, sipping on hot broth from the huge pot resting on the hob. They all stared into the flames like contented kittens.

Mug empty now, Lizzie climbed to her feet, yawned and stretched her arms.

"Bedtime, boy," she said, gently kicking the Chinese lad's foot. "You're stayin here tonight, we can talk about this later when I've had time ta think."

It was a statement of fact. She had given the order and expected them to obey as she moved off to her bed with a tired 'goodnight.'

Morning arrived too quickly. The children were still yawning as they ate breakfast, but Lizzie insisted they had to be at Johnson's bakery on time.

It was a hard day for both of them after their late visit to the docks. At the end of their run, all they could think about was getting home as quickly as possible. Missus Johnson gave each of them an extra piece of pie to take home and bade them goodnight.

"My gawd, that lass is a worker," Bill muttered, watching fondly as the tired youngsters left his bakery to drag their weary legs up the back alley toward home.

"Aye, but you just take note, Bill Johnson, that lass is going to be somebody someday. Just you mark my words, brains an drive, that's what young Lizzie has."

Chapter 3

Lizzie and Joe sat snuggled up together in Joe's big chair by the fire when she suddenly spoke.

"Tamorra, I want yer ta go an find them two sailors."

The old man cautiously waited, wondering what was coming next but she was silent.

"For what reason?" he asked.

Lizzie turned her big blue eyes upward onto her friend and smiled gently at him.

"Just ta renew old friendships," she said softly, then giggling as she gave him a tight squeeze. "An sniff out what's going on," she continued emphatically.

Old Joe laughed out loud as he returned the affectionate squeeze of the child at his side. She never failed to amaze him with the power of her thoughts and the decisive way she set out to get what she wanted,

"You little devil," he chuckled. "Av yer got a scheme in yer head?"

The small head nodded vigorously as she wriggled free of his arms, but without a word of explanation, she scampered off to bed with a cheeky 'goodnight' and a wave of her hand.

Sleep came easily to the rosy-cheeked girl, content with her lot and happy as a Christmas robin now that she had a family of her own—even if it was only Joe.

Joe sat staring into the dying fire, wondering what she was up to this time—knowing he would do whatever she asked. This girl was special—he had known it from the first day they met. Money has a way of gravitating toward some people like a magnet—and young Lizzie was proving to be a true magnet.

Walking over to the chest of drawers, he pulled open the top drawer, turned back the clean clothes and extracted an old tobacco tin. As he walked back to the fire and sat down, he slowly eased off the lid.

Reaching for the flat piece of wood, he used for a cutting board, he tipped out the tin's contents, sighing with surprise. This was their savings, all put together by the hard work and wily dealing of his young partner. Slowly counting until he reached sixty-four guineas, eight shillings and four pence, the old man shook his head in amazement, never having seen so huge an amount and finding its contents more than he had expected.

How did she do it? he wondered. He hardly ever noticed her putting money into it. He quietly closed the lid and returned the tin to its hiding-place.

During the next few days the old man searched the docks for his old seafaring mates but found no trace of them. After supper one night, Lizzie inquired if he had found them.

"Not a sign of them anywhere," he had to admit, looking puzzled and giving his head a scratch.

Lizzie looked up at him from her seat on the floor and smiled. "Yer lookin in the wrong place, lad," she stated, then went quiet for a while.

Joe could bear it no longer.

"Well, where should I be lookin?" he asked ruffling her hair.

"Try the government tax ships," she murmured, staring intently into the fire. "Could be the fox lives in the hen house!"

Joe Todd slapped his leg with delight and let out a mighty laugh.

"You clever little devil," he chortled, slapping his leg again. "I bet my braces yer right too, it's just the sort of lark them two would do."

So, it was decided that tomorrow he would take a walk to the government ship dock.

It only took one day to find information about the men. The dockside workers told the old man that Ben Thorn and One-Eyed Jack were at sea on their regular two-week trip to France, patrolling the shipping lanes looking for contraband and liquor smugglers. Joe managed to keep a straight face until he was well out of sight of the men. Now, he had something to report—the date and time they were due back at their dock.

Once he was around the corner and out of sight, he stood up straight and picked up his walking stick. He was pleased that their plan was a success—he had merely used the stick for effect and to gain a little sympathy from the dockworkers. It also gave him the innocent look Lizzie had said it would. Joe hadn't needed his stick for several months now, as Lizzie's constant care and massage had made him feel many years younger . . . after all, he was only 50 years old.

That night as the young pair left the baker's yard—wind howled almost to a gale and the rain poured down soaking them to the skin—it was almost impossible to stand upright. Lizzie screamed above the clattering so Quon could hear.

"Yer comin home wi' me tonight."

Grabbing Quon's hand, she leaned into the swirling force of the storm and the Chinese boy gripped her tightly as they tried unsuccessfully to use their small bodies against the wind.

Suddenly, old Joe was there with them, clamping a strong hand on their coat collars, and together the three of them battled their way homeward. Holding the children tight against the big wooden door of the cottage, he fought to get it open, and when it did open, they all fell inside. It took their combined effort to push it closed from inside.

"What a night!" Joe gasped, as they all hung their dripping coats behind the door and moved toward the fireplace for warmth.

From the floor in front of an enormous fire, Lizzie looked up at him, grinning through the water streaming down her face.

"Thanks for comin ta get us, you old luv," she said quietly.

The old sailor went beet-root red and busied himself getting their meal onto the table, to hide his embarrassment.

"Come on, let's look lively shipmates, outa them wet rags an inta sum dry'ns," Joe cried in mock anger.

The youngsters scampered off, then re-appeared in dry clothes, but they had found some of Joe's old sweaters and pants . . . and they looked a sight.

Gasping in amazement, Joe burst into laughter.

"Gawd, what a pair of rogues you two look," he said, wiping the tears from his eyes, "but no matter, sit an eat, that's me orders."

All that could be heard for the next ten minutes were three hungry mouths chomping on good nourishing food—the fruit of their summer toil had certainly been worth the effort—Joe's mutton stew was delicious.

As soon as they finished, Quon picked up the plates placing them in the big clay bowl that served as a sink. As Lizzie rolled up her sleeves, he filled it with hot water from the fireside boiler. But cleaning up the dishes turned out to be a long process tonight as Lizzie spent more time staring off into space. Quon had to tell her to 'stop dleaming' or he wouldn't help. Coming back to the present, she finished up, placing each dish neatly on the sackcloth.

Joe sat rocking gently in his chair, watching the youngsters with renewed interest now that his stomach was content. He noticed how well they worked together. Quon added more water to the boiler before going to sit cross-legged by the fire. The girl shook the water from her hands, wiped them on her dress and joined them by the fire.

Once she was comfortable, she turned to the old man.

"Well wot's yer news, sonny?"

The pipe in Joe's mouth wobbled for a moment before he removed it . . . spitting into the fire causing it to crackle and sparks to fly.

"Well, today I found them two scalawag mates of mine," he began, and quickly the girl's head swung up to face him. "But they're out at sea," he said, with a note of disappointment in his voice. Then he leaned over to tap the pipe on the top bar of the fire grate.

"Damn," muttered Lizzie, shuffling back a little, away from the heat.

A chuckle escaped Joe's lips.

"Tain't all bad youngen," he said, "cos I know the time, date, an place of their return."

The girl's eyes told him all he wanted to know, even before she replied.

"By golly yer a gooden, me old luv, just what we wanted ta know."

Quon Lee was resting his head on his hands, elbows balanced on his knees and listening with interest.

Joe leaned forward.

"An what do yer want next little madam?"

Lizzie grinned back at him and winked, "Why it's Christmas time, an we're goin ta invite 'em for a feed."

The old man sat up straight as he pondered over Lizzie's statement. He muttered something to himself, but the girl ignored him. So, he continued to puff on his pipe and rock contentedly.

The room went quiet for a while, each one mulling over their own thoughts until Lizzie giggled aloud and announced, "Tamorra 'am going ta start preparin."

Joe's chair stopped creaking. Quon Lee's elbow slipped off his knee causing him to groan with surprise and Lizzie started giggling again.

"Just hold on a minute, lassie," begged the old man, knowing full well that he would have difficulty keeping up with the speed of her thoughts.

Rolling over like a big cat, Quon looked up, shaking his head.

"She got long way-off look, Joe. Damn velly bad for us, me tinks!" But he was grinning and had that look of adoration in his eyes.

"Do yer think yer could maybe tell us about it then?" Joe asked, poking her with his foot.

The set of her jaw told her companions that she did have a plan.

"Well, for starters, we are goin ta sell vinegar and cider," she told them. The grin on the Chinese boy's face began to widen.

"How?" Joe snapped.

"By using the bread cart . . . we can put a little barrel of each on't back corners, with no trouble at all."

"But from where, lass?"

"Jack Shaw's cider works at the bottom of Goat Hill," she answered, matter of factly.

Joe started to ask more questions but she held up her hand and stopped him.

"Don't you worry yer head about it, I've taken care of the whole thing."

This time the old man just couldn't contain himself.

"But what about money, lass?" he asked gently.

She smiled at him and climbed onto his knee to snuggle with him in his big chair.

"Why it's all done wi' credit, me old luv," she murmured. "We put no money out, just draw on it . . . now don't that sound grand?"

Joe drew her close, tickling her face with his stubbly beard.

"Who in the name of hell would give a nine-year-old kid that sort of deal?" he whispered.

Pushing on his chest to escape the torment, she jumped off his knee to stand in front of him wagging her finger.

"Look here, sonny!" she snapped. "I think I'm ten, an I've worked like hell to get a good reputation with the trades people just so we can start dealing . . . for us . . . soon."

As was becoming a common occurrence for Joe, he was totally dumbfounded with Lizzie's statement. All he could do was hold out his arms. Lizzie came happily back into them and they sat rocking together quietly, each absorbed in their own thoughts.

Quon Lee's head cocked to one side as he watched enthralled by their display of affection.

"Velly stlange people you Inglis, velly stlange!"

Next morning at the bakery, Bill Johnson already had the cart loaded when the youngsters showed up. Neatly fastened on the back corners were the barrels and swinging under the side on hooks were two measuring jugs.

Lizzie looked it all over carefully before turning to Bill whereupon he handed her the list of customers. She studied it for a few minutes.

"Where did the measuring jugs come from?" she asked without looking up.

The baker patted her shoulder affectionately.

"Me, lass. Ye'll need 'em."

Chapter 4

It was a cold and damp day, as all December days tend to be in London, but Lizzie and Quon didn't let the weather daunt them. Under the girl's tuition, Quon had now become quite a salesman. They both had quick heads for figures, gave good full measures—never forgetting to ask for regular orders—and long before the day was gone, they were sold out.

The last order of bread had been delivered to one of the ships getting ready to sail that evening. As they unloaded, an argument broke out on board the vessel and Lizzie's keen ears heard the words 'salt pork'.

The ship's purser counted out the money owed, which she double-checked, before asking, "Is there anything else you might be needin, sir?"

The officer gave her a long hard look, scowling at her as he scratched his beard.

"What the hell can you get, at this time a day?" he asked roughly.

Lizzie smiled sweetly.

"Anything you might be needin, sir!"

He let out a great booming laugh.

"How about four barrels of salt pork?"

His scowl deepened as Lizzie cracked back her questions.

"Price? Size of barrel? Time we've got before you sail . . . sir?"

Seeing her business-like manner, he suddenly realized she was serious.

"We sail at midnight . . . 50-gallon barrels, and the goin rate is ten guineas a barrel," he answered quickly. A grin appeared on his face but quickly disappeared as soon as she spoke.

"And the commission for us, sir?"

"Gawd . . . you little bitch!"

Lizzie's eyes narrowed but she continued to smile.

"When ye've finished rantin, sir, my price is twelve guineas and ten shillings, delivered to the dock and paid for before they're loaded. Take it or leave it."

A voice from the ship called out, "If you can deliver, I will pay you 13 guineas a barrel."

Lizzie motioned to her partner and they quickly turned the cart. Quon Lee threw his weight into pushing and they were off at a run.

Racing into the baker's yard, Lizzie ran inside to see Missus Johnson, hurrying past the baker without even a greeting. Unbuckling her purse, she gasped, "Be back in two hours for me pay, mum."

Bill Johnson scratched his head as he watched them leave as quickly as they had entered, tearing off up the lane.

As they ran, Lizzie yelled, "Quon, get Joe, an meet me at the slaughterhouse."

As they reached the cottage, Quon turned into the garden and the girl took off up the track to the slaughterhouse. Into the huge stinking barn-like building Lizzie ran, heading straight for the owner's desk.

Panting fiercely, she demanded, "Twenty guineas for four barrels of salt pork, best quality."

The big butcher jerked violently with surprise and his mouth began to twitch nervously.

"Yes or no, move yer arse man. I don't have all day!" she shouted.

The fierceness of the demand from this young girl, quickly made him jump to his feet.

"Y-yes," he mumbled, "delivered to where and when?"

Lizzie ran at him and kicked his shins . . . hard.

"Now! . . . to the docks at bottom of Water Lane. Cash when we get there."

The barrels were being loaded as Joe and Quon arrived. They all climbed aboard, sitting in the wagon behind the driver and his helper.

Let's get movin," the girl screamed at the driver and they set off at a trot. As they reached the end of the track, Lizzie stood up to give directions. "Come on, move it! Down Water to Dock Street . . . then straight ahead, third ship on't dock."

The beleaguered horses were steaming in the cold evening air as they pulled alongside the ship. Before long, the sailors and their two drivers had the wagon unloaded.

"Wait for me over there," Lizzie instructed them, indicating some bales of wool farther up the dock.

Lizzie returned to the ship just as she heard the now familiar voice from the dark ship say, "Pay her an extra guinea a barrel, Jock, and find out how we get in touch when we return."

Her business finished, Lizzie walked up the dock toward the wagon, squeezing the fifty-six golden guineas in her tiny hand. She counted out twenty and gave them to the driver, who doffed his cap respectfully. Reaching into her pocket, she produced two pennies.

Giving one to each of the men, she said, "Well done, lads and thank you."

The men beamed at the surprise gratuity, the driver clucked to his horses and the wagon rumbled homeward.

"Home now?" Joe asked.

"Not yet, lad," Lizzie chuckled. "Johnson's bakery next, ta pick up me pay."

It was a nice crisp evening. Walking along at the old man's pace, they arrived quickly at the bake house. Bill and his wife made a great fuss of Joe as the children scoffed their usual sweets.

"What yer bin up ter, lass?" the baker asked.

Lizzie gave no answer, just smiled sweetly and asked for her pay.

Missus Johnson sat at the table and emptied the purse Lizzie had delivered earlier. Taking out the bread money and putting it to one side, she glanced up at the girl and asked, "Shall I take out the cost of the cider and vinegar?"

Lizzie nodded.

Missus Johnson scooped the remainder of the money back into the purse and handed it to the girl, who strapped it around her small waist.

"Now I owe you yer pay," she said handing some money to the girl, with a smile. "Are we straight now lassie?"

Lizzie grinned. "Aye, that we are, missus. We'll be off now," she said, moving toward the door.

"Don't forget yer bag, luv."

The girl stopped in her tracks. "Tell yer what, get me two barrels of cider for mornin."

Bill nodded. The Chinese boy picked up the bag and followed Lizzie out of the door as Joe smiled knowingly at the Johnson's and said his farewell.

Bill Johnson and his wife stood looking at each other as the door closed behind their visitors, surprise registering on their faces. Mrs. Johnson broke the silence.

"Told yer didn't I? Well mark my words well, Billy boy, it's started. Our little Lizzie is on her way up."

Joe unlocked the door, picked up a pail-full of water he had been carrying and entered the warm, fire-lit cottage. Quon dropped the bag of baked goods and went back outside, returning with two logs for the fire.

The burning logs soon sent sparks flying up the chimney, crackling fiercely as they rose into the air. Meanwhile, Joe filled three big tankards with hot broth from the cast-iron pan balanced on the hob and started to empty the bag of baked goods Lizzie and Quon had brought home with them.

Settling down in front of the fire, Lizzie suddenly blurted out, "Do you two know what we made today?"

Quon didn't seem a bit interested, but the old man shook his head, sipping his broth with a slurping noise.

"Well, let's see," the girl said, in an excited voice. Hopping onto her feet, she unbuckled the moneybag and emptied it onto the table.

Quon Lee sat bolt upright as the coins rolled, falling with a jingle on the tabletop.

"Wizzy make all dat?" he asked, in disbelief.

She leaned over to plant a kiss right on top of the Chinese boy's head.

He giggled with embarrassment, muttering, “Oh Wizzy!”

Joe lay back in his chair.

“Better not do that too often lass, yer goin ta give the little bugger a heart attack,” he said with a grin.

Counting out the money and meticulously stacking it in rows, she finally announced, “Eight shillings and tuppence.”

The old man took the last drop of broth from his tankard, and reaching for his pipe mused quietly to himself.

“That’s a hell of a lot of money for one day.”

Quon rolled over on the mat.

“So we lich, so what?” he said nonchalantly, resting his head on his arms and gazing into the fire.

“But that ain’t all, me shipmates,” Lizzie said coyly, “there’s money from the salt pork yet.

“Where?” Joe asked, sitting up in his chair.

“In me nickers!” she replied, giggling.

The old man shook his head in disbelief as Lizzie scooped up her dress and produced the golden guineas, holding them up for him to see. His pipe wobbled violently between his teeth, as a drop of spittle escaped onto his chin and the pipe dropped into his lap.

The girl laughed merrily as she counted out thirty-six guineas. She reached for a cloth from the other side of the table.

“Yer dribblin again, old luv,” she muttered, wiping Joe’s chin.

The old man was speechless at the sight of all the money. Quon Lee had no idea what was happening as he snored peacefully in front of the fire—being rich certainly hadn’t seemed to impress him at all.

Lizzie walked over to the drawer, took out their tin and brought it back to the table. Carefully packing the money away, she returned the tin to the drawer.

When Joe at last found his voice, all he could say was, “How?”

Again the young girl laughed. “Quick thinkin an salt pork, lad, that’s how.”

“But what are we going ta do with all that money?” Joe asked incredulously.

Lizzie slipped her arm around her friend.

“Well, we ain’t about ta start worryin about that. I’ve got a plan.”

The next few mornings were cold and windy, but the bread still needed to be delivered. The youngsters struggled through the streets, never missing a day; their vinegar and cider customer lists were growing in leaps and bounds.

One evening, Joe looked across the table at his wonderful little pal—this amazing girl who had changed his life. She beamed straight back at him, a merry twinkle dancing in her eyes.

"The government ship will be in tamorra, lassie," he said, softly holding his heat-blackened pipe in one hand.

Lizzie slowly moved her knife on the table, deep in thought. The old man watched her every movement, trying to perceive what was in her mind.

Finally, she was ready, eyes slightly closed and just a trace of a smile on her face, she began.

"Then tamorra, you will meet them on the dock and bring them home for a meal."

Joe looked a wee bit ill at ease.

"These are rough, tough sea dogs, lass."

Lizzie slammed her hand down on the table. The dishes and cutlery clattered about and Joe's pipe began to wobble again.

"Not as damned tough as me," she declared, thumping her still flat chest with one fist, "an I have logic and brains on my side, too!"

It was late the next afternoon when Joe caught up to them on their bread route.

Spotting Quon Lee dashing out of an alleyway on his way back to the cart, he shouted, "Tell her, they're comin tamorra."

The boy acknowledged him by shouting back, "Light Glanpop," as he filled his arms with long loaves of bread and scampered off up another alleyway.

Joe Todd hunched his shoulders against the cold and wound the long, woollen scarf one more turn around his neck. Gawd, that sounds like he wants ta set me on fire! he chuckled to himself.

Abe Kratze, the tailor, stood on the step of his shop and watched his old friend, Joe Todd, come up the street toward him. For a tailor, Abe wasn't much of a dresser, his clothes obviously rumpled beneath his open black smock.

"Drink of hot stuff, Joe?" the tailor inquired, as Joe came closer.

Startled, the old sailor's head jerked up as he noticed the tall man in the nearby doorway.

"Ah think ah were in a trance," he said with a nod toward his friend, when Abe repeated his offer.

Entering the shop, Abe shuffled off, leading the way into a back corner where behind a screen blazed a warm fire with a hissing kettle perched on one corner. Sitting on one of the two rickety chairs, Joe watched as old Abe reached for two small china cups and a bottle of clear syrup and placed them in the middle of the small table.

Sitting down, he poured a quarter cup of the syrup into each. Abe smiled broadly revealing broken and black teeth. He reached for the kettle, first wrapping the hot handle in a piece of fine cloth he picked up from the floor.

"Full?" he asked.

"Ah," muttered Joe getting a whiff of the familiar smell. "Peppermint," he commented, taking a sip of the hot drink.

"Good for a body, an cheap," Abe announced, using a spoon to gingerly taste his hot mixture. Letting the drinks warm them through, the two old friends sat in silence until the tailor asked, "What's she up to now?"

Joe turned his full attention on the tailor. His eyes were mere slits.

"Why?"

"Oh, she came in the other day to ask me how to buy property."

Joe's nose began to twitch.

"Buy property?" he gasped incredulously. Then he chuckled with amusement. "An did yer tell 'er?"

The old tailor looked as serious as a minister at a funeral but he nodded.

Joe observed his friend for a moment.

"Like you, old lad, ah'll have ter wait an see," he chuckled aloud making his way to the door. With his thumb on the latch, he looked back at his friend.

"She's a shrewd one, Joe!" Abe called from the back of the shop.

Joe merely nodded, quietly closing the door behind him.

That night after dinner, Joe and the children sat quietly in front of a huge fire.

"What about the lad tamorra night, lassie?" Joe suddenly asked.
"He stays," was the blunt reply.
"But won't that make 'em suspicious?"
"No," she said, slowly, "just the opposite. It'll throw 'em completely off guard, then ah'll get what ah want easy. Just you wait an see."

Chapter 5

The next day, a downpour of rain mixed with icy cold sleet made deliveries difficult. Customers too, were in a hurry making their special orders for Christmas, which Lizzie wrote down in her little book. Some were for the Johnson bakery . . . some were for cider. It all took time and effort, and tired her right out.

On the way home, she told Quon Lee not to speak until he was spoken to, because this was a special night and she needed her wits about her. He nodded his head, his eyes as big as saucers when he thought of the visitors coming to the cottage for dinner.

Ben Thorn and One-Eyed Jack arrived at six o'clock—clean, tidy, and smiling at the thoughts of a home-cooked meal. Joe introduced them to the children, simply saying he had unofficially adopted them both.

The meal was a tremendous success. The goose was done to perfection and cakes and pies from the bakery were enjoyed until no one could eat another morsel.

The men sat back and lit their clay pipes as the children cleared the table and washed up. There was much talk of old times, battles at sea, adventures in foreign lands and old shipmates.

The visitors were completely at ease and eagerly answered Lizzie's innocent sounding questions about their jobs on the government ship—telling how they often confiscated barrels of brandy and rum. When she asked if the captain made any extra money, they broke into peels of laughter. They told her their Captain Davis would sell his grandmother for a gold sovereign.

"Then I have a proposition for you, gents."

Silence hit the room like a sledgehammer.

"Why don't we all make safe money," she continued, "by having one place handle all the goods you can bring in?" She stopped, watching their faces for a clue to their thoughts.

"Too hard ta find that place . . . an people yer trust. Would tek years ta set that up," Ben Thorn offered.

"Tell us what y'ev got, an we'll talk ta the captain," One-Eyed Jack blurted out, his good eye twitching like mad. "Come on, Joe, tell it all."

Joe Todd stretched and pointing at Lizzie with his pipe stem.

"Tell 'em lass."

The girl slowly climbed to her feet, clasped her hands in front of her dress and, smiling innocently, proceeded to explain.

"We have a warehouse that's central and discreet, a distribution network already in operation and so nothing would be noticed. There is also one other thing . . .," she stopped for emphasis, letting the tension rise.

"What other thing?" Ben asked, leaning forward and reducing his eyes to slits.

Lizzie calmly looked him in the eye.

"The harbour patrol and the king's collectors are ready ta grab ya. They know what yer up ta . . . but not ta worry boys, Joe can keep 'em off yer backs if yer throw in with us."

One-Eyed Jack jumped clean out of his seat, grabbed his cap and began nervously twiddling it around as he paced across the room.

Ben was made of sterner stuff.

"That right, Joe?" he snapped.

The old man quaked inside not sure where Lizzie was going next, but he sat still and merely nodded.

"An if the captain goes for the deal," Lizzie continued, "the negotiations will be done here tamorra night or the deal is off. It's the law or come with us. Not much to think about is there? We shall expect you to bring the captain at seven in the evening." With that, she sat down, eyes cast on the fire.

The two sailors were eager to be off now. Thanking Joe profusely for the meal and the warning, they went out into the cold and rainy darkness.

Closing the door and turning the key, Joe walked back to his chair and collapsed into it. Sitting there in front of the fire, Lizzie grinned up at him with that devilish twinkle in her eyes that sent the old man's emotions spinning.

"You must be the cheekiest brat in Christendom!" Joe gasped, hardly having enough energy left to puff on his pipe.

"You long Glanpop, you long," Quon Lee said, shuffling in front of the fire. "Wizzy velly damn smart. She only tells 'em tings they cannot check up on and daren't take chance she right. They be back. Wizzy know best."

"I would never have thought two younguns could be so scheming," Joe said, grinning now.

The Chinese boy never even lifted his head as he countered, "Just Wizzy Glanpop, just Wizzy."

The old man nodded, looking down at the boy who had eyes for no one except his beloved Wizzy.

"Right!" Joe muttered, recovering his composure. "Better fill me in. Where in heaven's name have we got a warehouse?" He took a long puff on his pipe, then settled back into his chair. "And that bread cart ain't no distribution organization, lassie!"

The girl poked at the Chinese boy with her foot and giggled as she rolled onto her side, head propped on her elbow, looking up at the old man.

"Stir that fire, yer lazy little dumplin," she ordered, poking the boy again.

Rising to his knees, Quon complied by throwing a log onto the red embers. Rattling the poker through the bottom grate, he sent a shower of sparks into the space below. As the flames threw more light into the room, she gave Joe his answer.

"The warehouse is right behind the slaughterhouse, been empty and unused for years." Pausing, she watched the old man intently for his reaction.

Joe slowly reached for his pipe stem.

"Tom Burns is a devil ta deal with," he commented.

Lips pressed together but still showing the tiniest of smiles, Lizzie retorted, "No, he ain't. Once yer learn he's a greedy bugger, it's easy!"

Joe was silent for a long time while he marvelled at Lizzie's grasp of human nature. Finally, his next question came rushing out.

"How do we get the stuff from the dock?"

"Meat wagon."

Joe nodded, scratching at his beard and spitting into the fire, causing Quon to leap back from the sparks.

"Getting the stuff around the district, ahh . . . an without being noticed," Joe quietly muttered, more a statement to himself than to the others.

Lizzie's next answer left him with his mouth gaping open and drooling a little.

"Butcher cart, bread cart and you . . . the rag and bone man with pony and cart." Pausing to catch her breath, she continued, "An don't ask. We bought it yesterday from Mucky Frank. It's stabled up at the slaughterhouse right now."

Joe grabbed the edge of the table, as he came upright.

"For who?" he demanded.

"You!" Lizzie replied. "An it's only the first of many. Oh, look at yer, drooling again!"

Consternation and concern appeared on the girl's face as she took the cloth and wiped the old man's chin, kissing him on the nose when she finished. Standing there before him, she began to elaborate a little, her voice brimming with gentleness and her face shining with the special little smile she kept especially for her Joe.

"Don't worry, old lad, I have it all worked out. An as for Burns, the butcher, he just thinks he's smart. At the moment ah don't want ya to upset him, cos in six months we will own him!"

She paused, stroked his hair affectionately and leaning closer with her face very near to his, she quietly continued, "You just do it, lad, an let me do the thinking."

Captain Davis, master of the customs ship, *Falcon*, was a short, thickset, cheerless man, with a full black beard that hid a dark face and frowning black eyes. He sat in cap and greatcoat, listening intently as

Lizzie put the deal to him. He was a man of decision, used to making them in a hurry, with few words wasted.

"Done!" his voice cracked loudly as he pushed his chair back with a scraping sound. He motioned to Ben and Jack, who stood by the fire, that he was ready to leave, but before he could rise, the girl intervened.

"Not yet, sir."

A frown crossed the captain's face.

"Who buys the victuals for your trips?"

Davis studied her for a moment and scowled. "I do!"

"Then we want to supply your meat, salted pork and the like, again sharing the profits with you," Lizzie explained. "Makes it easier to load victuals on as we take your goods off."

If ever Captain Davis came close to smiling, it was now—the thump of his hand was enough to signify approval.

"One more thing, sir."

His head swung back to face her again.

"If we need a couple of bully boys, we can get Ben and Jack."

The bearded head nodded as he rose to go, holding out his hand to Joe to seal the deal. The door closed behind the seafarers and Joe Todd wiped the sweat from his brow.

"Gawd lass, ye've some gall!" he muttered as he slumped into the chair.

Quon Lee only had one thing to say as he stoked up the fire with more logs.

"Wizzy velly smart Glanpop, velly damn smart." Then he dashed out into the cold night air to bring in some more logs.

Lizzie and Joe sat discussing the new role he would be playing. Everyone knew who Mucky Frank was and his rag and bone cart were a common sight in the streets of this little piece of dockland.

Joe thought he would very much enjoy that sort of daily routine. He especially liked the part about meeting people and he was walking almost normally now—albeit not without some pain.

Christmas was only a few days away and there were preparations to be made—many cider and bread orders, still to be filled. Quon Lee had also secured a contract to supply meat on a regular basis to the small Chinese community, which ran the laundry service for the fancy hotels and the local gentry.

Two days before Christmas, One-Eyed Jack turned up at the dock with a message for Joe. It was a note ordering barrels of salt pork, some fresh meat, and letting them know there were two barrels of rum and three of French brandy for them. The three partners had prepared well; the whole operation was going as smooth as silk.

Tom Burns told Joe how pleased he was with the arrangement, especially his improved meat sales. The rag and bone cart became very popular as it delivered its liquid joy to the drinking fraternity and each evening, Lizzie and Quon poured over their book of accounts as the old man slept peacefully in his chair.

Chapter 6

It was the 25th day of December 1804 and preparations for Christmas were almost complete as the three partners warmed themselves in front of a blazing fire. It had been a bitterly cold day and the warm fire was especially inviting.

Joe's special dinner had been simmering all day while they completed their Christmas deliveries and they were all eager for a hot meal—their first real Christmas dinner—together. For Lizzie and Quon, it was especially exciting as this was the first time either of them had experienced any Christmas at all.

Tom Burns had seen to it that they had goose, pork and ham for the holiday meals, and Missus Johnson had done them proud, with bread and spicy fruit loaves from the bakery.

There had been Bill's deliveries to finish earlier in the day, but Joe with his pony and cart had agreed to help which made the job a whole lot easier. Even so, threading their way through a multitude of street vendors, open-fronted shops with barkers outside yelling whatever they had for sale, and the inevitable dandies acting foolish . . . along with the drunks, it was quite a day.

A dusting of snow had fallen turning everything white, and the wind had a sharp edge to it as it met them at each corner. Home was a welcome sight as Joe's flat cart slowed down as it neared the cottage, so the youngsters could jump off at the garden gate. Joe clucked at his pony and off they trotted up the lane toward the warehouse, behind the butcher's slaughter yard.

Shortly after, a huge log fire greeted Joe as he entered the cottage.

Now, hungry and ready for the meal, the unlikely trio sat around the table to eat Christmas dinner.

In between mouthfuls, Lizzie, always the leader, tapped the table for attention.

"Gentlemen," she said, addressing her two companions, "we have become a business now and we must have a name—any suggestions?" The room became quiet and her fingertips rested quietly on the tabletop. "All right . . . how about TLS?"

"What's TLS mean?" Joe asked, scratching his head.

"Todd, Lee and Short," the girl answered quickly, A thoughtful look appeared on her face and, with a faint smile on her lips, she muttered, "Maybe it means together for life for sure!"

"'Am for Wizzy all time," pronounced Quon.

She shook her head at the Chinese boy's ranting.

"There ain't no doubt of that lad. Ah think ye'd kill if anybody hurt your Lizzie, wouldn't yer?" Joe said happily.

Quon puffed out his chest.

"Yes!" he said, beaming with pride.

It was easy to see he meant it too.

In the weeks and months that quickly passed, it was soon springtime and winter was at last behind them. One day in April, Lizzie called to see Abe Kratze, the tailor. Old Mister Kratze was always pleased to see his favourite pupil, especially when she brought him fruit bread as a gift. They sat talking and sipped peppermint tea in the back corner.

"How can I be of assistance to you, my dear?" the old man asked through blackened teeth, studying the girl who, he now noticed, was beginning to grow quite tall.

She pondered the question for awhile before answering.

"I want you to find out how much we can buy the slaughterhouse for, who from, and teach me how ta do it."

Abe was flabbergasted.

"Yer mean just Joe's cottage don't yer luv?"

She looked at him with her bright, blue sparkling eyes. Slowly, she shook her head and smiled.

"No, I mean the whole lot, and the one acre behind the cattle buildings."

Pulling a stained kerchief out of his pocket with a bony hand, he wiped the flush of sweat from his brow. When he spoke, his voice croaked almost inaudibly.

"All of it!" His face had turned white as a ghost.

"Yes," she replied, "all of it!" Rising, she walked quickly toward the door shouting over her shoulder. "Quickly, my dear man. I shall expect to hear from yer soon." And she was gone.

Abe Kratze felt like he had just been hit with a sledgehammer. He was an old businessperson having had many stressful experiences during his life, but at this moment he felt he had just been outdone by this girl; and what was even worse, he felt obliged to do all she had asked of him.

Joe was working well at his rag and bone business. He had now acquired three carts with ponies and two other old sailors worked for him. Both had been injured in sea battles, so they were grateful for the work and loyal as the day was long. Captain Davis was happy with the arrangements but was having difficulty keeping Lizzie's orders filled with illicit liquor.

Quon and his Wizzy pushed their bread cart through the streets every day, keeping a watchful eye on their ever-growing empire. A tiny terrier dog had attached itself to the children, turning up every day to trot alongside their cart, accepting tidbits from people along the way.

No matter how they tried to get rid of the dog, it just turned up again, until finally they gave in, and took it home with them . . . like the men, it idolized Lizzie, following her everywhere.

Two weeks passed, until one day when delivering his bread, Abe Kratze handed her a note. That night, instead of going straight home from work, she called around at the tailor's shop, accompanied by Quon and the dog. A tap on the door brought the tailor scurrying to open it for them.

Quickly closing and locking it, he shuffled off into his back corner with the little group close behind. Lizzie sat facing the old man who clasped his bony hands together so hard his knuckles showed pure white. Gently, she reached over and took his hands in her own tiny pair.

"Tell me what's wrong, old lad?" she urged.

"It's the land, my girl. No chance, no chance at all," he muttered with a sad face. "I tried lass . . . I tried."

Lizzie smiled, her eyes soft and gentle.

"But who owns it, luv?"

"Oh, that were the easy part. It's owned by the church and they also run a couple of cargo ships to France."

The girl sat silent for a while.

"And what might their names be?"

Old Abe relaxed enough to have a chuckle as he began to explain.

"Aye lass, the names are *Minister* and *Bishop*. Great imaginations they have, them folk."

From his position, standing behind her chair, Quon's hand gently squeezed the girl's shoulder. Rising, she thanked the tailor for his efforts and bade him goodnight.

Back on the street, they heard the door lock behind them. Holding hands, they slowly walked home in silence.

"Where the hell have yer bin?" Joe asked. "Av bin worried sick ye'd met some harm." Feeding them quickly without noticing their silence, he announced that he had some work to do up at the stable but would be back in an hour.

During the washing up after supper, Quon deliberately splashed Lizzie. She splashed him back and the fight was on. When Joe walked in the door shortly after, they were both sitting on the floor, howling with laughter and wet through.

"What the 'ell!" he said, grinning.

"We wash for today, Glanpop, then we wash for tomollow," Quon quipped, causing even Joe to laugh.

"Is the custom boat in, lad?" Lizzie asked Joe, when they had calmed down and were sitting in front of the fire to dry.

"Comes in at noon," he replied, poking the fire into a glow, before adding a new log. "Why, luv?" a puzzled expression crossing his face.

"Gotta talk to Captain Davis an Ben Thorn after work."

Joe looked surprised, but offered to tell him when he was down at the dock.

"Aye, yer can do that," she said, winking at the Chinese boy.

Next morning, the youngsters were in a happy mood as they skipped off down the road.

Quon kept singing, "Wizzy is a tinkin, Wizzy is a tinkin."

When they arrived at the Johnson bakery, she turned to him with a stern look. "If yer don't shut yer trap, 'am goin ta thump yer!"

Bill Johnson heard the voices and looked up from his bread-making to see the strange goings on between his two employees. He was most concerned until he saw them grab each other and, giggling like mad, they rolled around on the floor—even their little dog joined in.

Turning up at the docks before daylight ended, Ben Thorn noticed them straight away from his position by the gangplank and he waved them aboard.

"Follow me," he said, stepping onto the deck and escorting them to the captain's cabin.

Captain Davis sat scowling at his desk as all three entered. Motioning to the chairs, Lizzie sat down but Quon stood behind her as he usually did . . . Ben remained standing by the door.

"Well?" Davis grunted, sourly letting his gaze pass over the youngsters.

"Do yer know the two ships, *Minister* and *Bishop*?" the girl asked.

Davis nodded, the black eyes showing no emotion at all.

"Well, is it possible to arrest one of those vessels, confiscate some illegal goods, then turn it loose while you consider what you will do about it?"

The captain thought deeply before answering.

"What's it worth?" he demanded bluntly.

"Twenty golden sovereigns!" she snapped back.

"Done!" Davis growled, his flat hand hitting the desktop with a mighty thud.

"When I have the arrest papers in my hand, I pay," Lizzie said, sweetly.

Ben Thorn helped them back onto the dock. He was beginning to have a lot of respect for this young girl. The grasp she had on a situation and the way she manoeuvred things into place was almost frightening. Heaven help the owners of those vessels when she had those papers in her hand, he thought.

The iron bar whizzed by their heads and rattled on the cobbles, narrowly missing the youngsters as they jumped back in surprise. The little terrier turned tail and ran away. Four dockland roughs stepped out from the dark alleyway, each one swinging a weapon.

"Now what av we 'ere?" the biggest and dirtiest of the rogues asked, slobbering through blackened teeth.

Lizzie squared her shoulders and stepped boldly forward to meet the scoundrels.

"You big, dirty louts had better not be tamperin with us," she spat out venomously.

"Oh, and why not, me uppity little madam?" one of the footpads inquired mockingly, shuffling closer.

"Because yer'll be sorry, if ya do," the girl snapped, without flinching.

Tiny feet sounded and the little dog appeared taking his place between Lizzie and the danger, yapping his head off.

One of the rogues swung his club at the dog, but the terrier easily jumped out of the way.

"Is that dog vicious?" the first robber asked doubtfully.

"No . . . but we are!" a new voice announced, as Ben Thorn, One-Eyed Jack and a few more sailors, stepped out of the darkness.

It was a short fight, full of grunts, groans and cursing but the rogues being no match for the sea-hardened mariners, were soon put to flight.

"Good little dog that is, came back and got us damn quick, I'd say," Ben Thorn muttered appreciatively, stooping to give the terrier a pat.

"An I thought he'd run off ta hide," Lizzie chuckled.

"Do yer want a couple of the boys to see yer home, lass?" Ben asked.

"Aye they can, but only if they keep out of sight."

Ben shook his head knowingly.

"Off yer go then, ye'll be safe now."

"Saw the captain, did yer?" Joe asked, attempting to gain an explanation for their tardiness when they arrived at the cottage.

"That we did, luv," she quipped innocently, shooting a glance at Quon as they sat down to eat.

"Anything important?" Joe inquired from the comfort of his chair.

"Just a little thing ah needed, lad," Lizzie answered, feeling the Chinese boy's foot kick her knee under the table, but taking no notice.

The old man filled his pipe, stuffing it tight with a stout finger end before lighting the tobacco. As the blue smoke curled upwards, he turned his attention to Quon.

"An what have ye ta say for yerself, lad?" he inquired.

The Chinese boy laid down his fork, folded his hands together, and announced, "Wizzy damn smart, my Wizzy is."

Joe laughed as he muttered, "Some day that little bugger will say something else, an shock the life outa me!"

Chapter 7

In the days that followed, Joe bought a new pony and cart from an old vendor who used to boil and sell tripe to the poor. Although, after some discussion, the trio decided they did not want to get into the tripe business. They had discovered a more lucrative operation with the rag and bone carts that delivered liquor, cider and meat from the slaughterhouse.

Joe already had a man for that job and he now employed a stable man to look after his ponies. They were all battle-scarred ex-sailors, fiercely loyal to the old man and Lizzie. Space in the building behind the Burns slaughterhouse was getting awful tight, Joe had commented, giving young Lizzie a gentle nudge to find larger premises.

One of the local ships ravaged in a sea battle off the coast of France barely managed to limp home with a reduced crew and many wounded aboard. Old Joe and his team of ex-sailors were the first on the dock, offering what help they could to the grieving widows and vowing to employ every one of the maimed. As Quon was apt to say, 'Good man Glanpop is, velly good.'

Three weeks passed when a message arrived from the customs ship for Joe. It was delivered by Ben Thorn, the ship's first mate, and informed them that there were goods to be collected and supplies needed. He had a list from Captain Davis with a note that said he needed to see Lizzie.

After the youngsters finished work at the bakery, Joe was waiting with his pony and cart to drive them down to the ship. Ben, who detailed one of the men to show Joe the goods, immediately showed them aboard then whispered to the girl that the captain was in his cabin.

Knocking gently on the cabin door, she waited for the gruff voice to bid her enter.

Once inside Lizzie and Quon took up the same positions as their last visit, while the captain glowered at them.

It was some time before he spoke.

"I have it! " he snapped, reaching for a paper from the side of his desk and holding it between his thumb and first finger.

The girl never moved a muscle though she strained inwardly.

"Tell me again, what's it for?" he asked, rising and pacing the floor.

Lizzie's eyebrows flicked in annoyance and Quon Lee tightened his fingers on her shoulder as a warning.

"I never said what I wanted it for," she snapped. "Do I question yer, sir?" She reached into her purse, brought out a handful of golden guineas and counted out twenty. She placed them neatly on the desk and held out her hand. "We have a deal, captain."

He strutted around his cabin menacingly, then suddenly stopped and handed her the paper. She read it immediately, nodding her approval. When she looked up, he was standing in the darkest corner glowering at her again. Lizzie smiled sweetly, bade him a good evening, and walked out of the cabin with Quon Lee close behind.

Joe was sitting on his cart patiently waiting as they came down the gangplank. He was smoking his pipe and talking quietly to the sailors, who were quick to give the youngsters a hand onto the cart. Shaking the reins, the old man soon had them trotting toward home, humming an old sea shanty in time to the clip clop of hooves.

After supper they were in a talkative mood, so Lizzie used the opportunity to ask a few questions.

"Ever bumped into the minister, Joe?" she began.

"Just once, that were enough," he replied, a puff of smoke rising to the ceiling.

"Didn't like him, eh?"

This time Joe bit hard. He removed the pipe quite deliberately before answering.

"He wanted rum for himself an rags for the poor, but he didn't want ter pay a penny piece . . . said it would do me soul good."

The girl leaned eagerly toward him to hear the rest.

"So ah asked him for his rags an bones," he continued with a chuckle, "an the unholy bugger told me ah were an uncouth excuse for a man, an stormed off!"

They all laughed heartily at the old man's outburst. His feelings certainly would not be hurt when Lizzie dealt her blow to the church. She tucked the captain's paper away safely, promising herself to deal with it very soon.

Sunday afternoon was sunny and warm after two days of rain. People were happy to be outside again and were milling about the streets as Lizzie and Quon walked to Abe's.

A carriage stood outside the shop with the driver holding the heads of two fine, light horses. From inside, giggling girls could be heard as the two young street traders peered in the window. Lizzie gasped. They were the very same girls from whom she had stolen the coat, on her first day of freedom that seemed so long ago.

Grabbing the Chinese boy roughly, she whispered, "Run back home an bring me the blue coat with the fur collar, hangin by the back door."

Quon, as usual questioning nothing, took off at full speed. The terrier followed for about a block before coming back to sit at Lizzie's feet. But she could not keep still. Pacing up and down the cobbles, she muttered to herself. As Quon came tearing down the road, she ran to meet him.

"Throw it into that carriage when I distract the driver for a minute," she urged the boy.

A not-too-accidental fall caused the driver to look her way, as Quon completed his mission . . . not a moment too soon.

Out of the tailor shop came the three squealing girls followed by the big, well-dressed man, she also recognized from her earlier encounter at the coaching house. They spilled into the coach making such a noise that once the door slammed shut the silence was deafening. Suddenly, the carriage door burst open again, as the man stepped out gingerly holding the coat out in front of him.

"Here girl," he said, addressing Lizzie. "Take this and be warm," he said, throwing the coat at her.

The carriage disappeared down the street and Lizzie laughed until tears ran down her cheeks. She hugged the coat to her little body as if it were a long lost friend.

"Wizzy gone clazy, me tinks," Quon muttered as they entered the shop.

"'Am ready," she told Abe, walking toward the back of the shop.

The old tailor, looking a bit perplexed, followed them.

"Ready for what lass?" he asked, standing by the table.

"To buy that property the church owns," she announced.

"But the minister said they wouldn't sell. Ah told yer that."

Lizzie looked at him sweetly and winked.

"They will now," she said, producing the captain's paper and handing it to him.

Abe adjusted his glasses and sat down to scan the paper, his head jerking up and down.

"They'll give anything ta keep this quiet," he said in a hushed voice. "How in heaven's name did you get it?"

But there was no answer forthcoming from the girl . . . only a grin.

"What was the going price three weeks ago, sir?" Lizzie asked slowly.

"Oh, I think in the region of three hundred and fifty, with the back acre," he said calmly, his eyes watching every move the girl made.

"Do they own more in that area?" she inquired curiously.

Abe thought for a moment then producing a piece of tailor's chalk, he sketched the area out and proceeded to mark several adjoining properties.

Both Lizzie and Quon Lee watched carefully, noting each area Abe marked.

Finally, Lizzie sat back, her eyes narrowing, "I will trade the deeds of every piece of that property ye've marked, for the note."

"That's highway robbery lass!" he gasped, wiping sweat from his forehead.

And you can tell the minister, I shall get just as much pleasure if he says no . . . when I present this paper to the military."

"Is there no point you will bend, girl?"

"None," she said, emphatically. "That's my one and only offer. Keep our names out of it, do all the paperwork, and there's two guineas in it for you." She folded the paper, slipped it into her shirt, wished the tailor a good afternoon and calmly walked out into the street.

Air from the Thames had a smell distinctly its own, and the high masts of sailing ships at anchor by the docks, always made it a wondrous place to watch sailors busy at work mending rigging and sails.

Dock workers could be seen busily loading barrels or bales of wool and rags, and other exotic cargo. Even cattle, horses, and sheep were being stowed aboard ships, en route to far off destinations.

Walking through dockland, observing everything with interest, Lizzie suddenly stopped.

"Can you remember the drawing old Abe made for us on the table?"

Her companion was about to throw another stick for the dog to chase, when he stopped. He turned around to face her, his brow furrowed in thought.

"Evly damn line," he said softly.

No more conversation passed between them until they arrived home. There in the garden, Joe was burning last year's garden rubbish, getting the area cleared for his new garden—the first since his accident.

Joining him in the warmth of the bonfire, Lizzie picked up a piece of charcoal and challenged Quon to do a copy of Abe's drawing on the outhouse door.

The boy walked over to the door and began drawing. Joe put down his rake and ambled over to watch.

"There," Quon said a few minutes later, standing back to admire his work.

"Oh no, me boy," she giggled, "what about the crosses?"

Joe gave them an inquiring look but the boy scratched his head and continued his drawing. Lizzie smiled as he drew in the adjoining properties putting the crosses in all the appropriate places. Finally, adding his signature, Quon Lee turned to the watchers, a pleased smile on his young face.

"That's better," Lizzie agreed enthusiastically, studying it intently. Picking up a long twig, she used it to point to the first cross. "Now it's your turn, me lad," she said, addressing Joe who looked at the drawing with a confused expression.

"I have no idea what it is," he confessed.

Lizzie laughed happily as the Chinese boy proceeded to explain.

"It's the plopelty, Glanpop," Quon offered, giggling at the look on Joe Todd's face.

The old mariner wrinkled his nose, scratched on his beard and asked, "What in heaven's name is plopelty?"

Lizzie stopped laughing long enough to explain, "He means property, this property," she said pointing to the drawing.

Quon nodded vigorously.

"Can yer see it yet, sonny?" Lizzie teased the old man, who pretended to take a swipe at her.

"Ah think ah can, but what are the crosses?" he asked, still bewildered.

"They are smaller places up that far side, adjoining this piece," Lizzie said, again pointing with her stick. "What we want to know is, who lives there, and do yer know 'em?"

Joe slowly walked up to the door and touched the black charcoal lines with outstretched fingers. "This," he said, tracing the outline of the shop and house on the corner of Slaughter Lane and Bent Street, "is Widow Riley's old place—bin empty for years. An that," he said, warming to the task now, "are a couple of broken down old cottages that need pulling down. Next is a row of four . . . ah think some of the slaughter men live there."

Stopping to fill his pipe, Joe studied the picture and began muttering again. "Tom Burns lives in't next one, it's a nice place folks say, about half acre ah'd guess." Picking up a twig, he prodded the brightly burning embers until the end caught on fire. He set fire to the tobacco in his pipe and sucked deeply on the stem. "That answer all yer questions, missy?" He addressed the girl with a look of satisfaction, knowing that his knowledge of the area shouldn't come as any surprise to Lizzie.

Lizzie had that glint in her eye that said there was devilment afoot. Slowly, she moved toward old Joe like a tiger ready to pounce.

"Ah feel like givin you a great big kiss!" she announced.

The old mariner started to retreat but it was too late. She jumped forward, threw her arms around his neck and planted a big, smacking kiss on his cheek.

"Stop that slobbering," he shouted, feigning anger and making a feeble attempt to defend himself. "Yer almost a woman now. Damnit, behave yerself!"

Lizzie let him go and stood back, a wide grin lighting up her lovely face.

Chapter 8

Almost a week went by before Abe Kratze saw the youngsters again.

"Need ta see yer lass," he hissed softly, without turning his head or slowing his stride, as they passed each other going in opposite directions.

She heard him, but showed no outward sign, being more concerned with the two well-dressed men in bowler hats and half capes, obviously following the tailor.

On their way back to the bakery that evening, they took a different route, one that took them past Abe's shop. Sure enough, there were the two men again, watching from the corner. The youngsters passed by showing no special interest, returning the cart to Bill Johnson's yard. Quickly completing their business, they walked out into the alleyway.

"Don't know what's goin on, lad," she said to Quon with a frown, "but we don't want them two ta see us visit Mister Kratze."

All the way home, they pondered the problem.

They ate in silence until Joe, in frustration, demanded, "Tell me!"

The youngsters looked at each other in anticipation.

"We need two gents distracted for half an hour," Lizzie blurted out.

"Where are they?" he asked.

"Corner of Mast, looking down Water Lane," Lizzie told him, then went on to describe the men to Joe.

"What's old Abe Kratze bin doing?" Joe wanted to know, casting his eye on the girl.

Her gaze met his as she put her hands up, palms facing the mariner, indicating she didn't want to answer any questions.

Joe stood up, walked over to the door and turned back to them. "Give me half an hour, then make yer move. Ah'll keep 'em away for an hour," he said quite seriously, as he went out the door.

Lizzie collected the paper the captain had given her and slipped four golden guineas into her purse.

"You be the timekeeper, dumplin," she said to Quon Lee, smiling.

"We go see," the Chinese boy giggled. "See how Glanpop make tings happen."

She smiled, nodding in agreement, as they slowly walked down the garden path.

Making their way down Pump Street to a back alleyway that led to a carpenter's yard and the backs of some shops, they climbed onto the low roof of a carpenter's workshop and hid behind the roof-sign. It had a clear view of the corner and the two men were plainly visible.

Soon they heard dogs barking and vicious snarling as down the street came a gypsy with four or five fighting dogs on long rope leads. Cats could be heard screaming as they made haste to get out of the way.

The two men watching the tailor's shop stepped out of a doorway into the streetlight, nervously looking up the street.

As the gypsy and his dogs approached, they suddenly crossed the street and headed directly toward the two men, who quickly moved off down Mast Lane with the dogs following a short distance behind.

"Now we go," Lizzie whispered.

Scrambling off the roof and racing around to the tailor's shop, they banged on the door. A curtain moved slightly, the lock clicked open, and they were soon safely inside.

"Give it to me quickly, Abe, yer being watched," Lizzie said, excitedly,

The tailor, with sweating hands, produced a roll of deeds and Lizzie laid her arrest papers on the table.

"The deal's done, but they'll kill yer if they find out who you are. That's what those men are watching for."

The girls laugh was cold.

"We can play rough too, Mister Kratze, here's four guineas for yer trouble."

Scooping up the gold coins with a bony hand, the tailor warned, "Go, but be damned careful."

Creeping out of Abe's door and into the street, they heard the dogs barking some distance away. They wasted no time, running home as fast as their legs would carry them. The garden gate clanged behind them and they hit the door with a thump, spilling into the room red-faced and out of breathe.

"Steady on now," Joe said, peering out of the dull light. "Nobody's chasing yer,"

Quon turned and frowned, a puzzled look on his face.

"How you know that Glanpop?" the boy asked.

"It's like this," the old man said. "Tonight I had you watched all the way, just for me own piece of mind."

Lizzie quickly slipped off her coat and heaped more fuel onto the fire. She hoisted her dress and stood warming her rear-end on the crackling flames.

"We saw no one," she murmured.

"Weren't supposed ta, were yer?" he asked, tapping his pipe on the iron fireplace.

Quon appeared satisfied, but Lizzie was obviously puzzled.

"Let's just take a look at what happened tonight, dumplin," she addressed the boy. "We saw one gypsy and his dogs." The boy looked perplexed, but said nothing as she carried on. "Gypsies are never alone, always two of 'em or more, an we didn't see the others did we?" Her question caused Quon to slowly shake his head. "That old bugger's right, yer know, them gypsies were watchin us!"

Joe suddenly burst out laughing.

"Yer got it absolutely right, lass. Just my way of looking out for yer." The old man let out a happy chuckle as Lizzie moved closer and gave him an affectionate hug,

Turning her attention to the roll of documents on the table, she carefully smoothed them flat and began reading.

"What yer got there, lass?" he asked, observing from his chair.

"These, my lad, are the foundation stones."

The Chinese boy at her elbow gave a tiny chuckle, his finger following the writing across the page.

Joe reached for a walking stick hung on the back of his chair. Grasping it firmly, he began poking at her ribs. Giggling, she hopped out of reach and began to tell him about the property. Without interrupting, he listened carefully until she had finished.

"We won't be able ta do a thing until we have something to stop 'em moving against us, yer know," he said, quietly.

A frown crossed the girl's face as she considered his statement.

Quon, who hardly ever said anything, suddenly blurted out, "Do again Wizzy, hold damn big rope over dem."

The smile on the girl's face showed both her approval and her amusement at Quon's easy solution.

"They won't be expecting ta be got at a second time," she bubbled excitedly.

During the week that followed, Abe Kratze delivered the arrest papers to the minister who looked at the tailor with increasing suspicion and contempt. Knowing he couldn't threaten Abe with anything religious, on account of his race, the minister resorted to his natural instincts, advising the old man to walk carefully, lest he have an accident.

Nothing raises the hackles of a Jew like being threatened and Abe quickly voiced his loud disapproval.

"May your God look on you with disfavour and heap on you the trouble so deserved," he announced tersely.

The minister was momentarily taken aback by the old man's outburst and his dark, gloomy exterior became distinctly blacker.

"Be gone . . . and I hope never to cast eyes on you again," were his parting words at the back of Abe Kratze as he disappeared through the door.

Things were going along quite smoothly when, one evening, Joe announced, "We have a big delivery tomorrow. Captain Davis is back in port."

"Tell him I'll drop in to see him after work, Joe."

Joe's head swung around quickly.

"Why?"

"Oh, there's a couple of things I need ta tell him, that's all," she answered casually.

Later that day, the youngsters arrived at the docks with a fresh smelling bag of breads and an apple pie and were quickly shown aboard. Ben pointed upward to the poop deck. There, at the rail standing quite still, staring out at nothing in particular was Captain Davis. Handing the bag of baking to the sailor, the youngsters climbed the stairs.

Whilst waiting for Davis to acknowledge their presence, they enjoyed the view from their vantage point high on the poop deck. They could see scores of ships all along the dock each tied up near a large warehouse from which men were loading and unloading various interesting looking cargo. They could also see down the great river and noticed some very glorious looking buildings and churches . . . it was a view they had never seen before and the youngsters were spellbound. When he turned toward them, the captain's face was a mask of rage.

"Those sanctimonious damn pirates!" he snarled. Letting his head drop forward, he began to march back and forth across the deck. He came to a halt directly in front of Lizzie and Quon. "What brings you two here?" his voice cracked angrily.

"We need you to do the same job again, but this time on the sister ship."

The captain threw up his arms and continued marching around the deck shouting into the wind, "I want to kill those religious monsters, the power peddling dogs." Then he reverted to his head down marching, occasionally screaming swear words at the sky.

Lizzie studied the situation calmly before stepping out in front of the irate captain. He raised his arm as if to strike her, but Quon Lee sprang into action. In a flash, he was between Davis and the girl, hands up and ready to fight.

The look on Captain Davis' face slowly changed until he was actually smiling.

"You little devil," he said in surprise and admiration. "I wish I had a friend like you!"

"Move over, dumplin," Lizzie said, nudging the Chinese boy's shoulder. Looking the captain square in the eye she declared, "You have a friend like that . . . me!"

A smile barely touched the mariner's face.

"Listen to me," she continued, "if we can catch that vessel loaded to the hilt, we will have two birds at once."

Davis cocked his head on one side, giving her his complete attention.

"How so?" he grunted.

"When we have the arrest papers, they daren't touch us until they get 'em back an destroy them . . . and we have all their untaxed goods."

The Captain threw back his head and laughed.

"Aye, an what's to stop 'em killing us, lass?"

The girl shook her head in frustration, sending her long curls flying about her face.

"If they did, the paper would come to light, an they won't complain to anybody, for the same reason."

Davis stroked his beard, searching his thoughts for a flaw in the plan.

"Goddamn it girl, me thinks yer right. We'll do it!"

Quon Lee headed for the stairs until Lizzie's hand stopped him.

"One other thing, captain," she continued in a quiet tone.

His eyes invited her to carry on.

"I do all the negotiating and hold the paper."

His meaty hand suddenly jumped out of his pocket to clutch her shoulder.

"Wouldn't have it any other way, lass," he rasped.

Down on the main deck, Ben Thorn, sitting astride a barrel, had renewed his friendship with their little dog. Lifting his head to smile at Lizzie as they descended the gangplank, he commented, "Never heard anybody make him laugh before or treat him the way you do, lass."

Quon Lee grinned, "Wizzy knows best damn stuff."

Ben cocked his head at Lizzie and asked what the boy had said, but he received no answer.

Chapter 9

Walking home, with the dog jumping and playing in front of them, was a pleasant interlude after the stress of the meeting with the captain. Quon found a stick and soon they were laughing happily at the little dog's silly antics.

Lizzie explained to her friend and partner that the deal they had made tonight was the best yet. It put them firmly in control. It had also made Captain Davis into an ally, one who could be very useful.

Joe was proving a master at organization and the number of old seamen he knew was never ending, especially the ones who limped or had a patch over one eye. One of them, Lefty, the one-armed man, was a messenger. He was always smiling although his missing arm must have been a terrible handicap.

A few days had passed, when Joe mentioned that the custom ship had put to sea and the minister's men were still watching Abe Kratze.

"How'd yer know who they are?" the girl asked.

"Oh, I ask around my customers. One of 'em happens to be the gravedigger at the church."

Lizzie's eyes flickered, showing a little interest.

"Bet he could tell some tales," she commented ruefully.

"Aye, an often does," Joe muttered, watching the girl screw up her nose.

"About graves? What's ta tell about graves?" Lizzie teased, giving him her doubting look.

"Not graves. He sees most of what goes on, an who comes an goes." The old man was getting annoyed, not sensing she was funning him until he spotted the twinkle in her eyes.

"An you had better listen," she warned. "Cos yer never know when that sort of information can do us some good."

Several weeks passed and although the three partners had speculated on uses for Widow Riley's old shop, Joe had definite plans for the two blocks of refurbished cottages. Tom Burns' slaughterhouse had increased its business so much, due to the efforts of Joe and the youngsters, that he decided to turn over all the meat deliveries to Joe and his team of ex-mariners.

Lizzie and Quon expressed their approval, urging the old man to take it a bit easier at work. Joe poo poo'd the youngsters, saying he never felt as well in his life.

A few days later, Jack Shaw, the cider brewer, had a disaster when one of his cider tanks gave way. Nothing could be done to save the brew, but Joe and the ship's carpenters in his team, quickly repaired the damage, one of the men being a cooper by trade. Joe soon displayed his newfound business acumen by negotiating the cider brewers' deliveries and the purchase of a stable of heavy horses and drays.

Lizzie and Quon Lee were both thrilled and amazed. The three of them discussed all possibilities, until several days later, they decided to send Joe back to negotiate a buyout figure with Jack Shaw. An elated Joe marched up the garden path one evening to inform the grinning pair that the deal was done. Naturally, they wanted the details as quickly as possible, so they listened in complete silence as Joe related the whole story.

"The price was good compared to the profit margin," Lizzie commented when Joe was finished, and Quon Lee pointed out that the building was a bit on the cheap side. But the old man passed it over by explaining it was in need of repairs.

Lizzie particularly liked the finances—half now and the other half in one year with Jack to stay the full year teaching them the business.

"I like that last bit," she said, giving the old man a huge bear hug. "Now ye'll have ta become an office man and organize from behind a desk."

Joe puffed himself up with an important air, filling his pipe as he savoured the thoughts running through his head. Suddenly, a cloud seemed to settle over him as he sagged a little at the shoulders.

"Now, what's yer problem?" Lizzie demanded, watching him closely.

"But ah can neither read nor write very good lass," he mumbled in dismay, his face a mask of disappointment.

"Yer daft old brush, you can learn just like I did."

The sad expression didn't change on Joe's whiskered face.

"It's a bit late lass, 'am past fifty year old."

Lizzie was mad now and Quon leapt out of her way as she rounded on the old man.

"You damn cry baby. Stop feeling sorry for yerself an get on with it." She paused, but only for a moment, before starting into him again. "We beat yer accident and yer limp . . . the minister, too. An we even bested Captain Davis . . . an if yer think reading and writing will beat us, yer wrong. So start practising right now!"

Joe flinched from the onslaught. Squaring his shoulders, he muttered more to himself than anyone, "Bossy little bitch." Then, with a smile on his lips, he held out his arms and she jumped into them.

Quon Lee shook his head and shuddered.

"Wizzy mad, me run damn fast," he exclaimed, causing a roar of laughter from his partners.

Chapter 10

The bread route finished for the day, the youngsters spent some time at the Johnson bakery, eating and chattering to the proprietors before setting off for the docks. Walking along Mast Lane, they noticed two strangers, men who were not from the area, this being evident by the way they dressed and the shiny boots they wore.

Lizzie nudged the boy, discreetly pointing at the boots. Quon stopped as he walked close to the men and released a handful of coloured pebbles. One of the men looked down as the shiny pebbles rattled on the cobblestones.

The Chinese boy gasped and fell to his knees, fingers scrambling after his treasured stones. The girl watched, puzzled by her friend's antics. Finding the pebbles, after crawling around the feet of the laughing men, Quon ran and joined Lizzie who took him by the hand. Together they trotted off down Water Lane to the docks.

Out of sight of the men, she spun the Chinese boy around, a frown on her face.

"Well!" she demanded.

"Boots Wizzy, boots," he answered, grinning.

"What about 'em?" she asked, looking down at her own feet.

Quon giggled, then began to explain.

"All bootmakers have mark, and like laundry, customer have number."

Lizzie listened intently, her interest now sparked.

"Go on," she whispered.

"Damn marks on pull tab behind heel, had to get down on floor to look."

The girl was astounded and her mouth dropped open in surprise.

"Did yer see it?" she asked urgently.

Quon Lee flashed a smile.

"A triangle with a 'q' inside it and the numbers '57'."

Lizzie nodded and began walking toward the docks again, squeezing her lips together in deep thought.

The boy trotted alongside, re-assuring her, "No tink so hard, Wizzy. Me find out, you wait at ship," and off he ran. The little terrier watched him go and obviously wondered why.

At the custom vessel, she was greeted warmly by Ben Thorn, and One-Eyed Jack waved a welcome from the far side of the deck.

"He's waiting in his cabin, lass," the big mariner informed her happily.

She noted a change in attitude but kept her wits about her, twisting her body under the stairway to knock on the captain's door.

"Come right in, missy," the voice boomed out as she opened the latch and there behind the great oak desk was a smiling Captain Davis.

Lizzie stopped in mid-stride, a little unsure how to deal with this turn of events. Waving her into her usual seat, he beamed down at her, chuckling at the surprised look on her face.

"Don't look like that, lass, we had a wonderful voyage. Caught the bastards red-handed!"

The girl began to smile as she remembered all the cargo on deck.

"But did yer get that paper?" she asked hurriedly.

"Aye, the arrest papers are here," he said, opening a drawer, removing some papers and slowly sliding them onto the desk. "But we got much more than that."

Lizzie's eyes narrowed.

"What?" she whispered.

Captain Davis was grinning from ear to ear as he lifted himself from the chair, resting his hands on top of the desk as he leaned toward her.

"We caught the damned bishop aboard a vessel leaving the enemy shores," he hissed.

The girl's frown disappeared and she began to laugh.

"They never expected you'd do it again!" Jumping to her feet excitedly, she exclaimed, "We got 'em cold, we got 'em now!" Reaching over for the papers, she set them straight, then tucked them away inside her shirt.

"They were so scared, they would have made me into a saint if that's what I had wanted." He stopped for a minute sitting down abruptly and fixed his eyes on the girl. Slowly and deliberately, he continued, "You were right, lass, in every detail, but you had me worried with the sheer audacity of your plan."

Later, they talked of many general things until Quon Lee could be heard running across the deck and Lizzie got up to go.

"Can I leave you with a thought, Captain Davis?" she asked, opening the door for her friend to enter.

"That you can, lass."

"Would you like to start your own shipping company with us as your partners?"

Davis grabbed the end of his beard and giving it a tug, replied, "Every mariner's dream . . . but alas, only a dream."

A little smile found its way onto the girl's face. "No taint, it's easy right now."

It was now the captain's turn to look surprised as he fumbled to find words. Lizzie levelled her eyes on Captain David, her mind working furiously.

"Fifty," she said, through clenched teeth, still staring hard.

"Done," Davis snapped holding out his hand to shake and seal the deal. "Now tell me how," he grunted, sitting back down behind his desk.

"Well," said the girl, "you told me we are at war again with France and Spain."

The captain looked puzzled.

"Aye, lass, that we are."

"Would it not be correct to say that you know the French ports like the back of yer hand?"

He nodded slowly.

"Could you sneak into one of those ports and steal one or two vessels?" she asked playfully.

The captain's eyes narrowed.

"One, maybe, if we were lucky."

Lizzie burst out laughing.

"I bet you could steal 'em all!"

Davis sat bolt upright, listening intently with screwed-up eyes.

"We have the sailors, all you need is a diversion . . . an innocent-looking diversion," Lizzie said, thoughtfully.

It was obvious from the expression on Captain Davis' face that he was giving the idea some deep thought too.

Finally, he rose from his chair. Shaking his head and mumbling to himself, he slowly made his way toward the door with the youngsters following.

"Leave me with a thought, you goddamn little pirate—more like a whole head full of thoughts!"

Chapter 11

The late evening sun made it a pleasant walk along the docks. Lizzie teased and poked Quon Lee, who giggled merrily. They casually wandered by big sailing schooners and little barks all quiet now as sailors and dockmen had ended their work for the day.

Up ahead they noticed the two men were still watching the tailor's shop, which reminded her of Quon Lee's mission to find out about the boots.

"Did you find out anything about those boots, dumplin?" she asked quietly, pulling him toward her.

As their young bodies bumped together, he giggled, "Did some."

Lizzie glanced sharply at the boy. They turned to run along an alleyway that led to the back of the tailor's shop. Although there was no back door to Abe's shop, there were entrances to other businesses and they saw a couple of men working on their nets and small boats, but nobody took any notice of them.

"Now tell me . . .," she demanded as she settled down on a stack of broken wheels awaiting repairs.

Quon sat on a block of wood at her feet and began his explanation. "The 'q' in triangle mean 'Mason,' the high-class bootmaker in

Shambles Way . . . and Number 57 is Charles Wentworth, an army officer attached to Accles . . . ee . . . astic Court of Bishop.

As she heard this news, Lizzie began to laugh. She laughed so hard she fell off her perch and almost landed on top of the startled boy. He quickly came to his feet and turned to face a now upright Lizzie who was trying hard to compose herself.

"Wizzy, what's wong?" he asked in a concerned voice.

"It's nothin dumplin," she gasped. "It's the Ecclesiastical Court of the Bishop of London . . . half an hour ago Captain Davis told me we have the bishop over a barrel, an that's the boss man of the men doin the watchin."

A loud bang over in the far corner of the alleyway took everyone's attention. Suddenly, from a second-floor window black with dirt and soot, appeared a head and the squeaky sound of Abe's voice called to them.

Lizzie quickly made some signs with her hands and the old man immediately dropped a basket tied on the end of a thin rope. The girl placed the paper Captain Davis had given her in the basket, weighing it down with a small rock. Turning her eyes upward, she waved to Abe—up went the basket, and the window slammed shut again.

Wandering down the alleyway, the youngsters stopped to watch a blacksmith as he shrunk an iron rim onto a wooden wheel—amid clouds of smoke and burning fumes—then, with a burst of scalding steam, he dropped the whole thing into a barrel of water.

Glancing up, Quon saw Abe Kratze motioning to them again from the window. A quick nudge with his elbow and he had Lizzie's attention. He pointed at the window. Running back to their spot below the window, Lizzie looked up to see that Abe was now smiling down at them.

"Copy an give it back tamorra," she shouted.

The tailor nodded, understanding perfectly, as he disappeared inside.

Arriving home, they found Joe had gone out and left their dinners balanced carefully on two upturned buckets in front of the fire. The youngsters smiled as they tucked into a good meal of Joe's tasty beef stew. The old mariner returned just as they finished.

"Had a good day, luv?" Lizzie greeted him as he flopped into his chair.

"Aye, even bin and picked up a load from the docks. Ben told me yer'd bin there."

"That were straight after work," the girl informed him.

Joe lit his pipe and puffed on it a couple of times to ensure it was burning.

"Down at the ship they were all laughing, even Davis was joinin in." He looked at the girl questioningly. "Ben wouldn't tell why though." Joe spat into the fire and patiently waited for an explanation, but the youngsters began washing up the dishes as if he hadn't even spoken.

When she spoke, it was to change the subject.

"If you had to put a crew together for a ship the size of the custom vessel, could yer do it?"

The furrows in Joe's brow deepened with concentration. He slowly nodded his head but his expression was questioning.

"Many times over, lass," he answered cautiously.

A big grin appeared on the girl's face as she knelt at the old man's feet, resting her arms on his knees and wiggling her nose at him.

"How many times? Ten, twenty or maybe seven?" she giggled.

"Seven," Joe answered abruptly, not wanting to be doubted.

The Chinese boy's eyes were mere slits as he watched Lizzie manipulate the old man by asking clever, innocent-sounding questions.

"Aye, but yer'd need a year ta do it," she said, slapping his knee.

"No, no, no, a month at the most," Joe insisted.

The girl twisted her body over and sat between his feet; a show of affection that the old mariner enjoyed, having missed it since they had all become so busy. He reached forward and quietly sighed, running his knurled hand through the hair of the most beautiful thing that had ever come into his life.

"Heard sumthin else," she muttered tiredly, gazing into the fire.

"What?" Joe asked, only half interested.

"Oh, sailors arguing if a big ship could be moved away from the dock, quiet like."

The old mariner thought for a moment before his authoritative voice responded.

"I could move anything on water, as quiet as a cat, if I had the right men." Puffing clouds of tobacco smoke, he leaned back in the chair no doubt enjoying thoughts of his distant past.

Lizzie called at the tailor's shop with the regular order of bread, noticing the presence of the two watchers at the corner. Abe called to her from behind the huge sewing table. Peering over his spectacles in the dim light, he handed her the arrest documents she had given him two nights before. In one swift movement, the papers disappeared into her clothing.

As she ran for the door, she called over her shoulder.

"The conditions, Mister Kratze, are under yer malt loaf."

She jumped down the two steps and the bread cart was on its way immediately, rattling over the cobbled street to its next stopping place.

A gypsy woman selling flowers walked by with a thin, whining child hanging to her skirts. Breaking a spare loaf in half, Lizzie handed the child the hunk of food; a thin wisp of a smile crossed the woman's face as she nodded almost imperceptibly.

In mid-afternoon, they had to race back to the brewery to refill the cider kegs—quite common when the weather turned warm and thirst overtook the many hard-working labourers on their route.

Lizzie only once let her mind wander to the ship stealing venture—there were more pressing things on her mind. She had no doubt Abe Kratze would find the perfect way to present her demands to the bishop, who, in turn, would observe her wishes and act on them. He had no choice—she had seen to that with the help of Captain Davis.

When the youngsters finished for the day, they pulled into the Johnson's yard in high spirits, only to be greeted by a tearful woman relative who was just leaving. She informed them that one of the many Johnson children was at death's door with some mystery illness.

They quickly parked their cart and entered the bake house. Seeing Mr. Johnson, they immediately realized he was not his normal, happy self. They had previously noticed that when he was rushed or under stress, he rather fiercely reverted to his native Yorkshire dialect, and this was no exception.

"Tell us what's wrong?" Lizzie pleaded, counting out the money and entering it into the big account book.

Bill looked up from the dough he was mixing and Lizzie saw the mournful look in his sad blue eyes.

"Take thee pay out, lass, we trust thee," he said slowly, "an 'elp yersen ta a bite ov what yer want."

Lizzie watched as the big Yorkshireman listlessly dragged himself around the bake house. She tugged on Bill's apron to get his attention and loudly asked, "Can we see the kid?"

He nodded, and pointed to the door across the bake house that led to their living quarters. Quon's eyes met the girl's as they moved toward the door and quietly entered. They could hear a deep moaning sound coming from one of the rooms, but it didn't sound like a child.

Tiptoeing closer, they observed a stuffy smelling, dimly lit room off to the left. In a corner was a mound of blankets, under which they soon realized, lay the child. Mrs. Johnson sat beside the mound holding the tiny hand of her little son, while her body rocked gently back and forth and she wept with a sort of mournful singing.

"Don't come any closer, it might be the cholera!" she cried out, becoming aware of their presence.

Quon pulled on Lizzie's arm as he backed away, and kept pulling until they were back out in the yard.

"That give yer a fright, lad?" the girl asked in a concerned voice.

The boy shook his head.

"No, no, Wizzy, me know China doctor man," he said excitedly. Him velly good man."

"Where?" Lizzie snapped, and began moving toward the lane.

"Under Tower Blidge."

"Well, what are we waitin for?" she shouted, as they broke into a run.

Chapter 12

By the time they reached the steps leading down to the riverbank, they were completely out of breath and soaked with sweat. It was a good half-mile from the bake house to the bridge and they had run all the way. They flopped down onto the sidewalk to rest for a minute but were soon ready to be on their way again.

"Where to now?" Lizzie asked.

Quon pointed to the steps and issued a warning.

"Follow me and no spleakin. Big danger here."

She looked at her friend doubtfully but knowing she could totally trust him, she nodded and followed him down the long stone stairs and onto the muddy bank, heading for the arch under the bridge.

Suddenly, from out of the darkness stepped several fierce-looking characters in an odd type of dress. Quon reached behind him to grasp her hand and said something in Chinese to the leading man who abruptly stopped moving toward them. Holding his hand up for them to wait, the boy began chattering in Chinese again. This time the lead man walked quickly back into the darkness of the arch.

They could hear Chinese being spoken between two people in the darkness. As the man reappeared, they could see he was carefully carrying a stone jug, which he handed to Quon. This was followed immediately by a stream of jumbled words as he pointed to the stairs.

Quon grabbed Lizzie by the sleeve of her coat and began to pull her across the muddy bank. Then hand in hand, they slowly retraced their steps until they were back on the road.

"What the hell was all that about?" she demanded, when they reached the top, but Quon was on a mission and it wasn't finished yet.

They were almost back at the bakery when Quon finally slowed down to catch his breath. He handed the jug to Lizzie to carry for a while and she saw her chance again.

"Told yer how to use that stuff, did he?"

"Man of Tong say we no go dere again, but dis time he give clazy water for sick boy."

"And who is Mister Tong?" she said, puzzled that she had never heard of him before.

"Not Mister Tong," he laughed. "Man of Tong, dem plenty bad if dey mad."

Lizzie cast her eyes upward in frustration.

"I don't understand it at all."

"Den weave it, Wizzy, weave it," he said, with an understanding smile.

The youngsters had again worked up quite a sweat as they arrived back at the bakery carrying the precious crazy water.

Bill looked up at them in surprise as they came through the door.

"Forgot sumet, did yer?" he asked, continuing to knead the large batch of dough on his large worktable.

"Not really. Bill, we went to see a doctor for that sick kid of yers," Lizzie answered carefully, watching the Yorkshireman's reaction.

"Yer did what?" Bill asked, his big fat hands slowly coming to a halt, as he stared at them in amazement.

"An we got some medicine for yer, too," she continued excitedly.

"Oh bless yer hearts . . . ye are both little treasures," he exclaimed, seeming flabbergasted by their gesture. He quickly wiped his hands, removed his soiled apron and moved toward the doorway of their living quarters.

Quon handed the jug to Bill . . . quickly explaining how to use the medicine water. Bill, still muttering his thanks, disappeared through the door.

Very pleased with themselves and completely tired out, Lizzie and Quon headed for home. As they passed the corner of Water and Mast Lanes, they barely glanced at the two men still watching the tailor's shop.

Entering the cottage, they were greeted by an unfamiliar sight causing them both to stop dead in their tracks.

There, by the table, sat a woman they had never seen before. She was small, modestly dressed, and pleasant looking, and had a beaming smile on her face. In the corner of the room lay a cradle with a tiny wrapped bundle inside, obviously a baby by the sounds it was making.

"My but yer late!" the stranger said, gently.

"Who are you?" Lizzie asked, in a tone that was both calm and friendly.

"Come, eat my dears. We can talk as you enjoy supper," the lady insisted. "It's all ready and the master will be back quite soon," she said, busying herself with the meal as the youngsters watched suspiciously.

It was not long before Joe returned, gave both his charges a hug and sat in his chair at the head of the table, motioning the woman to sit at the other end.

There was no doubt about it—this lady, whoever she was, could really cook and Joe knew a lot more about her than he was saying—the delicious nature of the meal kept talking to a minimum, except for the sighs of approval and the rattle of cutlery.

When the meal was over, Joe, at last, gave them an explanation.

"Our new friend here is Missus Ada Mason, widow lady of the navigator from that ship that came in a while ago." He paused to let his words sink in.

The faces of his young partners showed their grief and they looked sadly toward the young woman.

"I saw she could use some help," Joe continued, "and knew we were getting to the point of needing someone to take care of us three. So I decided to offer her a job and a home."

The old man stopped, reached for his pipe and began to stuff tobacco into the bowl. Occasionally, he glanced up at the youngsters to check their reaction.

"What about the baby?" Lizzie's concerned voice piped up.

"He's a bonus," Joe said, in a matter-of-fact way. Then, remembering something else, he tapped the table with his pipe stem, "We have another bonus as well, Missus Mason is both a schoolteacher and a bookkeeper."

The youngsters' faces lit up with the thought of being able to continue their education. It had been sometime since their last lesson with Abe Kratze.

"Just one other thing ah want you two ta remember," Joe said, tapping his pipe again. "This is your home as well as mine now, an if yer don't want her, out she goes, baby an all!"

The horrified look on the youngsters' faces at the mere thought of throwing the baby out, was enough to tell the old man that he had won the day.

Down at the baker's yard the following morning, Bill Johnson was in a much better frame of mind as he helped them load the bread cart.

Quon was never one for talking, but this was an exception.

"Clazy water do good, Mister Bill?"

The baker stopped and looked seriously at the boy. His face broke into a smile.

"Yes, lad, thanks ta you two." He reached over the cart to grasp their hands, a tear slowly finding its way down his face.

"There's another thing yer can do, Bill," Lizzie said, pulling her hand away.

"What's that?" he asked.

"Tek the lad up to our garden when it gets warm. Let him sit in the sunshine and get some fresh air."

"That's a damn good idea, lass. Ah'll tell the Missus and we'll do that."

An air of merriment seemed to follow the youngsters around all day and they had exceptionally good sales with hardly any problems. Pulling their handcart up Water Lane at the end of the day just didn't seem as hard with the warm sunshine on their backs.

A few days later, they were approaching Mast Lane, leaning into their task as they pulled the cart up the slight incline. The thunder of a fast-approaching carriage as it rattled over the cobblestones warned them of iron-shod hooves bearing down on them.

Turning the cart into the gutter, the youngsters jumped safely off the road and watched as the snorting horses rounded the bend from the waterfront and slowed their fevered pace. Instinctively, the youngsters pulled themselves into a protective position hidden from the view of anyone on the road.

At the corner, two bowler-hatted heads were seen peeking around the building. When they saw the carriage, they immediately stepped out to meet it. The carriage ground to a stop. An arm appeared from inside, holding a cane that cracked the side panel with a bang.

Loud, unintelligible words were shouted, and suddenly the carriage drove off again—showering sparks from the scrambling hooves. The men quickly disappeared around the side of the building again.

The stunned youngsters looking questioningly at each other, pulled the cart out of the gutter, and slowly went on their way.

"What was that all about?" Lizzie puzzled out loud. "Looked like they were told to go," she said, glancing at the boy.

"It was the bishop's calliage, me damn sure," Quon answered slowly.

The girl sprang to her feet, grabbed the cart shafts and let out a yelp, "Push yer little bugger, push."

Bill Johnson looked startled at the speed at which they shot into his yard—Quon Lee sliding his feet to slow the cart to a quick stop. Into the bakery they ran with Bill shouting to them from outside.

"Do the cash, lass, me wife's up at your place with bairn. He's a hell ov a lot better today."

Lizzie did what he asked, while Quon acquired mugs of cider and two hunks of apple pie.

"Are yer goin straight 'ome?" the baker asked, smiling at the youngsters wolfing down his apple pie.

"No . . . one stop to make yet," the girl said, crumbs falling from her mouth as she talked.

Soon, they were finished and moving out of the yard with the loud 'goodnight' called by the baker, ringing in the distance.

They met Missus Johnson returning down the lane, and she stopped to show the youngsters how well her boy looked.

"It's a miracle, it is," she said, fussing over the child as she proceeded along the lane with something of a spring in her walk.

"Run!" Lizzie urged her partner. "Let's get out of here and call at Abe's."

"No!" Quon said emphatically, pulling to a halt. "You wait tomollow, might be one damn big tlap."

The girl stopped . . . turning to face her partner. She looked at him quizzically.

"Yer right dumplin, as usual, I think we'll just go home," she muttered.

Now in no hurry, they sauntered up the road toward home, looking in shop windows and chattering about friends and customers.

The Jennings' Harness Shop was a particularly interesting place, with its strong smell of oiled leather seeping out into the air, the sound of rivets being hammered to metal and the jangling of chain. It was always a busy place.

A little farther along was the Foundation Emporium, its small square windows decorated with frills and lace. From the open door, a hint of perfume crept into the street, perhaps coming from the flower-strewn objects in the window. This was a corset shop with its discreet displays, but it amused and interested the youngsters, sending their imaginations spinning wildly. They couldn't figure out how those things worked, or the reason for them, but it usually caused great eruptions of laughter.

Soon they were at Joe's garden gate. The new Spring flowers grew in a rambling sort of way, helping themselves to whatever space they could find in the narrow border and looking as pretty and fresh as they were able. The cottage could do with a coat of paint but it had a homely look about it.

Missus Mason was there smiling a greeting from the open doorway. Lizzie had to admit that arriving home certainly gave her a nice warm feeling and she sighed with contentment.

"We had visitors today," Ada told them, beaming with pleasure. "A really nice lady and her sick son," she said, busying herself with the food cooking on the open fire.

"Oh, that would be Missus Johnson," Lizzie explained. "She's the baker's wife, comes from Yorkshire and talks funny—we told her she could bring her little boy and sit in the garden."

"What you two did for that woman was right charitable," Ada continued, smiling a greeting as Joe walked in, hung his cap behind the door and flopped into his chair. "Did you hear that, Mister Todd? We have a couple of little heroes, I would say." She waited expectantly for his comment.

The old man smiled gently, his eyes fastened on his young partners—pride shining from them like beacons.

"Maybe I should tell yer sumthin, lass, before yer get too carried away," he said, as a little frown crossed Ada's face. "Them two are a law unto themselves, do what they want, when they want—smart as whips they are, and I warn yer, they're as crafty as a forest full'a foxes—ye'll see."

Looking pleased with himself, he tapped his pipe out in the cinder tray below the fire. Ada Mason wore a puzzled expression as she lay supper out, but posed no more questions and the meal got started. A tinge of redness touched her neck at the occasional compliment that came her way, and she quickly excused herself to attend to her son, Willie.

"Heard sumthin t'day," Joe muttered, recovering the still-smouldering pipe from a scorched waistcoat pocket.

He had Lizzie and Quon's instant attention as they waited for him to continue.

"Them fellers watching old Abe won't be there any more," the old mariner said plainly.

The youngsters' eyes met across the table.

"What's that all about?" Lizzie asked.

"As if yer didn't know," Joe chuckled, pointing his pipe at the innocent-looking girl. "Ah have a strange feeling that you set that up somehow."

All he received in reply was an almost angelic look from Lizzie, a smile and then, out of pure devilment, she blew him a kiss across the table.

Ada, who had been desperately trying to hear the conversation while she settled Willie, now looked slightly perturbed as she returned and began to clear the table.

Joe glanced at the lady and burst out laughing.

"Don't you take this to heart, Mother Mason," he teased Ada, "wait til yer know us better, then ye'll understand."

Lizzie reached over to take Ada Mason's hand, and winking at her murmured, "He's an old grump, me an Quon will take care of yer, luv."

If the baby hadn't stirred—causing them to talk more quietly while Missus Mason rushed over to coo at him—their silly conversation could have gone on and on.

Turning from settling the child, Ada was surprised to find both Lizzie and Quon sat on the floor at old Joe's feet, and he with a hand on each of their shoulders. The bond of love between these three was becoming more obvious everyday and this little scene tugged at her heartstrings.

She couldn't help herself and she let out a little gasp, whispering, "Oh, my . . . oh, my."

By now, the evenings had turned into wonderful learning sessions with their very own teacher in residence. Lizzie soaked up the knowledge like a sponge, with Joe and Quon battling along at their own speed.

Ada even knew about ships and navigation, which she had picked up from her husband . . . and a multitude of other things, which she imparted to the enthralled girl.

Chapter 13

As the youngsters went by on their bread route the next day, there was no sign of the men on the corner watching the tailor's shop. So, they decided they would call on Abe Kratze when they finished work.

Everything seemed normal at the Johnson bakery. Missus Johnson had made a special friend of Ada Mason, and continually sang her praises.

"That woman is a saint," she would say, repeatedly.

"Funny what happens ta folks when yer do 'em a little kindness," Lizzie remarked to the boy.

"Not funny at all," Quon muttered. "Life like wheel—do good tings an good tings come back."

The girl laughed at the odd way her partner put things and his funny way of talking.

"Oh you do tings," she giggled, imitating Quon, and then directed a playful kick at him.

Abe Kratze peered over his spectacles as he heard his bell jingle. He saw who it was and neatly lay down his sewing on the worktable. His black and broken teeth quite obvious as he produced the faintest of smiles to greet the youngsters.

"I think this deserves a drink," he murmured, moving toward the table in the back corner.

Lizzie sat, with Quon standing behind as usual. The old tailor pushed two half mugs of cider across the table, before filling one for himself.

"We drink to success," he said, taking a gulp of the cold liquid.

"So, you obviously got to the right people with our demands," Lizzie commented thoughtfully.

"Aye, an damn quick, that paper were a godsend—don't want to know how you got it though!"

"Good," she said, coyly, "cos ah wouldn't tell yer anyway!" causing the old man to smile at her abruptness. "Now, you have more work ta do, cos ah want you ta register the titles, too."

She paused as the old man reached for chalk and a board.

"To TLS and Company, address is Joe Todd's cottage." Reaching for the mug, she drank the contents, and prepared to leave.

"Do I get a fee for all this work?" the tailor whined.

"Don't yer always get a fee from me?" Lizzie snapped, pushing her chair away from the table. "I want it all done by the end of the month," she calmly ordered, opening the door and stepping out into the evening sun with Quon close behind her.

Watching the youngsters go, Abe couldn't help but think of how much Lizzie had changed in such a short time. He noted that his lessons had obviously improved the girl's grasp on the English language, however, when she got excited, all seemed to be forgotten. He sighed and returned to his work.

Ada and Willie had been at the cottage for many days now, but Joe still felt awkward when called on to look after baby Willie. Awkwardly cradling the little fella in his arms as he rocked in his chair, he held him close . . . but the lad seemed so fragile.

"Not so tight, Joe," Ada chided him as she attended to her cooking.

"Dammit, he's tiny," the old mariner exclaimed, gently rocking his body back and forth.

Running feet could be heard outside on the garden path, just before the door burst open and the youngsters raced in.

"Hey you two," Ada admonished, "slow down now!" Her voice reflected her schoolteacher days, and a startled Lizzie pulled to a halt in front of Joe and the baby.

"Just look you here, dumplin," she said, grinning at the baby and pointing to Joe. "That's our bad-tempered old daddy playing nursemaid."

Joe scowled, pretending to growl fiercely at the youngsters and Ada watched with interest at this interplay of affection. She considered herself so lucky to have been accepted by this odd family of misfits whom, she had no doubt at all, would be loyal friends for life.

The month end came without incident. Joe told Lizzie they were acquiring too much money at home, and he had put away five or six tins under the floorboards in the back room, for safety.

The girl nodded staring off into space. "Well, yer'd better get ready for spending some of it."

Joe had no idea what she meant as his attention was taken up with other matters—accounts to be collected, bills to be paid, and horse feed that had to be ordered. Although Ada was a great help, it was an extremely busy time for all of them. Lizzie knew that and left him to his work.

Abe Kratze was expecting them when they hurried into his shop at month end.

"Done it all, have yer?" Lizzie asked, flopping into the old chair as the tailor locked the door.

Quon watched Abe suspiciously, as they moved to the table. Abe took his time setting out the documents in their correct order, then without saying a word he sat down. Coughing to clear his throat, he began by caressing the documents with his long, thin fingers. He explained each one in detail, pushing them over toward the girl, who listened intently.

Finally the last one was passed over, and the old tailor's hands began their incessant rubbing.

"Now, can we discuss my fee?" he pleaded.

Lizzie was only young, but her grasp of business and her clever, manipulative skills scared the living daylight out of old Abe.

"You will receive a fee of five golden guineas for this work, Mr. Kratze, and I have another job for you, too."

The tailor groaned in anticipation but listened patiently, his eyes flicking over her shoulder at the unblinking Chinese boy who stood watching everything. What a pair! Abe thought, quaking a bit inside.

Staring hard at the old man, she began.

"We shall need a distribution chain set up to cover all of London."

The tailor looked startled.

"Fast, efficient and quiet . . . can you do it?" she asked abruptly.

The old man spluttered, drumming the tabletop with his fingers.

"What are the goods, lass?" he demanded.

"Anything we might have," she snapped back.

Abe Kratze looked bewildered as he rubbed his lower lip with a finger, deep in thought.

A smile flashed across Lizzie's face and disappeared immediately into a frown.

"Might be cheap corn for the poor folk."

The tailor almost had a heart attack as he jumped to his feet.

"Good gawd girl, ye'll get us all hung," he complained, referring to the recent laws relating to the sale of corn, as he snatched a cloth from his pocket and mopped his brow.

Lizzie laughed at the old man, having acquired the reaction she had expected.

"Hang never, soon we'll be too powerful ter touch . . . can yer do it?" she snarled fiercely."

Aye, but ah need time."

"You've got exactly two months," Lizzie said through clenched teeth. As an afterthought she added, "Joe will take care of all deliveries, cash on the barrel from your end."

The girl drew five golden guineas from her pocket and dropped them on the table.

Quon Lee drew back Lizzie's chair, allowing the girl to stand. She nodded to the old man and the youngsters made for the door; the boy unlocked it and they disappeared into the lane.

Running like rabbits all the way home, the dog bouncing along beside them, the twosome looked a picture of innocence.

Joe and Ada were patiently waiting for them. Supper was a quiet affair . . . no one seemed to want to spoil one of Ada's wonderful meals by talking business.

When they finished and she was busy clearing the table, Ada turned to Lizzie and asked, "Was it business that made you late tonight, love?"

"Yes," the girl said, blankly, "urgent business."

Lizzie glanced over at the old mariner.

"Yer got any plans for that property yet?"

Joe had to shake himself from his deep thoughts.

"What property?" he asked, looking a wee bit puzzled.

"The property we, or should I say our company, TLS, owns."

The old man sat bolt upright.

"Legally?" he gasped, almost dropping his pipe.

Both the girl and her Chinese pal smiled.

"Aye, legally," she said, and before Joe could interrupt her, she started talking again. "Better let the tenants know that you will be collecting the rent from now on, an that goes for Tom Burns, too."

Lizzie paused to let her words sink in. Ada gasped, causing the girl to look over at her.

"You mean . . . you own property," she uttered in disbelief, all the colour having drained from her face, "but how?"

Lizzie smiled through tight lips.

"Yes, we do . . . lots of it, and it's none of yer business to ask how, so I shan't be answering that one just yet."

"Easy, lass," Joe gently chided the girl, turning his attention to their stunned housekeeper. "Best you just listen, Missus Mason, because what you are about to hear can greatly affect the rest of your life."

Ada sat down visibly shaken, her hands trembling. Joe rose from his chair, putting his arm around her to offer some comfort. Meanwhile, Quon Lee scrutinized the situation from eyes that were narrow slits.

"It's time," Lizzie said, deliberately, "that we heard her oath—that anything she hears from us never gets repeated to nobody—not even a priest."

Both Joe and Quon Lee nodded their agreement.

"Are yer Catholic or Protestant, lass?" Joe asked the woman.

Ada gulped, taken by surprise at the turn the conversation had taken. She certainly hadn't expected this sort of treatment . . . especially from a girl.

"P-p-protestant," she stammered, as she tried desperately to get a grip of herself. "And you can have my oath right now, young lady," she said, her voice barely a whisper.

Quon quickly produced a Bible and with Joe directing, the job was soon done.

"Now yer one of us," Lizzie said with a chuckle, laying the sheaf of documents on the table in front of the woman. She noticed that Ada's shoulders were now beginning to relax. "An yer can start by explaining some of these documents ta our adopted dad."

Joe's head came up with a jerk.

"Ah haven't adopted either of yer," he said, looking puzzled.

"Didn't have to old lad, we adopted you," the girl said, giggling.

Chapter 14

In the week that followed there was much activity around the slaughterhouse land. Men brought in huge loads of lumber to be stacked neatly according to size. Digging had commenced on the foundations of a new stable block, behind the old one, controlled by the critical eye of an ex-sailor of Irish descent named Mick.

Ada Mason had proven to be a fully-fledged bookkeeper, demonstrating her ability to keep track of everything—the men marvelled at her patience, and she revelled in the goings-on about the property. Joe had offered her the tenancy of one of the cottages they now owned, but she declined, explaining it would be better to stay as she was, always available for them and feeling like one of the family. However, Ada was now far too busy with the accounts, to find time to tend to other tasks around the cottage, so Joe was now looking for a new cook.

Meanwhile, down at the cider brewery, Jack Shaw was proving a little temperamental. One evening, the partners decided to let him out of his contract and it was left to Lizzie to negotiate the terms. Again, Ada Mason proved her worth. Having a grasp of interest rates, production figures, and growth projections was becoming most important for furthering Lizzie's business education.

The only trouble was that Jack Shaw would not discuss business with a woman. Immediately, old Abe was brought in and under strict instructions from Lizzie, drove a hard bargain. Thus, Ada Mason got a first-hand look at this young girl's abilities, and the unusual bond between her and the Chinese boy, who rarely left her side. It became blatantly evident that it was the girl who controlled everything, not old Joe Todd, which was what she had previously thought.

Martha, a relative of Bill Johnson's, came to them highly recommended. She was a north-country woman, who had been employed as housekeeper and baby-minder for a family who had moved to Sussex. She was a woman of middle age, homely and of huge proportions, but possessing a kind and friendly disposition. She also had a reputation of being an excellent cook. She had an obvious love of children, which immediately prompted Ada to accept her as their new cook.

Angus McClain, a widower, had worked at the cider brewery for a number of years, attempting to raise his two children under extremely difficult circumstances. Joe was well aware of the Scot's home situation, having had on many occasions, the chance to talk with him—being impressed by his knowledge of the cider trade. Joe also took special note that Angus' rough exterior masked a gentle, helpful nature.

The old mariner offered Angus the position of manager at the brewery, which the Scot accepted with quiet gratitude. It was made crystal clear to him, that he would have to work closely with Ada Mason on the accounting, live in the brewer's cottage that Jack Shaw would be vacating, and acquire some further education. Agreeing to all the conditions, a frowning Angus had honestly expressed that he had no idea how his education could be expanded, considering the responsibilities he was shouldering—it left him very little free time as it was.

Joe reassured him that it was all taken care of—he just had to be open to taking the opportunity when it was offered. The Scot nodded, understanding very little of what the old mariner was saying.

At supper that evening, it was suggested to Lizzie and Quon Lee that it was time to give up their bread route. The youngsters studied the suggestion for some time, before the girl spoke.

"Yer got somebody in mind, have yer?"

"No, not really," Joe replied, stroking his beard and puffing on his pipe.

Quon's eyes flicked onto Lizzie's face as if his thoughts were being transferred by magic to the girl. She nodded almost imperceptibly just as Ada looked up from feeding the baby and noticed the exchange between the youngsters. Ada watched with rapt attention, until Quon slowly turned one hand palm upwards keeping the other palm down.

"We can talk about it if yer want," Lizzie said, smiling at Quon and winking at Missus Mason.

Ada's mind began to spin—he's talking to her in sign language, she thought, no wonder they seem to know what each other thinks.

"Well, that new manager at the brewery has two younguns, ah could put one of me old jack tars with 'em, then you two would be free ta do what yer want," Joe explained. Sticking his pipe back into his face, he began puffing.

Ada watched carefully as the Chinese boy turned both hands face up on his lap.

"Sounds good ta us, but we'll have ta ask the baker if it's all right with him," the girl said, reaching out with her foot and pushing Quon over from his cross-legged sitting position in front of the hearth. His hands quickly went into a position with palms together as if in prayer.

If I hadn't seen that with my own eyes I would never have believed it, Ada thought as she cleaned Willie's face.

Joe removed his pipe, balancing it precariously on the fireplace.

"Let me hold him for a while," he said, holding his arms out for the child. His chair slowly began to rock backwards and forwards in a comforting motion and soon Willie was fast asleep.

The McClain youngsters were not very bright and so were never offered the job for bread deliveries. Instead Lizzie took Billy, one of the waterfront children without a home, and a crippled sailor with one leg named Tom Day, and trained them in a week to work fast and efficiently together. (She made it very clear that they had better be honest or they would have her to reckon with.)

A place to stay was found for Tom and Billy, not far from Joe's cottage. Joe's part in organizing the terms of their employment was to insist that the lads stay together and eat their meals with the other employees. They were also required to check in with Ada every night to account for their sales and deliver any snippets of news they might have picked up during the route.

Eating had become quite an event for the now growing staff of TLS. Joe also provided the evening meal for the disabled sailors in his employment—an old leaning-shed that he had equipped with a huge cooking stove, table, and benches, served the purpose. All along one wall, hooks were loaded with serviceable clothing. Gleaned from the company rag carts that roamed the area, these clothes were free to anyone in need.

Within a month, Tom Burns decided to retire to a place in the country, allowing Joe to buy all his equipment at the slaughterhouse. Most of the workers stayed on to work for TLS, but the supply of farm animals to keep the slaughterhouse busy, looked like it could be a problem. The difficulty was solved when one of Joe's gypsy friends offered to supply them regularly.

Lizzie and Quon now had time on their hands to think about the future. They spent many interesting and pleasant hours at the docks, learning about ships and their capabilities. They studied the cargoes they brought, who bought them, and many other little details that would come in handy later on. From the sailors they learned about the war between England and the French/Spanish alliance.

Captain Davis added some small cannon to his vessel to give the look of being armed but he swore they were useless peashooters—hardly a threat to anyone except his own gunners.

One day, Ben Thorn told them they had been to a little Spanish port—one that was building new ships ready for some big battle (little did they know it was the Battle of Trafalgar for which they were preparing). Quon asked for a map of the Spanish coastline where the ships were being built and Captain Davis rolled one out on his chart table for the youngsters to study.

"When are you going to sea again? " Lizzie asked.

Without looking up, he answered, "Day after tomorrow, noontide."

Quon nudged her on the arm to urge her on.

"Will you be goin close to that port you showed us?" she asked innocently.

The captain, not feeling any motive in the girl's question, replied absentmindedly as he continued to gaze at the chart.

"Aye, lass, should be off their coast at dark, an we could sneak in for a look." Suddenly, the thought hit the captain like a thunderbolt, his head jerking upwards. "What the hell are you planning now?"

Lizzie smiled innocently.

"Won't be any danger in that, will there?" she purred.

Davis was scowling now, his eyes almost closed.

"Depends on what you have in mind, you little pirate!"

The girl sat down at the chart table, her finger tracing the coastline on the map. The captain's eyes followed her every movement, watching closely until her finger stopped at a tiny cove.

"What's there?" she asked, without looking up.

"Not a damned thing," he said. "It's all sand an rocks—barren, no good for nothing."

"Just what we need," Lizzie stated enthusiastically. Then, carrying on before the captain had a chance to reply, "We can land men there after dark and nobody would be any the wiser."

Davis' mouth dropped open with surprise.

"Why?" he muttered.

"Because," she said, forcefully, "we are going to steal all the vessels that we can get our hands on in Zarauz."

The captain's face twisted into a little smile of pure devilment as he warmed to the adventure.

"It's so crazy, lass, it could work . . . with lots of planning," he said, smoothing the chart with heavy hands.

"You'd be a hero," she whispered.

"Aye, an if yer were a lad, yer'd be right there with me."

Lizzie laughed and Quon slipped his hand onto her shoulder. She automatically reached up and held it for a moment.

"We will be there, Captain Davis," she snapped, "we will be there!" a harsh tone creeping into her voice.

"Oh no, you won't," he said weakly, needing to sit down—his face displaying his doubt.

Lizzie jumped off her chair, smiling brightly as if nothing had happened, and headed for the cabin door. Her hand grasped the latch but before opening it, she turned back to face him.

"When yer in that harbour next, captain, count the vessels that are finished, cos we are goin ta get 'em!"

With those parting words, the two youngsters ran across the deck, down the gangplank and onto the dock.

On the way home, they called at the Johnson bakery, where they stopped to enjoy some of Bill's delicious apple pie.

"Hey, Bill, can I ask you a question?" Lizzie asked.

"Aye, lass, yer can," he answered, dusting the flour off his hands and onto his huge apron.

"Well, how would yer move a vessel from the dock . . . quietly?"

Bill studied the girl for a moment.

"Yer not going ta get yerself in trouble are yer, lass?"

"No," the girl replied nonchalantly, watching the baker through pinched-up eyes, "but if ye've no ideas it's all right, we can ask somebody else."

Bill slowly walked over to his bags of flour and pointed to the rafter above, where rope blocks hung above a big hook.

"Rope and blocks would do it ah reckon," he said, slowly.

Thanking him, the youngsters made their exit.

Out in the lane, Quon stopped and turned to Lizzie.

"No good, Wizzy, no place to fasten lope."

Lizzie nodded her silent agreement as they slowly walked to the corner. Abe Kratze, standing in the doorway of his shop, saw them turn the corner and waited to be noticed before motioning to the youngsters.

"I have news for you, girl," he said, backing into his shop and removing his spectacles to clean them. "We are ready when you are." Then glancing over his readjusted glasses, he shuffled to the back of the store. "And no stolen goods, if you please!" he muttered.

Lizzie followed along behind until the old tailor reached his chair. "Just tax free," she replied, with a chuckle, watching Abe's reaction, which was virtually non-existent—only a slight nod. "We shall need the list and some detail of what they specialize in, so everyone can get the best price possible," she said, in a very business-like manner.

Abe rolled his eyes toward the ceiling as if in frustration—she's doing it again to me, he thought, beginning to feel uncomfortable under her scrutiny.

Suddenly, the atmosphere changed as Quon touched Lizzie's elbow and her face brightened.

"Know any ship movers, Mister Kratze?"

The change in conversation threw the tailor off his stride for a moment.

"No, no, 'am cloth not ships, girl," he retorted, a little disturbed by the question. The youngsters giggled at his obvious discomfort.

Back out in the fresh air they raced over to the stone trough from which the horses drank. Taking the tin ladle off the hook and pushing the froth aside, they drank their fill. This was natural spring water, the most beautiful tasting, clean water for miles around, due to the fact it was always running. No one could remember this trough ever going dry.

Chapter 15

Around the corner came four horses pulling hard on iron-shod hooves which clattered on the granite cobbles. Lizzie and Quon saw the dray careening toward them and jumped out of the way just as the driver pulled the horses to a stop—allowing them to take a much needed drink from the nearby trough before continuing. On the dray were several huge stones, which were much too heavy to be moved by ordinary methods. Lizzie approached the driver carefully testing his friendliness—this proved fruitless—the man was as rough on the inside as he was outside.

"Wonder where they're goin," the girl mumbled aloud to herself.

Quon shrugged his shoulders and muttered back, "We watch, plenty qlick we see."

Lizzie smiled at his sensible answer and nodded. As they watched the horses struggle up the incline, they wandered along behind—it soon became apparent that the dray was heading in the direction of the slaughterhouse.

Turning into the track that led directly to the front of the buildings, the youngsters ran by and secured a good vantage spot on top of a pile of lumber that allowed them to see all that went on. Someone called

Mick, the supervisor, who came bounding over with great energetic strides, his long muscular arms swinging at his side.

Mick was a man amongst men, absolutely in charge and leaving no one in any doubt of that fact. Lizzie was impressed—this was the first time she had seen the big Irishman in action. Joe and Ada Mason had talked constantly about his abilities to organize and control men, always having a watchful eye on costs. This was an up-and-coming company man—a real find—Ada had said, admiringly.

Backing the dray into the required position for unloading turned out to be quite a task and tempers began to fray as the youngsters watched with fascination. As the bad-tempered driver swung his whip at one of the older workmen, the reaction from the big Irishman was instantaneous and brutal as he leaped onto the dray and bodily hurled the driver to the ground. Lizzie and Quon came to their feet with excitement. However, it all subsided as quickly as it began—a mere look from Mick doing the job.

Now, thought the girl, how will they get those huge stones off the dray? The horses were unhitched and led over to one side as men hurried to wedge a great log under the back wheels. Next, under Mick's direction, the horses were hitched at the back of the dray to long ropes tied to the front, and then the horses were urged into motion.

It was almost an anti-climax as the dray began to tip onto its tail, and the stones slid off smoothly and easily onto the ground, landing some distance behind the horses. Rearranging the team of horses and the dray took hardly any effort at all, and soon the disgruntled driver was moving on down the track and off the property.

"Didn't learn much here, did we?" Lizzie grumbled, jumping off the pile of lumber. Quon Lee just sat there watching the Irishman stride away. The girl stopped, and looked back at her Chinese partner.

"Well?"

"Him damn good . . . him qlick. Him for us, I tink."

Lizzie looked thoughtful as they walked back toward the cottage.

"I think yer damn right, my lad."

Without another word, they both turned around and began walking toward the building site. They stopped to observe the slaughter men hard at their work with their blood-soaked leather aprons slapping against their high-booted calves. They watched fascinated, as meat cutters yelled for more trays, sausage makers screamed for lengths of gut, and amongst it all, the delivery men went running in between the rows, trying to load their wagons.

"If that isn't pure bedlam, I don't know what is!" remarked Lizzie, backing out of the stinking building.

Around the back, they found the rag shed had been moved to the outer fence line, conveniently separating it from the new stable site.

"Somebody sure has got things movin around here," Lizzie muttered, trying to see where the supervisor had disappeared. A clap of hands brought her attention back to Quon, who was pointing to Mick in the far corner of the building.

Making their way toward him, they noticed he was always on the move . . . and never slowly. It turned out to be quite a feat catching up with the Irishman, who greeted them with a rough grin, as he swept them up in muscular arms to set them down outside the building line.

"Taint a place for the likes of you two, me darlins," he said, quietly, turning to go.

"But we need ta talk to yer," Lizzie shouted after him.

"Later, after supper, lass," was his fading reply as he disappeared again.

"Him for us, him stlong body and mind," Quon said, decisively, taking her hand to tug her back toward the cottage.

Once inside, they immediately noticed the extra chairs that had appeared, though nothing else was out of place. Martha Johnson, the new cook, was busy making supper and attending to baby Willie, who gurgled happily every time the huge lady passed close by.

Lizzie sat down at the table, unfolding a drawing of the Spanish coastline. As she began to study it, Quon turned back outside, collected an armful of fire logs and returned to neatly stack them in the hearth.

Joe arrived home red-faced and panting. The concerned youngsters watched him carefully as he settled into his chair. Lizzie jumped off her seat and walked over to the old man, removed his cap and gently smoothed out his hair, planting a tender kiss on his brow. Quon dropped to his knees, unlaced Joe's heavy boots and carefully removed them.

"Want yer baccy, old lad?" Lizzie asked, receiving a nod in reply.

By the time Ada arrived home from the brewery, accompanied by Angus McClain, Joe had made something of a recovery. As he sat puffing on his pipe and blowing blue smoke toward the ceiling, Martha called out that supper was almost ready.

A knock at the open door revealed a grinning Irish Mick. The old man waved him in, to the surprise of the youngsters.

The Irishman walked in, greeting everyone warmly, a special little twinkle in his eye for Ada and the baby. As their eyes met across the room, Angus rose to shake hands quite formally across the table.

Glancing down, Mick observed the map Lizzie was studying.

"Ah, San Sebastian," he murmured, with interest.

"Yer know it?" asked the girl, trying not to appear excited.

"Should, lass, lived there for a while a few years ago. There see, that's Beacon Rock," he said, pointing to a small mark at the entrance to Zarauz harbour. "Never used now, it has huge rings set into the rock—the Spaniards used them to tie up ships many years ago."

Martha began to set the table for supper—Lizzie folded her map and put it aside glancing at her Chinese partner who, in turn, was watching her carefully. As their eyes met and held, the boy slowly raised his hands, palms facing outward. The girl gave him a wink and a smile and they all gathered around the table.

Talk this evening was pleasant and convivial, never getting too serious or business-orientated. Many compliments were directed at Martha, who took them with a giggle, a tinge of embarrassment brushing her cheeks. After the meal, the women, eagerly helped by Lizzie and Quon Lee, affected a cleanup. The three men sat smoking their pipes, quietly passing their views on politics, religion and the war with France.

Martha finished her chores and asked Joe if there would be any more need of her services. The old man smiled, shaking his head as the cook disappeared out of the door. Ada brought several large books to the table placing them neatly to one side, adjusted her chair and sat down.

"Well, gentlemen, shall we begin?" Ada's well-cultured voice broke the silence. The men moved their chairs into better position and sat down again. Lizzie and Quon sat close together on Joe's right.

"May I begin?" Ada directed her question at Joe, who nodded his assent but kept on puffing his pipe. "First, I would like to introduce the owners of the company, TLS." She paused for a moment, then turned again toward Joe. "You gentlemen both know Mister Joe Todd, who serves as the company figurehead."

Angus and Mick nodded courteously to the old mariner. The Scot began to speak, but was stopped immediately by Ada's raised hand.

"Later, Mister McClain, please," she gently chided the manager of the cider brewery. A frown crossed the Irishman's face but he kept quiet, apart from shuffling his feet, as Ada continued. "The boy is Quon Lee, also one of the owners—he doesn't say much, but he thinks an awful lot."

The surprise was now showing on the men's faces, as Ada Mason pressed on.

"The other one," she said, smiling, "is our Lizzie . . . Lizzie Short, to put it correctly."

Old Joe reached over took one of the girl's hands and said fondly, "My Lizzie."

"My Wizzy, too," Quon Lee piped up, taking the girl's other hand.

Joe could not help but smile.

"Gentlemen," Ada said, "you can see the bond between them—be advised, they are as one."

Mick blew his nose to disguise the tear in his eye, his soft Irish heart touched by this demonstration of affection. Angus stroked his chin, scowling into the tabletop.

"There's more," Ada said, quietly, drawing the attention of the two men back to her.

"Lizzie Short thinks she is maybe ten or eleven years old, I think she is probably closer to thirteen or fourteen, but that's just my opinion." She paused to get mugs of cider for everyone, and took a much-needed drink herself before carrying on.

"Now, gentlemen, comes the shock for both of you." Looking up, she saw the anticipation on the men's faces, and noticed the wide grin Joe Todd was displaying. "It is our Lizzie," she said, quietly, "who controls every aspect of this company, and its future direction. Gentlemen, believe me, she is a genius at business."

Both men sat bolt upright with surprise.

"Ach, look ye here, lassie, 'am ah tae understand that bairn is the boss?" the brewery manager asked, somewhat affronted.

Lizzie smiled sweetly at the Scot.

"Tell me, Mister McClain, are you better off than you were three months ago?" she asked.

His temper was instantly reduced by the nature of the question and he reluctantly nodded.

"That ah am."

"And are your prospects for the future better than they have ever been?"

"Ah feel that would be correct," he agreed, his temper by now having totally subsided.

That's when Lizzie lost her smile—sitting bolt upright in her chair and snarling fiercely enough to cause the Scot to shrink back in surprise.

"Then tell me how you have suffered by my hand, sir?"

Angus McClain shook his head, beaten by the hard logic of this innocent-looking girl.

"Ach, but it's highly unusual, hoy be thinkin."

The girl came at him again with controlled anger.

"If I do yer wrong, tell me, but don't be so stupid as to think women have no brains, or I will reduce you to dust, quick as a flash!" Sitting back and displaying her sweet innocent smile again, Lizzie took a sip of her cider and patted Joe's hand reassuringly.

Ada quickly intervened at this point.

"Are you satisfied, Mister McClain, or have you more to say?"

Angus McClain stared at the table for a moment, squared his shoulders and coughed to clear his throat.

"Ach noo, lass, ah'v been put in ma place, an rightly so, too." He coughed again, then gently thumped the table. "I offer my apology for doubting you, young lady. From this day hence, ah'll go to hell an back for ye, take my word on that as a Scot." He sat back down, forcing a smile, obviously drained of emotion.

Ada was grinning from ear to ear as she turned to the big Irishman.

"Well, Mick, now it's your turn," she purred invitingly.

"Not on your goddamn life, girl," Mick chuckled, addressing Lizzie. The room erupted in laughter at the big man's reaction. "I'll go to hell for yer along wi that daft Scotty." Another round of laughter broke out, subsiding as the Irishman held up his hand for silence. "Sure, yer can rely on me darlin . . . an I'll kill any man that does yer wrong," he added quietly.

A hush came over the room knowing Mick was serious with his promise. Again Ada came to the rescue, wiping tears of laughter from her eyes.

"Now we have another surprise for you gentlemen," she said, as both Angus and Mick came to attention fearing the worst. "This is the good part," she said, gently. "The owners would like all three of us to be members of the board of directors. I already have agreed, how say you two?"

Angus answered immediately. "It would be ma pleasure, ma' am."

Mick was nodding vigorously, grinning. "Ah, that hoy will." Then before anyone else could speak, he quickly added, "Hoy would be scared ta death ta be agin yer!"

Lizzie jumped off her seat, ran around the table, and belted the big Irish man across his mighty arm.

"Cheeky bugger," she laughed.

All the excitement over now, the rest of the evening was taken up with building problems and production figures. A disturbance from Willie, who needed some immediate attention, brought a halt to the meeting for a short time allowing the men to fill their pipes and puff for a while.

Ada soon came back to the table and quickly ended the proceedings. Angus said he needed to be going as he had left his children in the care of a minder and Mick sat talking to Joe whose eyelids had begun to droop.

Lizzie noticed this and motioned the Irishman to the table where she had the Spanish map spread out again.

"Talk to me about that coastline, please Mick," she asked.

Mick fondled the map with his hand, trying to recollect details back to the time he spent there.

"Just a small shipbuilding village," he mused quietly to himself, stroking his chin. "Beautiful work they turn out though, it's kind of a hook harbour."

Ada suggested Mick tell the girl all about the harbour, village and the surrounding countryside, in as much detail as he could remember.

Glancing up at Ada, the building supervisor frowned but turned to Lizzie.

"Now why would yer be wantin all this information, missy?"

The frown deepened as he studied the faces of the youngsters. Again, Ada came to the rescue as once more she sternly chided Mick.

"Just do it, you great lump," she said, her face breaking into a smile, "it must be important to her, and maybe if you're lucky, she'll tell you why; if not, you will have to wait and see, won't you now?"

Mick stood up and stretched his back before answering.

"I think you need ta meet my Aunt Jemima," he said slowly.

It was the youngsters' turn to look surprised now, as Quon clasped his hands together with the fingers interlocked.

"Why would we need ta do that?" Lizzie asked, grinning at her partner, while Quon smiled back at her.

Ada, by now, was standing watching the youngsters intently, trying to read their sign language without success.

"Because me beauties," Mick continued, "my aunt is Jemima Nicholas, the old gal who captured the French mercenaries at Fishguard Bay."

Joe, who had evidently been listening, although he seemed to be asleep, opened his eyes and sat up.

"Fill my pipe, lass," he said, offering the blackened object to Lizzie.

Then, turning his total attention to the Irishman, he asked, "How can that be lad? She's Welsh . . . an a national hero ah'd say."

Mick smiled at the faces eagerly awaiting an answer.

"She's my mother's sister," he said, "and will be here next week to see me for a day or two."

"Now, there's a feisty lady to model yourself on, Lizzie," Ada interrupted excitedly.

Mick reached for his coat and prepared to leave.

"Thank ya all fer yer kindness and generosity," he said, smiling broadly. "Hoy'll be wishin yer a good night now. An don't yer be worryin, Lizzie me darlin, yer just like Jemima, brave as the devil himself an I'm with yer all the way." His little speech over, the Irishman left, still chuckling to himself as he walked down the garden path with his big lopping strides.

Chapter 16

During the days that followed, the youngsters quizzed the Irish building superintendent doggedly, often causing an involuntary chuckle from Mick as he tried to answer every detail. It soon became apparent that they were very serious in their quest for knowledge of the Spanish village and the surrounding area.

Ada watched fascinated as the youngsters made a model from clay scraped up from the building site. Each day, they added some new little feature from their many talks with Mick, until one week later they were ready to show off their model.

Aunt Jemima Nicholas arrived at Irish Mick's during the weekend, and was duly presented to the household at Joe Todd's cottage, having been invited to Sunday supper.

She was a tall, slim lady of approximately 54 years, stern looking, but very sprightly and mentally quick for her age . . . also forceful, pushy and a little bit inclined to be nosy! She wore a Welsh bonnet, smoked a long, clay fisherman's pipe and had a tendency to speak her mind.

Lizzie questioned the Welsh lady about her feats of bravery at the Fishguard affair.

Jemima, not knowing the girl yet, began to explain. "Just because thou art a she doesn't make thee useless, and the sooner men realize that the better they'll be."

Lizzie nodded in agreement, smiling sweetly at the lady.

Quon made another of his silent signs to the girl, receiving back the predictable slight nod. Ada watched, quietly aware that the youngsters were working to a plan. Lizzie continued to lead the conversation, working it skillfully around to the time Jemima spent on the Spanish coast. The Welsh lady was quite unaware that the sweet-smiling girl was manipulating her into a position of giving up all her thoughts and reflections on the village of Zarauz.

Even Mick began to smile as the questions came thick and fast, though his aunt really seemed to be enjoying the attention. A nudge from Lizzie's elbow sent the Chinese boy scurrying off, soon to reappear struggling with the clay model. The Irishman quickly came to his assistance and together, they slid it onto the table.

"What's this now?" Jemima asked, frowning. She took her spectacles from the case, adjusted them on her sharp nose, and peered at the model.

Lizzie leaned closer. "It's our attempt at reproducing the village of Zarauz, and nearby coastline."

Jemima was enthralled, turning the model this way and that.

"It's not quite right, you know," she said, in her clipped way of talking, addressing her nephew and rubbing her pipe stem across her cheek. Then, suddenly pointing her finger at the model, she asked, "Have you got some more clay handy?"

The Chinese boy leapt from his seat and tore off outside, to the amusement of the gathering.

While the boy was gone, the old lady began to explain, pointing a long, bony finger at the model.

"There's a hill missing, and a long wooden building in a little valley back there."

Mick looked over her shoulder at the place indicated by her poised finger.

"By gee's, yer right, an that shed made black powder for cannon if moy memory serves me right."

Quon Lee returned carrying a big ball of fresh wet clay and, without further ado, the old lady disposed of her heavy woollen cardigan, rolled up her sleeves and started to work. She took the piece of clay, slapped it around with excited energy, pulling a small piece off, and attached it to the model with deft strokes of her thumb.

She repeated her action with another piece, and another, finally placing the building in position.

"There you are, that's better." The old lady was really into this now as she turned happily toward her nephew. "Ah haven't enjoyed meself so much for a long time, lad." Then looking directly at Lizzie, she spoke sharply. "Want ter know anything else, lass?"

The girl smiled. She was really beginning to like this feisty old lady.

"Yes, there is," Lizzie confessed, watching Quon's hands make a series of movements. She glanced up to catch Ada watching carefully, too. "Can you tell me about the people who live there—are they excitable, have they a leader, do they follow him, and are they lost if he's not there? Is it a very quiet place, are there soldiers, do they get drunk, and how far to the next military garrison?"

"Hold it, hold it, girl!" Jemima squeaked in delight and all present watched and listened with undivided attention. "Let me get a word in, an ah'll tell you."

The baby stirred in his crib, temporarily pulling the attention his way. Mick scooped him up and cradled him gently under the watchful eye of his mother. Joe held out his arms and the big Irishman sat the child on the old mariner's knee—as the chair began its comforting rock, Jemima began again.

"Yes, you could say they're excitable, but what Spaniard isn't? Yes, they have a leader in Alfonso Demingo, a great carver, very clever with his hands but leaves his brains in his workshop. Loves ta strut around looking important—as daft as a ballast rock when it comes to other things." She paused to sneer scornfully before taking a big drink of cider and glancing at the interested faces surrounding her.

"Oh yes, they will follow him to a man," Jemima said with a wicked grin, "but not to a fight. Lost without him you say, lass, why they're more lost with him. Aye, it's quiet, an only three drunken soldiers in the damn place, but they have a warning beacon . . . it's right there," she pointed to a hill on the model. The old lady glanced up at Lizzie and, with a wink, whispered, "but they never have a guard on it, an it's a long rough ten miles to the garrison at San Sebastian."

Jemima Nicholas sat back on her chair, recharged her pipe and took a big puff. All faces turned toward Lizzie, who simply smiled sweetly and thanked the old lady—who only listened to a few words before interrupting.

"What in heaven's name is there that would interest anybody?" she asked, turning to Joe Todd.

Joe handed the sleeping baby back to his waiting mother.

"Ah have no idea at all!" he said, obviously puzzled, too.

Mick suggested it was time to go and his aunt readily agreed, quickly slipping into her coat and Welsh shawl.

"Well," Jemima said, at the door, "this has been the highlight of my trip to see Mick." Then, turning to Lizzie, she said, with a little chuckle, "Good luck, lass, you show 'em what we women are made of!"

After Mick and his aunt had gone Quon and Lizzie made off into the back room with their model, returning only to say goodnight to Joe and Ada.

It was then that Joe, in his gentle manner, broached a question.

"You two want ta tell us anything yet?"

The pair merely grinned impishly at each other. Ada watched as the Chinese boy turned both hands face down.

Lizzie immediately replied, "Not quite ready yet, Dad."

Joe could only shake his head as the pair disappeared into their rooms. He knew he could trust his young partners. They must have a good reason for keeping their plans to themselves, but nonetheless, he would be happier when they gave him an explanation.

Chapter 17

While checking the docks the next day, they learned that Captain Davis and the patrol vessel would arrive soon—they had been spotted out in the channel escorting a merchant vessel. Lizzie and Quon knew the way Captain Davis operated and so were quite sure there would be a load of confiscated goods to dispose of.

"Better talk to Joe, an see if he's ready to do a fast delivery . . . an pick up that list of drop-off points from Abe at the tailor's shop, we need that bad now." She neither received nor wanted an answer but Quon was nodding profusely to everything she said.

They made good time as they left the docks, crossing the Thames riverside road and up the hill to Abe Kratze's shop. The bell clanged vigorously as they bounced through the door, but they immediately skidded to a halt when they noticed the tailor had a visitor. There, at the back of the store, Abe was in deep conversation with a small, fat man with a round face bordered by a pair of mutton-chop sideburns. He was a complete stranger to the youngsters.

"Beg pardon, sir," Lizzie said, backing toward the door.

"No, no, come right in, lass," Abe quickly shouted, standing up from the table. "Come and meet my cousin, Nathan."

Warily, the youngsters approached the stranger who had an infectious smile.

"So you are the two that Abe has been telling me about, hey?" he said, with the merriest twinkle in his eye that Lizzie had ever seen.

Relaxing a little, the youngsters allowed the little man to put an arm around each of them and shepherd them to the table where he offered them a seat. Mister Kratze introduced his cousin as Mister Nathan Goldman, cargo merchant and insurer from the Inner City. The youngsters were suitably impressed, though they didn't have a clue what all those titles meant.

"We called for that list you were getting for us," the girl said, with a smile. The tailor shuffled off to get it, leaving them alone with his cousin.

"I have been wanting to meet you, my dear," he purred pleasantly. "We are going to be involved together, in the distribution of . . .," he paused, still smiling, trying to find the right words to explain his position. "Shall we say . . . recently acquired goods?"

Neither Lizzie's eyes nor her facial expression gave her thoughts away, as their new friend studied her carefully. A quick glance at the silent Chinese boy with his hands clasped tightly together told her to take some care—her right elbow gently nudged the boy's arm in acknowledgement.

Nathan Goldman's eyes unintentionally displayed a little surprise.

As the smile halfway slipped from his face, Lizzie had to bite her lip to stop herself from giggling, but the Inner City businessman recovered quickly.

"Sir," the girl said, pleasantly, "we are but children. We take messages here and there or run errands for the TLS Company," she explained as Abe Kratze returned, handed her the list and sat down.

Quon was already halfway to the door when Lizzie stood up and politely said goodbye to the men.

The rattling of the old door had hardly stopped, following the youngsters' quick exit, when Nathan began to speak.

"Damn it cousin, you're right, she's a cool one, that Lizzie. I thought it would be smart to test her reaction to my involvement."

Abe's wrinkled face looked blankly at his cousin.

"But I lost . . . the little devil beat me at my own game," Nathan chuckled.

"Yer daft ta even try," the tailor mumbled. "She and that Chinese boy are never apart, he never speaks, but something goes on between 'em." Abe paused, looking up at the ceiling and shaking his head. "She's too blasted smart for the likes of me," he continued, then as an afterthought, he muttered, "an the likes of you, too, cousin."

Nathan laughed aloud, his fat little belly wobbling like jelly on a plate. "I have no misgivings about dealing with that little lady, and dealing straight, too. We will do a lot of business together soon." He wiped the tears of mirth from his face and rose to go—they kissed each other on both cheeks and the little man quickly went out the door.

Meanwhile, out of sight, the youngsters sat on the curb talking.

"Who was that man?"

"Him weader of gloup."

"Leader, of what gloup?" Lizzie giggled. "I mean group."

"Big damn business gloup. Him another Jew, smell money, come to test Wizzy out . . . but we beat him good!"

The boy took Lizzie's hand and gave it a squeeze, bringing an instant smile to her face. They walked up the road toward home holding hands, like the two innocent youngsters they were supposed to be.

Missus Johnson, the baker's wife, saw them as she came out of one of the stores and had to show off her little boy, the one who had recently been sick.

"Look at im yonder," she said, pointing at the boy who was now happily playing with their little dog. "Picture ov health he is, thanks ta you two. Be in yer debt forever me dears. Oh, av just left yer a big apple pie at 'ome, bin up ta talk ta Ada for a change. Gotta go now."

She called to the boy, waved goodbye and they hurried toward the bakery. The dog followed them for a few steps until Lizzie called him and he quickly ran back to her, running around her legs until she bent down to give him a loving pat.

Martha finished up quite early and left for home—supper had passed over fairly quietly, there being no extra guests this night. Joe settled into his old chair with a fully charged pipe of tobacco, belching its blue smoke toward the ceiling. Ada, attending to Willie, suddenly informed them that Mick was calling around to discuss a few things with the family. Joe nodded and carried on rocking with his eyes closed.

A chalkboard lay across the tabletop and the two youngsters vigorously made marks on it, discussing something in whispers as a gentle knock came at the half-open cottage door.

"Come in," Ada called, turning from her accounting books, which she worked on endlessly.

In stepped Mick carrying a small bunch of flowers, which he awkwardly offered to Ada, mumbling, "These are for you."

Ada looked surprised and delighted.

"Why, thank you, Mick," she said, graciously, noting the embarrassment the big Irishman was displaying. As she relieved him of the flowers, she quietly commented. "That was very thoughtful of you, Mick."

"And where are my flowers, you big lug?" Lizzie asked with a giggle, causing Mick to turn beet-root red once more as he spun around in mock anger and pretended to grab for the girl. Quon was off his chair and in between them in a flash, hands up ready to fight.

"Now, would yer be lookin at that!" Mick exclaimed jokingly. "She's got herself a bodyguard now. Peace, friend, hoy'll not be tackling a man loyk yerself," he said, backing away.

"Sit down, dumplin," Lizzie commented with a smile.

Quon returned to his seat, muttering, "My Wizzy, my Wizzy," a wary eye on the Irishman.

The Chinese boy's actions hadn't come as a surprise to Ada Mason. It only served to re-enforce her suspicions that he would die before letting his friend get hurt. You didn't see that kind of devotion very often, in a lifetime.

The old man sat up in his chair. "Gotta problem, lad?"

Mick shook his head. "No, not really, but by this weekend we won't be needin all the men, an you said not ta lay anybody off until ah talked ta you or Lizzie."

Joe got up from his chair by the fire and came to join them at the table. He removed his pipe and very deliberately used it to accentuate his next statement.

"What do yer think, lass?"

"No one goes," Lizzie said sharply, her voice all business now. "We can employ some of them cleaning out the old shop on the corner, then doin it up." Pausing, her eyes turned fierce as she glanced at Quon, his hands were open, face up. "Mick, I want you to start training six skeleton crews for me. You pick 'em, you train 'em, an they had better be good!"

Lizzie's demand dropped like a bombshell on the dumbfounded group and they were struck speechless for what seemed an eternity.

Joe finally managed to splutter just one word, "What!"

Ada, who was carefully observing everything, was the first to collect her wits."

That's what the model is for isn't it, Lizzie?"

The girl nodded. "Don't have all the details yet, but we will have this week, I hope."

"Good gawd, yer plannin ta raid that Spanish village, aren't yer?" Mick gasped.

"We are, and I want every detail worked out before we strike 'em," the girl said, in a voice that left them in no doubt she was serious, and that she was also the general in charge.

"But why?" asked Joe, still in shock.

A wicked little smile flashed across Lizzie's face as she spoke through clenched teeth.

"Because they have something I desperately want."

Again, Ada interceded.

"But even if it can be done, it's going to take a lot of planning." Her eyes pleaded for an answer, which came quickly, but from an unexpected source.

"Wizzy damn done it. Wizzy say go, we go."

Mick smiled, though his mind was in a whirl.

"How soon do yer want them men trained?" he asked, still disbelieving.

"Well, as soon as possible—remember, they're all sailors, so it shouldn't be hard—let's say two weeks."

Before the Irishman could object, Joe, who had hardly said a word, began talking, and it was obvious he was going along with the idea.

"They're all good men, lad, an they know the sea—yer biggest job will be pickin the crews." As he finished talking, he stuffed the clay pipe back in his mouth and began puffing furiously.

Ada had to sit down and think. She had just seen a whirlwind at work, actually witnessing Lizzie in one of her most intense moments;

the way no one argued with her was a demonstration of her power over people. That girl could take over the world if she wanted it—of that Ada had no doubt at all.

"Oh, there is one thing, Dad," Lizzie said, gently smiling at the old man. "We make cider at the brewery, why don't we make whisky?"

Joe hadn't thought too much about this, as he had been so busy of late. "Don't know, lass, but ah'll ask Angus if he knows owt about it. Yer think we could sell it?"

"Absolutely positive, with the set up for distribution we have."

"Just a minute," Ada almost whimpered. "If you go on expanding at this rate, I'm going to need some help with the books."

The girl and Joe nodded almost simultaneously.

"Then train somebody," Lizzie said sharply, immediately asking a question of her own. "Do we have cash on hand, is everything making a profit?"

Ada sprang to her feet with an indignant look.

"Yes, missy, we have cash on hand, we don't owe a penny piece to a living soul and everything we have is making lots of money. It's time you came up with an idea what to do with it all."

Lizzie laughed, slipping her arm around the boy's shoulders.

"You just watch, it'll take care of itself one of these days."

Ada frowned and sat down, not understanding it at all.

Soon things settled down in the little cottage and Ada left the room to tend to her crying baby. The men talked of buildings comparing mental notes on some of the workmen, their capabilities and the jobs that they could handle. Joe knew a lot of the men from his seafaring days, and so knew their strengths and weaknesses, their leadership abilities and most of their disabilities, which many of them had proudly earned in battle.

Lizzie and Quon had long since departed into their back room when Mick said his goodnight and began to leave. Ada rose and walked him down the garden path. Closing the gate gently between them, they stood talking for awhile. Ada thanked Mick again for the flowers, trying to make it plain to the big Irishman that his advances were welcomed.

Mick's embarrassment came flooding back again and he quickly changed the subject.

"She's an amazing girl," he proffered quietly.

"More than that . . . she's a genius and her understanding of business and people is uncanny," Ada added.

"Is she serious about the village of Zarauz?" asked the Irishman.

Ada reached out to touch his hand.

"She's absolutely serious and I can assure you, will do it successfully," she paused momentarily, " . . . if it can be done at all."

Mick was becoming fidgety and wished her goodnight, leaning over the gate to brush her cheek gently with his lips—this time it was Ada's turn to blush, watching him stride quickly away.

Chapter 18

As the sun started its daily climb in the July sky, giggling and frolicking, Lizzie and Quon raced along the roadway leading to the local church. They pulled to a halt at the iron gates, peering in before opening them. Slowly moving the heavy gate, their creaking was so loud they only opened it wide enough to squeeze through. Amid more loud creaking, they swung the gates shut and made a dash for the bell-tower. Once inside, they felt safe.

Up the winding stairs, around and around they went, finally reaching the top. From this vantage point, they could see far down the old Thames River, across the jumbled rooftops with their crazy peaks and garret windows, past the smoking chimney pots, and far into the distance. Quon produced Joe's spyglass, which they had borrowed when no one was looking, and rested it on the rail of the walkway.

Peering way down the river and seeing the *Falcon* in the distance, he cried excitedly, "He damn come long way near yet."

Lizzie chuckled. "How the devil can he be a long way near? Dumplin, yer priceless." Taking the scope and looking for herself, she continued, "Won't get here 'til tamorra."

She handed the scope back to the boy who took up the rear and they began to make their descent. The smell of tobacco filtered through the old belfry door, as the youngsters peeked through a crack before opening it.

It was the gravedigger, who sat smoking his pipe and grinning at them with smoke-blackened teeth.

"Oh, it's you two," he said, recognizing them. "Better scarper off quick, the beadsmen are here today and the minister's about. Use the southgate, he won't see you then."

Moving quickly and giggling at the peculiar old man who dug holes in the ground for dead bodies and kept Joe informed as to the goings on at the church, they made their way back to the slaughterhouse and building site. Mick saw them coming and waved, deliberately pointing toward the cottage.

"He wants us to go home," Lizzie muttered, a bit puzzled with the instructions, as they turned for home.

Drawing close enough for them to see into the garden, they were surprised to observe Ada and Joe sitting on the grass by the side of the cottage enjoying a mid-morning snack. The youngsters had no idea what was going on as they flopped down to join them. Martha noticed their arrival from inside the cottage and quickly arrived carrying mugs of cider and huge pieces of apple pie for the twosome.

"Mister Mick not here yet, sir?" the cook asked the old man respectfully.

"Will be in a minute," Joe answered pleasantly, not quite being able to come to grips with this boss and employee relationship—he was a lower-deck man and always had the urge to treat people well no matter what their station—it was his nature and always would be.

Just then Mick came bounding up, dispelling any more conversation as to his whereabouts. As he dropped down beside Ada and the baby, Martha poured him a drink and stood back holding the large pitcher in both hands. Mick's first drink finished the whole tankard. The supervisor's lips smacked with joy and delight. The cook grinned and poured him another as his big hand reached for the apple pie.

"What's the party for?" Lizzie inquired, still puzzled.

"Oh, we just wanted everybody to meet a relative of my late husband, he'll be here in a short while," Ada said with a smile, without a trace of the emotion that once was so visible when she thought of her dear husband.

Lizzie and Quon Lee glanced at each other, neither having a clue to the real meaning of the get together, but becoming increasingly suspicious of the whole affair. Then through the gate hobbled a young man on crutches, his dark complexion adding to his boyish good looks.

Swinging toward them, he flashed a smile showing pearly white teeth set almost perfectly straight in his mouth. The girl jumped up to give her assistance.

"Don't bother, lass," he said, waving a crutch in the air. "I'm well used ta these things."

Ada smiled as she passed Willie over to Mick, who quickly deposited the child into Joe's outstretched arms.

"Ah sure he'd rather be with his granddad," Joe chuckled, gently holding the baby close to him.

"This is my husband's younger brother, Charles—Charley for short," Ada began, as she gently laid her hand on the young man's arm. "He's here for your benefit, my girl," she said, clearly addressing Lizzie.

Quon made some movement with his hands that Ada missed and Lizzie smiled her most disarming smile at the newcomer.

"You've come ta carry me away on yer blinkin fine white charger!" she giggled sarcastically, delighted at her own words.

Charley thought the statement was hilarious; laughing so hard he had to wipe tears away with his sleeve.

"Gawd, fancy me on a horse. How the hell would I be able ta stick on there?"

"That's enough young lady," Joe said, sternly. "Mind yer manners an listen ta what the lad has ta say."

Lizzie clamped her lips together like a vice, knowing she had been chastised and deserved it. Ada smiled, fully aware the girl's silly sense of humour had no malice attached to it.

"Tell her what you are, Charley," his sister-in-law coaxed gently.

"Oh, that," he replied, grinning. "I'm an Engineer."

Ada shook her head in frustration.

"And what do you specialize in lad?"

This time Charley became serious.

"Moving heavy weights," he said, watching the girl's face, which lit up immediately with anticipation.

"Like ships?" she whispered expectantly.

"Aye, like ships," he answered slowly.

Lizzie's hand instinctively clutched Quon's arm in excitement.

"We found im dumplin, we found im!" she chortled.

Mick coughed to draw their attention.

"Na, don't yer go getting excited yet, lassie, he moy't be changin his mind when yer done with yer explainin. Do yer want me ta come fer supper now?" he asked, turning to Lizzie as he prepared to leave.

The girl grabbed at the offer.

"Yes," she snapped, "an don't be late!"

Mick smiled, moving off toward the building site shouting over his shoulder.

"Show him yer model that'll sure give him a chance ta study the problem." Then he was gone.

"Think I'm your friend now, missy?" Ada asked, as she and Joe prepared to go back to work at the brewery where they had a long afternoon of bookwork ahead of them.

"Thought yer were before," Lizzie retorted, jumping to her feet.

As Joe and Ada left, Lizzie and Quon ran toward the house to get their model. Returning quickly, carrying it between them, they placed it carefully on the grass in front of Charley. Then lying down beside him, they proceeded to explain their problem using the model to illustrate their story. When they finished, they eagerly awaited Charley's reaction.

"Shouldn't be too hard ta do that," he said confidently after some consideration, rubbing the aching stumps of his legs. "It looks like a job for reduction pulleys," he muttered, drawing imaginary pictures on the grass with his finger. Suddenly his voice grew louder, "Let's take a trip down to the Thames, an check a few things." The youngsters were on their feet in a flash and stood watching Charley's tremendous struggle to get back onto his, finally making it with a gasp of effort.

"Yer know, Charley, " Lizzie said, thoughtfully, "if yer such a good engineer, can't ya find a way ta beat that problem?"

He looked at the girl almost helplessly.

"Haven't thought much about it, luv."

Quon tugged on the girl's sleeve.

"Like bled cart, we damn lide him."

She understood and nodded, pointing to the slaughterhouse. The Chinese boy grinned and took off at a run.

"What the hell did he say?" Charley inquired, scratching his head.

"He said that we're going ta ride ya," Lizzie answered with a chuckle.

"In what? I'm not riding in no wheelbarrow!" Charley was adamant.

"Just you wait, we can go like the wind with what he has in mind."

Racing into the main building, Quon spotted the old sailor in charge of deliveries.

"Need handcart damn qlick," he gasped.

The foreman pointed over to a corner. The Chinese boy grabbed the shafts and was away at a trot, the weight of the cart pushing him down the slightly inclined lane, swinging wildly around the corner and skidding to a halt in front of the startled engineer.

"Well, ah'll be damned," Charley Mason whistled in surprise.

"Just a minute," Lizzie called, as she scampered off and disappeared into the cottage. Some muffled talk was heard between Martha and the girl, then both of them came out and disappeared around the back of the building, to return quickly carrying an old torn and tatty easy chair. With Quon's help, they struggled to lift it up onto the top of the handcart.

They all stood back, breathless, to admire the new transport.

"Fit for a king," Lizzie declared, to the laughter of the others.

Getting Charley into it was no problem at all—he scrambled, they heaved, and up he went. Folding the legs of the contraption up under the cart's flat bottom, the youngsters were off down the road, leaving the hand-waving cook standing at the garden gate.

Part 2

Chapter 1

More than a few heads turned to watch the unusual handcart as it travelled down the cobbles of Water Lane, bumping and jolting to the merry tinkle of the youngsters' laughter. Charley was enjoying himself immensely, waving to anyone who would wave back. As they flashed by, a cheer went up from a group of sailors who sat on the wall overlooking the river. Slowing to a halt halfway along the dock, Lizzie and Quon Lee set the legs on the cart to prevent it tipping and turned to talk to their passenger, who was looking all around as if in search of something specific.

"What yer lookin fer?" the girl asked, "cos we know where everything is."

Charley smiled. "How about a blockmaker?" Then he chuckled and the youngsters looked at each other and shrugged their shoulders.

"What's a blockmaker?" Lizzie asked, frowning.

Charley Mason wriggled out of the chair and swinging his useless legs out over the edge of the cart, balanced on his two crutches and lowered himself to the ground.

Hopping over to a barrel, he pulled himself up onto it and began to explain. "A blockmaker is a very special type of carpenter, he works in solid oak and carves rope pulleys."

Quon's face lit up as he nudged Lizzie, excitedly.

"Wumpy in Blown's Yard."

Slowly she nodded, trying to recall the workshop. "But he's a blacksmith, ah think," she answered, wriggling her nose.

"That's right," Charley interrupted, "but what did he say, lass?" pointing at Quon.

"Oh, he told me of an old man called Lumpy in Brown's Yard."

Charley let out a surprised chuckle. "Did he really say that?" he asked, almost in disbelief.

From their position on the dock, the trio watched the traffic on the old river and the young mariner commented on some of the vessels and their capabilities. Lizzie found it most educational, interrupting to ask questions of tonnage carried, most likely cargo, seaworthiness, how many hands to man them, repairs generally needed and on and on, until finally Charley cried a halt to the stream of questions, swearing she had tired him right out.

So, once more loaded onto his transport, with the help of two hefty soldiers who happened to be passing, they were off at a gentle trot.

"Can we call at Brown's Yard?" Charley shouted against the breeze, banging the woodwork with one of his crutches when they took no notice of his request. He received no reply until they stopped at the horsetrough halfway up Water Lane and offered their passenger a drink from a tin ladle hanging on a post.

"Lumpy will be in the ale house by now," the girl offered.

"An flubbered," the Chinese boy added with a smile.

Charley chuckled. "Ah hate to keep askin you, but what did he say?"

Lizzie flashed Quon a grin, as if there was some private joke between them.

"Oh, he means old Lumpy drinks a lot, an when he's fallin down drunk, he calls it being flubbered—sounds better than drunk, I suppose."

The young cripple laughed at the candor of the pair.

"Say it as you see it," he muttered, then asked for a drink.

Quon started to comply and then stopped. He looked back at Lizzie and pointing toward the brewery in the distance, he clutched his throat with one hand. Charley watched in fascination at the boy's theatrical antics.

Lizzie nodded and turned back to their passenger.

"Would yer rather have a cider, sonny?"

Charley's immediate reaction was to swing his crutch at the girl, who nimbly stepped back out of reach. Pretending to be angry, Charley shook his fist in the air and swore at Lizzie.

"You cheeky little bugger!"

Laughing, she curtsied grandly. "Does that mean yes, sir?"

Grabbing the shafts, the cart began to move forward again, prohibiting any further discussion on the subject. Moving quickly along Mast Lane, around the corner into Corn Street, then sharp left into Bell's Yard and the entrance to the brewery—they came face to face with a huge delivery dray.

Pulling to one side, well out of the way of all the activity, they parked the cart. Instructing Charley to wait, they disappeared into the building, returning quickly with a man carrying three mugs and a wooden bucket full of cider.

"How the hell do you do it?" the engineer inquired, scratching his head in amazement at the antics of his companions.

"By the way, sir," said the man with the bucket. "My name is Angus McClain and I be the manager here." He held out his hand, shaking Charley's vigorously. "Enjoy yer cider now, for it's the best there is."

Charley was now flabbergasted—all he managed to utter in reply to Angus's greeting was a halting, "Ada's . . . brother-in-law . . . Charley Mason," before Angus disappeared again back into the building.

A giggling Lizzie handed him a mug of the finest cider and went to sit against the wall beside Quon. Charley was amazed at how interested these young people were in all that was going on around them, often whispering to each other although the Chinese boy didn't seem to talk much to anyone else.

A huge dray pulled into the yard loaded with barrels of apples and proceeded to manoeuvre to an open door. Suddenly, a third floor door flew open and a head popped out.

"Ready Jack?" a voice shouted, as the hidden man on the third floor hung a pulley onto a gantry arm. Charley immediately came to attention, watching every movement.

A rope was lowered and slings attached to one of the barrels as four strong men appeared to heave on the loose end of rope.

"Watch this, you two," Charley barked in a voice that brought the youngsters to his side in a hurry.

"What's the matter?" Lizzie asked anxiously.

"Look at the rope, it's hooked on that barrel, up and around the pulley above, then back to those four big men pulling on the end. Now observe the effort they need to lift that barrel."

In complete silence, they watched the scene developing in front of them. Slowly, the barrel began to lift amid the grunts and groans of the straining men. Angus came out of the building and walked over to Lizzie's group, his eyes carefully following the ascending barrel as he moved toward them.

"Do you have any more blocks?" Charley asked, an urgent note in his voice.

The manager answered half-heartedly, concentrating on the still rising barrel.

"Och aye, lad," he said, turning to walk away.

"Don't go!" snapped Charley in a commanding tone. "Show me your pulleys," he said, sliding off the cart onto his crutches.

Angus glanced at Lizzie doubtfully.

"Do it," the girl instructed.

Angus led Charley inside, as the youngsters watched the men land the barrel high above, instantly swinging it out of sight.

Soon Charley was back hopping along on his crutches and grinning from ear to ear. Loud talking could be heard from above, then the creaking of the gantry arm being moved.

Angus stuck his head out of the upstairs doorway and shouted at the men below to let go of the rope and it was quickly pulled up and out of sight. Ten minutes went by and suddenly the rope came hurtling back down, but this time there seemed to be something unusual about the configuration.

"Right, come on," Charley called to the puzzled youngsters, hopping over to the rope. Then he instructed the men to stand back. "You two take hold of that rope," he ordered Quon and Lizzie. They gave him a very doubtful look but did as he said. Then, looking up, he yelled, "Hang a barrel on."

Suddenly, a barrel swung out in mid-air and the youngsters braced themselves for the expected weight.

"Hold tight, an let it down . . . easy . . . now," he instructed, but it came down gently with hardly any effort at all.

The youngsters began to laugh now that they saw how easy it was.

"Don't laugh yet," Charley commanded, "you're going ta pull a full one up now."

The look of disbelief on Lizzie's young face said it all.

"Yer daft, we can't do that!"

"Just do it, an don't argue with me, " Charley replied sharply. The men on the ground hooked the barrel on, chuckling as they waited to see what would happen next. The engineer gave the command slowly and deliberately. "Now . . . pull . . . and don't let go!"

Slowly the huge barrel began to lift. Up, up it went until at last it was level with the doorway where strong arms pulled it in to safety. A great cheer erupted from the men in the yard below.

"Right, we can go now," Charley said, scrambling back onto his seat in the cart, carefully keeping his back to the younguns so they couldn't observe his excitement.

Angus McClain came running out of a doorway, red-faced and puffing a little.

"If ah'd noo a seen that wi me own eyes, ah'd noo av believed it! 'Am in yer debt, sir, and ah'll be thankin yer profusely," he said, shouting to the men to get back to work.

Lizzie eyed the young engineer from behind a frown.

"Tryin ta tell us sumthin, weren't you?" she muttered.

All she received in return was a grin from the elated Charley, who importantly tapped the cart with his crutch and pointed to the way out.

"Home, boss," he shouted with a chuckle, settling into his tatty throne.

Chapter 2

On the way home, the youngsters quietly discussed what had happened.

"Heavy load lift easy, damn," Quon Lee reflected. "How he do dat?" he asked, wrinkling his brow as he tried to understand.

"Sumthin ta do with pulleys," the girl mumbled, pulling hard on the shafts as they crested Water Lane. "Yer goin ta get off here?" Lizzie asked their passenger as the cart stopped at Joe's garden gate.

"Aye, might as well," Charley replied pleasantly, quickly sliding off his transport and onto his crutches.

"We won't be long," the youngsters shouted, trotting away to return the cart to the slaughterhouse.

A voice boomed out as they approached the building.

"Leave it outside, yer might need it again." It was the foreman, who had watched their approach from inside the doorway.

Lizzie nodded and Quon pointed to a small outside shed where they deposited it neatly.

"Let's take a quick look at the new buildin," the girl suggested, moving toward the corner, knowing the Chinese boy would be following right behind her.

Not expecting to find anything of particular interest, she walked around the corner and stopped dead in her tracks—there in front of her were five distinct groups of men, all standing to attention and listening intently to the Irish supervisor. They found a comfortable observation spot and quietly watched.

"Do yer want to go to sea, one more time?" Mick's voice boomed.

The chorus of replies was a unanimous, "Yes, sir."

"Have you selected yer crews?" Mick yelled.

Again, the chorus was unanimous. "We have, sir."

Mick stood and surveyed the men before adding, not quite so loudly. "Be sure ya can handle the work, now."

A hush fell over the assembly until a peg-legged, younger sailor stepped forward.

"No sir, we ain't good fer the climbing, but add three able-bodied men who know the trade, to each crew, an then we can do it."

The rest of the men agreed with shouts of, "Aye, aye, shipmate."

Again, silence descended on the gathering, as the sailor stepped back into line and Mick began again.

"Some might not come back," he reminded them with a serious look.

"Beggin yer pardon, sir, but Master Joe's bin good ter all ov us, an we're all loyal TLS men now—if any man crosses the master, we fight," another sailor shouted as a murmur of agreement passed through the group.

Mick waved his hand toward the cookhouse to dismiss the gathering and quickly flick the tear that escaped one eye, and threatened to run down his weathered face. These men might be short a limb or two, but their backbones were still as hard as ever and their loyalty was without question.

The Irishman walked slowly over to the youngsters.

"Well, ya heard 'em now, an in moy own opinion hoy'll be tellin yer missy, hoy'd ride ta hell an back wi men loyk them."

Lizzie looked up at him with sad eyes that were somewhat clouded over.

"They're all good men, aren't they, Mick?" she whispered, also finding their display of loyalty very touching.

"Yes, they are," he said seriously. Then smiling, he changed the subject.

"Hoy'll be changin me clothes an washin, then hoy'll be joinin yer fer supper, lass."

The youngsters slid down from their perch and watched Mick as he walked away.

"Him damn good man," Quon muttered to himself, but received no comment from Lizzie except a nod and a scowl. She was obviously in one of her thinking moods, so the boy bothered her no more with conversation as they walked back down the lane to the cottage.

Supper went well, with lots of laughter and stories of earlier sea voyages. Joe had invited Angus McClain, who simply had to tell of the engineer's feats at the brewery earlier in the day. Charley became quite embarrassed with all the praise the brewery manager was heaping on him. Mick wanted to know how it was done and listened very carefully, only interrupting with a nod of understanding, here and there. The old man sat in his chair, rocking the baby, not understanding a word of the long drawn-out explanation.

Lizzie had also been listening intently.

"Can you move a ship that way, Charley?" she asked casually.

Both Mick and Angus shot heavy glances at the girl, neither of them having been told the plan for the raid on Zarauz, so they had no idea why she would want to know that.

Charley Mason answered the question readily.

"Need a fixed point, lass, that's all. You can move London Bridge if you've enough pulleys!"

Ada asked the supervisor how the new building was coming along, and he was only too willing to tell everybody in great detail.

At the end of his description of the new stable block, Mick added, "And I think we have the makins of five good crews, just need Joe ta go over 'em with me."

The old man looked up, his eyebrows almost knitting together, as his gaze settled on Lizzie.

"Yer goin ta tell us soon, young lady?" he asked quietly.

"About another three days should do it," she said breezily. "Then I'll tell you all." She slapped Quon on the back, pushed her chair away from the table and rose. "Come on," she said to the boy who was already moving to follow her.

At the door she suddenly stopped and looked back, Quon Lee almost fell over her.

"Don't you go away anywhere Mister Charles Mason, I need yer," she said emphatically.

"Where we go, damn?" Quon asked, catching onto her sleeve once they were outside.

"Have yer got the spyglass?" Lizzie continued, ignoring the boy's question.

"Can do," he said, turning to run back inside the cottage, as the girl kept on walking. Soon the patter of running feet told her he was on his way back and she speeded up to a jog.

The church soon came into view as they slowed to a walk—a flowering yellow gauze bush bringing the girl to a halt.

"Now what?" Quon Lee asked, with a puzzled expression.

"Get yer knife out an cut me some of those pretty flowers."

A knife appeared in his hand and he cut four or five of the tough gauze branches and handed them to her. Lizzie tied the flowers together with a piece of tough grass, set her face with a solemn expression and marched toward the gate in the church wall with the Chinese boy trotting alongside.

An old couple, coming out of the churchyard, held the gate open for them. Noticing the flowers, the man doffed his hat at the children, in respect for the departed.

"Bless you children, carrying flowers to a loved one's grave, are you?" the woman commented with a kindly smile.

Lizzie nodded, her head bowed as they walked on up the path.

The Chinese boy was becoming quite mystified by Lizzie's actions but knew her reasons would become apparent if he was patient. With their heads still down in a reverent manner, they rounded the side of the church and Lizzie quickly lay her flowers down on a nearby grave.

Then, as they passed the belfry tower, she grabbed the boy's arm and pulled him inside. Quickly closing the door, she stopped and turned to face Quon. Pressing her finger to her lips, she stood very still and listened.

"Quiet now," she whispered, then began tiptoeing up the stairs to the bell tower.

Once at the top, she again gave him the sign to remain silent as she reached into his coat and extracted the spyglass. Resting it on the parapet rail, she searched the length of the river for a sighting of Captain Davis and his ship, *Falcon*, then turning excitedly and pointing, she pulled the boy forward to look for himself.

"Captain home late tonight, damn," he said quietly, stuffing the spyglass back into his coat.

Down the old wooden stairs they crept, as quietly as possible, until they reached the door. Lizzie almost had her hand on the latch when they heard the voices. They sounded angry and were headed in their direction. Quickly scooting in behind the door just before it opened, they stood holding their breath—Quon Lee put his arm across the front of the girl in a protective stance.

The door was quickly pushed open . . . but only halfway, and someone threw a pick and spade inside. Lizzie and Quon tried hard not to breathe and it seemed an eternity before the door was pulled shut once again. They remained quiet until the muffled voices became so soft they couldn't be heard anymore.

Waiting a few minutes, the youngsters apprehensively opened the door . . . just a crack, listening intently for sounds of anyone who might still be in the area. Hearing nothing they slipped out, pulled the great door shut behind them and ran for the gate.

"Close one that time, dumplin," Lizzie ventured with a sigh of relief, noticing that Quon Lee's skin was almost as white as her own. Without waiting for him to say anything, she grabbed his hand and they took off down the road at a run.

Mick and Ada were standing at the open garden gate, deep in conversation, as the youngsters came hurtling toward them. Charley, hobbling up the garden path from a different direction, stopped to talk to Mick and Ada and was almost bowled over by the excited twosome.

Laughter and apologies were exchanged and nothing more was thought of the incident.

"Where be yer stayin, Charley?" Mick inquired.

"At distant relatives, about half a mile away."

"Fancy a ride home, then?" Mick asked.

Ada looked puzzled, but said nothing, as she watched Lizzie's reaction.

"On what . . . you a horse now?" the girl asked quizzically.

The Irishman laughed, kneeling down.

"Jump on lad," he commanded.

Charley hesitated for a moment until encouraged by the girl's somewhat authoritative command.

"Do it, Charley!" Lizzie encouraged, grabbing hold of his crutches.

Now having his hands free, Charley did as he was told, climbing aboard Mick's broad back. Mick effortlessly climbed to his feet—Lizzie handed him the crutches and away they went. Long, easy strides quickly took them out of earshot and Lizzie muttered, "He's so big, Charley won't even be felt."

"Charley's a good lad," Ada mused quietly, "and desperately wants somebody to need him,"

Lizzie looked hard at Missus Mason, a tiny crinkle of amusement. playing around her mouth.

"Well, he's found a home then, ain't he . . . cos we need im!"

Ada slipped an arm over the girl's shoulder and they walked up the path together.

"You, young lady, are somebody special, too—goodness knows how you became so old, while still so young, it fairly mystifies me."

Down the road, Charley and Mick were getting to know each other better as they strode along. Deep in conversation, the big Irishman hardly noticed the burden on his back.

"Ever been to sea, Mick?" asked the engineer.

"Aye, lad, that ah have."

Mick adjusted Charley's position and asked the next question somewhat less eagerly.

"What happened ta yer legs, Charley?"

Mick thought he could feel some tenseness in the body on his back. In the short pause before Charley gave Mick his answer, Mick had a fleeting thought that he probably shouldn't have asked such a personal question.

"Cannon ball bounced off me," was Charley's simple reply.

Mick knew they were almost at the cottage and decided not to pursue the matter.

Arriving at the home of the young man's relatives, Mick slid his passenger off onto the garden wall and sat down beside him. They sat talking for a while about nothing in particular, simply enjoying a pleasant evening and good company, when a jovial looking man of about forty came walking toward them from the direction of the little cottage.

"Found a handsome horse ta ride, did yer, lad?" he chuckled, introducing himself as Dan Duffy, master blacksmith, second cousin of Charley's mother.

They exchanged a few pleasantries and soon Mick announced that he had to go, promising to send someone for the engineer in the morning. Then the big Irishman strode off into the waning light of the evening.

"Seems a good-hearted sort," Dan Duffy commented, watching Mick disappear up the road.

"The best," Charley answered, as they entered the house and he began to tell Dan of his latest adventure.

Chapter 3

Dawn found Lizzie and Quon Lee scurrying down Water Lane to the docks and, sure enough, there was *Falcon* tied in her usual berth, but tied alongside was another vessel—an unfamiliar one.

"Don't recognize that other ship, do yer?" the girl asked her partner.

"Damn foliner, me tink," Quon spat out in disgust, causing Lizzie to burst out laughing, then they hurried back home for breakfast. A knock at the door, just as they were finishing the meal, brought Ada quickly to her feet.

"Oh, it's only Mick," she said, stepping back to allow him to enter.

"Missy," he said, addressing Lizzie, "I brought yer cart down for ya."

The girl scowled at the building supervisor aware there was more to it than this.

"Well, I sort of promised Charley," he continued apologetically, pausing to find the right words.

"What did yer promise him?" the girl asked sharply.

"That somebody would come and get him, ta be savin the lad a long walk," Mick blurted out, a little embarrassed.

"Oh, now ah see," Lizzie said, staring at the Irishman. "An you want us ta keep yer promise for ya!"

"Now you just stop that young lady," Ada admonished the girl, wagging her finger. "Take no notice of her, Mick, she's just roastin yer for the fun of it."

Mick backed outside, cap in hand. He was extremely glad to be out of there but as he closed the door, he could hear Lizzie laughing.

It was another sunny day as the handcart bumped and bounced over the deep-rutted road; the youngsters charged along at full speed toward Charley's lodgings, arriving amid a cloud of dust, dirt, and laughter.

"Time yer got here," the waiting engineer grumbled, "we don't have all day, you know."

A jovial Dan Duffy picked Charley up bodily, plunking him into his seat.

"Tek the bad-tempered little bugger away from here!" he grinned.

Turning the cart around in the road, they were soon on their way back to Brown's Yard—the speed these two youngsters travelled almost shook their passenger out of his seat several times, unable to avoid potholes during the hair-raising ride.

At last, they were on cobblestones and as they pulled into Brown's Yard, Lumpy, the carpenter, watched with a definite look of fear on his face and his pipe began to wobble in tune with his dithering jaw.

Charley straightened his cap, winked at Quon Lee, and shuffled off his perch onto his crutches, feigning dizziness.

"Thank you for a wonderfully smooth ride, although I am inclined to arrange my own transport back to your cottage when I'm finished here!"

He made an attempt at bowing to Lizzie, who smiled sweetly back at him, and then walked over and gave him a hug.

"Yer a good sport, sailor, we'll be back for yer."

Lumpy stood back watching, regaining his composure. Taking his pipe out of his mouth, he grunted, "What the hell do you want wi' me?"

The engineer looked him over carefully.

"Better be civil my man, this is an official request," Charley snapped, as the pipe began to wobble again in the carpenter's mouth. "It is also top secret and no one is to know what we are doing or who I am—is that understood?"

Shock registered on the old man's face and all he could manage in reply was, "Aye, sir," in a very fearful, humble tone.

"Right, let's get at it then," Charley said, knowing he had won all the co-operation he would need from the old man.

He produced a piece of chalk and handed it to the carpenter who scratched his head and frowned, then dropping everything, he went to work with a vengeance, skilfully preparing the drawings Charley needed.

Everything the old man did showed his skill and love of the wood with which he worked—his use of tools was like watching an artist. One or two adjustments were made here and there as each of the two men used their particular skill in complete collaboration, and slowly the huge pulleys began to take shape.

Down on the docks meanwhile, Lizzie and Quon had happened on some unexpected goings on. Soldiers had surrounded the government vessel and were rounding up some foreign-looking sailors.

"Who are they?" she whispered to one of the many bystanders gathered near Captain Davis' ship to watch this unusual display of military force.

"It's the French merchant ship, *Le Canard*," the man answered, moving in behind the jeering crowd now following the soldiers as the captured crew was led away.

Despite the fact there was a major war going on which greatly affected the people in other areas of England, the poor people down here in dockland, were rarely reminded of its devastating effect. Few poor people were able to read, and the only news came by way of travellers and the occasional ship that came to their area of the Thames.

But Lizzie and Quon were aware of what was happening in the outside world, thanks to Captain Davis. As the dock cleared of the excited crowd, Davis spotted the youngsters and waved them aboard, meeting them at the head of the gangplank.

"Tell Joe to bring as many drays as he can find, at ten tonight—now go, we have guards on board 'til six," he said quietly.

Quon tugged at her sleeve and they left the dock at a run.

Finding Joe in a hurry could be a problem at this time of day. Dropping the cart in front of the tailor's shop, they dashed in. Abe Kratze looked up from his sewing—his glasses balanced precariously on the end of his nose, as was usual—and peered at them inquiringly.

"Don't move," the girl panted. "Just called ta tell yer, we have lots of goods ta be delivered startin tamorra." She then spun around and left in a hurry.

"Blewely," Quon Lee suggested as they picked up the cart and moved off again—the girl nodded her head in agreement.

They were in luck as Joe was just leaving the brewery on his morning rounds of inspection. They delivered the message, adding that they had already alerted Abe Kratze.

The old man sucked hard on his pipe, shaking his head.

"It's all right, luv, we're ready ta go anytime ya say," he chuckled, moving off at a slow walk.

"Amazin," Lizzie mused, "he hardly ever gets flustered anymore, just takes things as they come."

Quon cocked an eyebrow at the girl.

"Our big flend is Joe . . . our dad," he said proudly.

"Aye, an yer my dumplin, yer little devil," she said, kicking him gently in the rear and causing him to giggle. "But we gotta go, so come on," the girl urged, picking up a cart shaft and moving off.

Back to Brown's Yard they trotted, being careful not to rattle the six stone jugs of cider they had begged from one of the men at the brewery as a gift for Lumpy. Lunchtime was almost upon them as they turned into Brown's Yard—there stood the old carpenter in close conversation with Charley Mason, obviously discussing the huge wooden thing in front of them.

"Well, what do yer think about that?" Charley asked, pointing at Lumpy's handiwork.

The youngsters shrugged their shoulders.

"What's it for," the girl asked, adding cheekily, "but it looks luvly!"

Quon Lee grinned. "It's a big ballel lift, damn."

Even old Lumpy let out a chuckle—it was the very first time they had ever seen a smile on the old man's face.

"This time I know what he said," Charley chortled, banging his crutch on the cobbles. "That thing is just what you need my girl," the engineer stated in a serious tone.

Lizzie looked at the contraption with a frown, wrinkling her nose. "I'll bet it could move a ship, it's big enough . . . but could two men lift it?" she asked, cocking an eyebrow at Charley.

"No, but four can, and if we make it in pieces, two can."

"It's lunchtime," Lizzie announced, changing the subject abruptly. "Are you coming home or staying here?"

The engineer was quick to reply. "Staying here."

The youngsters quickly unloaded the cider explaining it was for Lumpy, and began to move off.

"Pick me up for supper," Charley yelled, without getting a reply from the fast-disappearing pair.

Trotting off down the road, the youngsters heard Charley yell, but simply smiled at each other and decided to have some fun with him. Charlie was a nice fella and he was able to take a ribbing as well as most.

Ten minutes later they pulled into Bill Johnson's yard. The baker looked out to see who had arrived, and waved.

"Nice ta see ya," he called to them, his face breaking into a large grin. He shouted for his wife to come into the bakery.

Missus Johnson poked her head around the door which connected the house to the workplace. She squealed with delight as she saw who the visitors were, rushing out to wrap her huge arms around each of the youngsters in turn.

"By gum, but it's nice ta see yer both," she declared in her best Yorkshire accent. "Is this a social call, luv?' she asked, and without hesitation she produced a slab of pie, cut it in half and placed each piece onto a plate for the youngsters.

"Well, not really," Lizzie admitted, watching the Chinese boy wolf into Bill's always superb apple pie, her mouth watering in expectation.

"Can we get two of yer Yorkshire meat pies, an maybe an apple pie as well, for two hungry men?"

Missus Johnson pursed her lips. "Of course ye can, luv."

"I'll pay for 'em," Lizzie said, as she began eating her own piece.

Always the businesswoman, the baker's wife simply nodded in agreement and asked for and received three pennies in payment. A basket was produced and the pies were stowed safely inside. Both youngsters cleaned up the last of their pie, thanked the Johnson's for the delicious treat, and with a cheery wave and a shouted goodbye, they were on their way again.

Brown's Yard was unusually quiet as they drew closer on the return journey that afternoon. With some suspicion, they slowed to a walk, and parking the cart outside in the lane, they proceeded quietly. They stopped to peek around a tall entrance post before proceeding, and there, right in the middle of the yard, sat Lumpy and Charley talking quietly head-to-head like long-time friends.

"He's sure tamed that grumpy old bugger," Lizzie commented in a whisper, shaking her head in amazement.

Sneaking back to the cart they returned a second time making a normal noisy entrance, causing both men to look up startled by the intrusion.

"Don't you two do anything quietly?" Charley snapped, accepting the old man's help to get to his feet and balance on his crutches.

"Don't lose yer temper just yet," Lizzie snapped back. "We brought yer something ta eat," she said, scooping the basket off the cart and gingerly throwing it at him.

Old Lumpy deftly stepped forward to catch the flying object before it hit Charley, flipping the basket's cover off to reveal the food inside. A grin spreading across his face, he announced, "Time to eat, master," and the youngsters turned the cart in preparation to leave.

"You can leave it here if you like," Charley directed, blowing crumbs from a mouth full of food, "an pick me up about five."

Taking the shortcut up Goat Hill, they meandered past some tiny cottages and waved to a couple of people in one of the nearby gardens.

"You hungry?" Lizzie asked casually.

The Chinese boy grinned.

"Me big full apple pie, damn," rubbing his stomach to emphasize the point.

"Right then, let's do a little snooping on our own," the girl suggested, a merry twinkle of devilment in her eye.

Quon Lee's answer was totally predictable.

"Wizzy go, me follow," he said, as they broke into a run.

As they jogged toward home, Lizzie instructed the boy to get their spyglass. The order sent him racing ahead to comply. As she neared the cottage, Lizzie could see Martha in the backyard taking in the clothes, and called out to her as Quon arrived back at her side.

"We need ta be on the roof of Abe Kratze's shop, facing the docks," she muttered, pondering the problem and wrinkling her brow. "An without him knowing what we are planning," Lizzie added secretively.

Down Pump Street and into the back alley off Mast Lane they turned, slowing to a walk as they took notice of everything around them. A group of small children were playing happily in a corner—not a single adult was in sight. Slyly, they checked all the windows to make sure there were no prying eyes watching. Only when they were perfectly sure no one was aware of their presence, did they make their move toward the rickety stairs leading to the roof.

Stealthily the young pair crept up the stairs and onto the roof. Once there unnoticed, they knew they were safe from detection. Quon Lee stayed just out of sight at the parapet wall, peeking over just far enough to make sure no one had followed them. After a while, he joined Lizzie, who had taken up a perch between the two tall chimneys, from which vantage point they had a clear line of sight to the docks and the deck of the government vessel.

Quon Lee lined up the spyglass to the *Falcon*'s deck, studying the area silently but thoroughly. A tap on the shoulder from the girl and he handed the spyglass over without a word. Lizzie swung the instrument onto the deck of the French prize tied alongside and whistled through her teeth.

"What see?" her partner demanded, excitement in his voice.

"I see One-Eyed Jack and the crew of the patrol ship unloading barrels of brandy from the French ship's hold. Wait now," she said, concentrating hard, "there's bales of silk on the deck." Slowly lowering the spyglass, she thoughtfully rubbed her brow. Handing the glass back to Quon, she whispered, "Time to go dumplin."

Dropping to their knees, they crept silently back to the head of the stairs and Quon carefully peeked over—there below were three soldiers, just standing there, smoking their long clay pipes and, no doubt, hiding from their officers.

"Tlouble," Quon Lee whispered, pointing them out to the girl.

With their heads ducked well below the parapet, Lizzie began planning their escape. Looking around, she spotted a piece of wood and two clay bricks, probably left on the roof by workmen long since gone.

"Listen now," she whispered, grabbing his shirtfront, "take those two bricks and throw them off the far corner of the roof into the street below, but don't hit anybody with 'em."

The Chinese boy nodded, understanding the situation completely. Stealthily, he crossed the roof and followed Lizzie's instruction. As the bricks crashed into the street, it seemed to startle the soldiers but they quickly gathered their wits and ran to see what the noise was all about.

Quon ran back across the roof to rejoin Lizzie and they quickly scrambled over the parapet wall, dashed down the rickety stairs at full speed and were soon safely out into the back alley unnoticed. Casually strolling down the lane trying not to attract any attention, they dared not look back. Behind them, they could hear loud voices, as the soldiers tried to understand how two bricks came to be in the middle of the street.

Chapter 4

Making their way through back alleys toward the river, the youngsters decided to take a look at one of the other docks. A couple of times, they stopped to talk with some of their old bread customers, also bumping into Tom Day and Billy on their rounds.

"You all right, Tom?" Lizzie called, as she spotted him limping into a shop, breadbasket loaded. It never ceased to amaze her how well Tom got around on his pegleg.

"Just fine, Miss Lizzie. My Billy's o'er yonder," he announced, pointing down the lane.

Billy soon arrived back at the delivery cart and let out a yelp when he saw the visitors. Flinging his basket onto the cart, he threw his arms around Lizzie in a tremendous hug.

"Don't like yer job, eh?" the girl asked, teasing the young boy.

"Oh, but ah do, ah do," Billy cried in alarm.

"It's all light lad, she bad one, just funnin," Quon quickly interceded. "You stop doin dat, Wizzy," he scolded the girl in mock anger.

"No, no, Billy boy," Lizzie said, smiling and hugging him, "we're right pleased with yer lad."

Tom returned with a now empty basket, wiping the sweat from his face.

"Sorry, missy, but we gotta go," he said, picking up the cart shafts. "We just ran out of cider—gotta go get more." The delivery cart rumbled off with Billy pushing from the rear.

"We pick good pleeple, damn," Quon Lee chuckled. His partner nodded, watching the cart disappear around the next corner.

Arriving at the Thames' dock, well below the bridge, the youngsters wandered in amongst a large group of top-hatted shipping owners and agents standing around discussing cargoes and vessels. Seating themselves on an empty crate, they began to throw pebbles into the water. The group closest to them took no notice whatsoever and continued talking loudly enough for Lizzie and Quon to overhear their every word.

"Gawd, I wish we had some empty ships in dock," said the big man with his posh city accent.

"But, Daddy, the rag trade into Scotland will wait," a pasty-faced young dandy replied.

"Only because no one knows about it yet, you fool," the older man snapped impatiently.

"But, sir, we won't tell them," snivelled the young dandy, tapping his silver-tipped stick on the cobbles for emphasis.

Lizzie glanced at the Chinese boy and winked. He grinned back and nodded to confirm that he too had heard the conversation. As they walked farther along the dock, they listened carefully to all they heard.

They soon became aware that French wines were in great demand. Dockside buyers seemed ready to bid premium prices against each other for the precious liquid. There was much talk of the war amongst the upper class and how it was making a mess of business transactions with French merchants—ruining their lucrative profits.

Strolling back toward the shopping area in the mid-afternoon sun, the youngsters discussed what they had heard.

"I wonder why they want rags in Scotland?" the girl asked, pondering the question but knowing full well she wouldn't get an answer from Quon.

The Chinese boy shrugged his shoulders and changed the subject.

"Captain Davis will know how to get Flench wine. You see Wizzy, we ask," he muttered confidently.

Turning quietly into Brown's Yard, they were surprised to see Charley and old Lumpy leaning on the handcart, obviously in deep conversation, each with a mug of cider in front of him.

"Ah, there ye be," Charley said, smiling happily as he slapped the old man on the back and thanked him profusely for the great help he had given. "How soon can you finish the others?" the engineer asked the carpenter.

"Well, we av all't patterns now, reckon it depends on't number yer want, sir." Lumpy scratched his whiskered face and added, "Ah can do two full sets a day if ah can get yer help."

Charley reached out and shook the old man's hand.

"My, oh my, you're a real gent, Mister Lumpy, an a pleasure it is to be associated with you. Tell me what your charges are for today, and the cash will be in your hand first thing in the morning." Then, hopping onto the cart, he wriggled into his seat and waited for the reply.

After some pondering, Lumpy answered.

"Would two shillings and tuppence be all right, sir?" He paused for a moment and added, "That be time and lumber."

"Aye, shipmate, it would," the engineer said, urging his transport into motion and calling for them to head for home.

Speeding through the streets and back alleys with their passenger waving his crutches at all the passers-by, the cart was soon pulling into Slaughter Lane. Slowing their pace, to dodge the heavy traffic, they pulled up at the door and backed into the place where they parked the cart.

"Thought yer might want to have a look around here," Lizzie said, helping Charley to the ground.

"Right grand idea, lass," he muttered, "but I don't want a guided tour, just leave me to wander on me own, I'll come for supper in a while."

The girl smiled, motioning with her head for the Chinese boy to follow her.

"Let's find Mick," she said, running off around the corner toward the new stable block.

Mick was sitting on a log watching the roofers finish their work. A curt nod was the only greeting he gave them as they sat near him on the ground. One of the workmen leapt down from the roof, landing like a cat in front of them.

"Just av ta back-point that ridge now, then she be done, sir," the young man reported, moving off to get a bucketful of lime.

"What's yer problem, me beauties?" Mick asked, never taking his eyes off the men on the roof.

"Just wondered if ya had the five crews picked yet?" Lizzie said nonchalantly.

The supervisor grunted before answering.

"No missy, but give us just another day an I'm sure we'll av all seven ready for yer," he said, still not taking his eyes off the workmen,

"What yer watchin for?" the girl asked, puzzled by his intentness.

"Look at the agility of them two men," Mick muttered, scratching his chin.

"How many men to a crew?" Lizzie asked, changing the subject.

The big Irishman turned slowly to face her, a frown wrinkling his brow.

"Gettin urgent now is it, lass?" He was almost whispering.

The girl nodded.

"Thirteen for luck," he added with a chuckle, referring to the size of each crew.

"Ninety-one extra men," Lizzie mumbled, deep in thought as she climbed to her feet and walked slowly out of the stable block. Quon hadn't taken his eyes off of her. Then she abruptly stopped. "Come on lad, we've a lot to do tonight."

Quon leapt to his feet and raced after her as she picked up speed.

The cottage had taken on an air of excitement and supper was a noisy affair. Joe and Ada discussed the coming night's work and Charley and the youngsters talked excitedly of their productive day. Martha was asked to stay the night and look after the baby so they had no interruptions. She agreed willingly, asking only that someone tell Bill at the bakery that she wouldn't be home this night—Lizzie quickly volunteered.

Everyone was making preparation to fulfil his or her tasks with efficient enthusiasm. Joe was leaving to organize the dray teams—nothing must be left to chance tonight but he had a question for Lizzie.

"How many teams and drays do we need?"

She answered smartly, her quick brain snapping into gear to meet the challenge.

"Everything we've got! Send 'em in relays an put a rider out to run yer messages fast—liquor goes to the brewery. Better alert Angus McClain—he'll need men there, rest of it comes here behind the slaughterhouse. Tell Angus ta keep a tally down there, Ada keeps one here."

She paused for a breath looking around at the silent, attentive faces.

"I want a quick, clean, and quiet job done tonight. This is a big one, so let's do it right." She paused again. "Me and my shadow will be here, there and everywhere, so don't look for us."

The old man left the cottage, nodding his agreement.

Ada had remained silent throughout the whole thing, just a nod or two of approval here and there, but now she had something to say.

"I never thought in my wildest dreams, that I would ever hear a general talking to his troops before a battle . . . " then she hesitated, her eyes on Lizzie, full of admiration, "but I just did, except the general was a she, not a he!"

Quon Lee's face was grinning from ear to ear.

"Dat my Wizzy," he whispered and Lizzie belted him across the shoulder.

"Enough of that stuff, let's get going, dumplin," she snapped, heading for the door.

Up to now, no one had taken the slightest notice of Charley who sat off to one side carefully taking it all in. Not wanting to be left out of what was shaping up to be a very exciting evening, he suddenly spoke, catching Lizzie in mid-stride just before she lifted the latch on the door.

"Can I help in any way?"

Without a backward glance from the door, the girl hesitated only briefly.

"Aye, help Ada, yer good with numbers," and she was gone with Quon Lee close behind. Bang went the door, as it shut in a hurry, and the patter of feet on the garden path faded away.

"Seems to know what she wants, that girl does," Charles Mason commented sarcastically.

Taken aback by her brother-in-law's comment, Ada suddenly turned on him.

"Maybe I should paint you a little picture, my lad," she said sharply. "That was the big boss talking and you had better not step one inch out of line tonight." She hesitated, watching Charley's face turn suddenly pale. Then very quietly and menacingly, she continued, "We're all fiercely loyal to that girl and will do whatever she says without question . . . and so will you!"

Charley spluttered and coughed to cover his embarrassment.

"But she's only a young girl!"

Ada's lips were clamped tight in anger.

"So, because she's young and a girl, you think she's no match for you men?"

Again, the mariner looked embarrassed.

"Well, let me tell you my lad, she's more than a match for any man I ever met. Lizzie has more brains than ten men put together—that's why we all listen to her when it comes to business. And that's my last word on it."

Down at the bakery, the youngsters were talking to Bill Johnson and his wife, explaining that Martha wouldn't be home tonight. Suddenly, the baker turned to Lizzie.

"Ee bye gum, lass, ah had an interesting young fella in't shop today."

"Who?" she asked, her interest sharpened.

Bill stopped what he was doing, laid his big hands on the table and leaned toward them.

"Patrick Sandilands, from Aberdeen in Scotland," he whispered, almost reverently.

"So, what's important about that?" the girl shot back.

"Cos I told him ta go see Joe."

Lizzie began to look a little frustrated not understanding where this could be leading. Knowing Bill liked to be prodded, she implored, "Come on, Bill, tell me it all, then maybe it'll make some sense."

Missus Johnson burst out laughing. "Ain't he maddening, tells yer bits an pieces 'til it sends yer crazy. Yer goin ta have ter drag it outa him, lass."

Bill pretended to pout a little, then grinning from ear to ear, he began to explain.

"He's a papermaker from Scotland lookin for rags, an he's comin ter see yer tamorra."

A controlled smile moved slowly across Lizzie's face as she glanced at Quon whose hands were pressed firmly together, thumbs pointing upwards.

"Oh, I see," she said, "he wants ter buy a few rags."

Bill coughed. "A few," he spluttered, "a whole damned shipload!" The baker was getting so excited, he could barely finish and Lizzie giggled at his reddening face.

Quickly leaving the bakery, the youngsters discussed the sudden turn of events. A big buyer of rags turning up out of nowhere was something they decided to be wary of, at least until he produced some credentials, or they found someone who would vouch for his authenticity. To the best of their knowledge, they knew no one from Scotland, except the cider brewery manager, Angus McClain.

Angus worked long and dedicated hours, so it was no trouble finding him. True to his nature, there he was out in the yard with four of his most reliable men, counting and moving barrels and generally getting prepared for the brandy and French wine deliveries later in the evening.

"Comin ta see me are ye, lassie?" he asked smiling, using a big cloth to mop his sweating brow.

"Aye, that ah am," Lizzie answered mimicking his Scottish accent and giggling at the result of her effort. "Ah'll be wantin ta know if yer aware of a Scot by the name of Sandilands?"

The manager furrowed his brow.

"Aye, yer could say all of Scotland kens the name."

The girl began to look a bit bewildered. Now this was interesting news, she thought, but was it good news? She leaned forward, eagerly waiting for him to continue. But Angus was in no hurry. He straightened his back and stretched with a groan. Just as Lizzie was about to explode from anticipation, he continued.

"The Sandilands' are one of the most respected families in all of Scotland . . . honourable men and true ter their word every last one of them."

Relieved, Lizzie whispered, "How do yer know all that?

A grin broke out on Angus McClain's face.

"Ach, it's been that way fer at least four hundred years, lassie," he concluded, beginning to walk away and shouting orders to his men.

The youngsters slowly walked away, each deep in their own thoughts, considering the manager's little lecture. Quon spoke first.

"Me tink we tlust dis one, damn."

Lizzie nodded her head in agreement and the discussion was over.

Chapter 5

It was well after supper, and all along the docks there was quiet—just the occasional delivery wagon making its way over the cobblestones. As they looked for a particular ship in the growing dusk, they found Captain Davis and Ben Thorn sitting on the deck of *Falcon* talking quietly.

"Come aboard, me hearties," the captain invited, quickly rising to his feet and ordering Ben to bring drinks into his cabin.

Scampering up the gangplank, Lizzie was soon seated in front of the massive oak desk with Quon Lee standing in his customary position behind her. Ben arrived with the drinks, put them down on the desk, and left again quietly closing the door behind him.

"So, you all ready, girl?" Davis asked, his eyes scrutinizing the pair.

"It's all arranged as you expected it would be," Lizzie answered curtly.

Quiet settled between the two facing each other across the desk—almost imperceptibly the Chinese boy's fingers tightened on the girl's shoulder.

"Did yer get a peek into the harbour at Zarauz?" she asked.

"Better than that," the captain said grinning, fully expecting this question and knowing the answer was going to please his Lizzie. "The merchantman we captured—that was his home port—an he told us everything we wanted to know."

Excitement did not often cause Lizzie to forget her position and revert to childlike actions, but this time she could not contain herself and she bounced off her seat, eagerly approaching the captain.

"Tell me what he said . . . about the ships in dock?" she asked leaning eagerly over the desk.

Davis leaned back in his chair and roared with laughter. As he calmed down, he began to chuckle.

"It gets better and better, lass. They have six lovely mid-size barks almost ready and one brig with the repairs due to be finished in two weeks."

Lizzie sat back down in her chair unable to hide her total surprise and excitement. Quon patted her shoulder gently urging her to calm down.

Davis started to laugh again. "Now, godamnit, yer little pirate, which two do yer want?" he demanded, rubbing his hand through his beard.

The girl bounced forward again and snarled at him fiercely.

"The whole damn lot, sir!"

This time it was the captain's turn to be surprised and a look of shock quickly spread over his face, turning it quite crimson.

"What!" he bellowed. "It will be a nightmare getting two, but 'em all . . . yer must be a lunatic!" Leaping out of his seat, he proceeded to stomp around the cabin, muttering to himself in violent torrents.

"Sit down and listen!" Lizzie yelled, her voice jerking him to a sudden halt and bringing him back to his desk. "I have the crews, all experienced sailors, and a master engineer who has worked out how to move 'em out of the harbour quietly. All the equipment can be loaded in two day's time. I have the man to run the whole damned show . . . and I have only one question," the girl snapped. The captain's eyes narrowed even more as he silently waited.

"Can you carry a hundred men across the channel to Zarauz and glory?"

Rubbing his beard vigorously, the captain's eyes shone with the vision of the adventure.

"I goddamn will," he said, thumping the table.

There was a sound like the rumble of a dray's iron-rimmed wheels on cobblestones outside, followed by many running feet on deck.

The captain jumped out of his chair.

"Organize it, Lizzie. We leave in five days," he flung back at the girl as he disappeared out onto the deck to oversee the offloading of goods and, no doubt, to carefully keep his own tally sheet.

By the time the youngsters left, one dray had been loaded with ten barrels of the best French brandy. The four huge Shires strained under the load as they moved off down the docks and the second dray was just pulling into the loading area. Lizzie and Quon stood for a moment watching all the activity, marvelling at the speed and efficiency with which their men worked.

"We go, Wizzy, big day tomollow, damn," Quon Lee urged the girl.

They had only gone halfway up the dock when they heard someone calling to them. There, sitting on a half-barrel was One-Eyed Jack, looking very sad and holding a dirty cloth to his face.

"Are ya hurt?" inquired Lizzie, with instant concern.

Jack slowly removed the cloth from his face revealing a great swelling on his jaw.

"My gawd, what's happened to yer?" the girl asked, as Quon cringed at the sight of One-Eyed Jack's grotesque face.

"It's me rotten tooth," Jack slobbered, not being able to talk properly.

"Yer should go to that new teeth doctor."

The sailor looked up, his face a mask of pain and suffering, as he whimpered, "What new doctor?"

Lizzie put her arm around her distressed friend.

"We'll take ya first thing in the morning," she said, patting his shoulder.

"We go right now!" Jack spluttered, jumping to his feet.

"But it's after ten, he won't be doing his teeth work at this time a night," the girl argued.

"Oh yes, he will," Jack muttered, drawing a wicked-looking dagger from his high-topped boot.

Lizzie shook her head in mock disgust.

"If yer show im yer pig sticker, ah reckon he will . . . come on then."

Chester Street was more than a mile away, though the long walk in the cool night air seemed to ease the pain in One-Eyed Jack's tooth. They arrived just as the big Parliament Building clock chimed a quarter to eleven.

It was a normal shop front with big signs in the window, advertising dentistry by Doctor Burges. It also said he had acquired all his training in the art from Professor Grot of Hamburg, Germany. In an upstairs window, a lantern burned, casting an almost orange-coloured glow back into the room.

Bang . . . bang . . . bang . . . the door vibrated as the hammer fist of the mariner struck blow after blow. The second-floor window grated and began to rise as Jack stepped back into the street to get a better view. The head that showed itself was wearing a white nightcap, complete with a tassel.

"What do you want at this late hour?" a voice whined, obviously in fear of his life.

"We have urgent need of your expertise, sir . . . and the cash to pay for the service," Lizzie assured him in her most persuasive tone.

"My expertise, eh?" the voice said, more confident now that he realized they were only late customers. The payment would be a small reward for the disturbance.

"Wait there, I shall attend upon you with all haste," he called, slamming the window down with a crash.

Five minutes later, the light of many lanterns lit the interior of the dentist's office and the heavy locks could be heard clicking open.

"Come in now," the voice called. In the middle of the room stood a very low dentist's chair with a sloping back, topped off by a headrest.

Doctor Burges was a tall skinny man of around thirty-five, with long, thin fingers, goatee beard, and a moustache. He was still dressed in his white nightgown and matching tasselled cap.

"Get in the chair," the doctor ordered, and Jack quickly complied. "Lay back and open your mouth," Burges ordered, fiddling noisily with his instruments.

One-Eyed Jack silently slid the long dagger out of his boot and held it with both hands on his chest. The dentist noticed it immediately. He turned away from Jack and his whole body began to shake—his mouth tried to make words, but none came.

"Thought that would improve yer damned manners," Jack spluttered through his swollen lips.

The girl's voice brought the dentist's attention back to the job at hand.

"Better get on with it before he gets mad an sticks yer wiv it!" she warned.

Burges composed himself, keeping one eye on the dagger. Working fast and silently now, he quickly found the offending tooth. "Pelican, pelican," he muttered, reaching onto his table full of wicked-looking instruments. Turning back to his patient, he locked the instrument onto a tooth, gave a sudden twist and a jerk.

Jack's dagger flew off his chest as he gave one mighty scream and leapt out of the chair, cannoning off the wall onto the floor.

"God Almighty . . . yer had better av got it, cos we ain't doin that no more," the mariner snarled, blood now dripping from his mouth.

Lizzie and Quon were laughing so hard they had collapsed onto their knees. The good Doctor Burges was standing admiring the rotten tooth, clasped firmly between the jaws of the instrument he called a pelican.

Jack picked himself up off the floor, recovered his dagger and put his hand out mumbling something inaudible.

Doctor Burges dropped the offending molar into the outstretched hand, and said, "That will be two guineas, sir, for a job well done."

The big mariner dropped two coins into the dentist's palm and, being unable to speak, urgently grunted through the blood, words that sounded like, "Brandy . . . brandy . . .."

Burges left the room, returning almost immediately with a bottle of cheap liquor. One-Eyed Jack grabbed it, pouring it into his wide-open mouth; then sloshing it around, he spat it out onto the floor, only to refill his mouth and swallow it this time.

"That's better," he said, just before he put the bottle to his lips and drained it completely.

Doctor Burges looked shocked at the display, but managed to point at the empty bottle.

"Don't worry, we will replace yer booze tamorra, an with good stuff—come on you two, let's get outa here," Lizzie commanded, as she herded her two companions back outside and into the street.

On the way home, Jack mentioned his pain was now subsiding, but he hoped he never had to make another visit to Doctor Burges. Too many shocks like that could kill a man.

"He must av done his training with the torture chamber at the Tower of London," he announced sardonically.

By the time the youngsters climbed into bed, it was almost midnight.

Martha had scolded them thoroughly for being so late home, and could not understand what was so funny about a man going to the dentist. The rumble of heavy-loaded drays and the snorting of horses on their way up the lane to the warehouse were like music to their ears as sleep overtook them.

"A wee bit late this mornin," Martha clucked, in her broad Yorkshire, at the sleepy-eyed pair. "I'm not a bit surprised, stayin out half the night. Mister Joe and Missus Mason haven't come home yet," she said, busying herself around the fire and her cooking pots. The baby began to cry and good-hearted Martha scuttled away to attend to his needs.

"Tink she adopt us, Wizzy?" Quon muttered sleepily.

"I don't mind if Martha adopts us, dumplin," she said smiling ruefully, through mouthfuls of breakfast.

There was no answer from the Chinese boy as he busily mopped up the bacon fat on his plate with a big chunk of bread, then wiped his greasy chin on the back of his sleeve, grinning with total satisfaction.

Joe and Ada, accompanied by Charley, walked in as the youngsters were lacing up their boots ready to be off. Lizzie told them of her talk with Bill Johnson and the impending visit of Patrick Sandilands.

"He'll need checking out," Joe muttered tiredly, shovelling breakfast into his hungry face.

"Already done it," was the girl's instant reply.

"You can deal with it then, Lizzie," Ada intervened wearily.

Quon's hands began to move as the girl watched him intently, nodding ever so slightly when they stopped.

"Tell Quon, yes, I'll give you the prices we need and all the relevant details—you will have to figure out the shipping," Ada said sweetly, smiling at the look of amazement on the youngsters' faces.

"You understood what he said?" Lizzie asked.

"No, just a good guess," Missus Mason replied, reaching across the table for more bacon.

Charley looked up from his plate, his tired eyes meeting Lizzie's.

"Yer quiet, lad," the girl commented.

"Aye, lass, 'am fair done for. That slave driver worked me like a dog all night," he said sarcastically, referring to his sister-in-law, Ada Mason, who simply ignored the jab and went on eating her meal.

Lizzie looked around the table at the tired faces.

"We go to Zarauz in five days," she informed them all quietly. It took several seconds for the statement to sink into their tired heads.

Ada reacted first, her fork clattering onto her plate as she repeated, "In five days!"

Lizzie giggled at the shock she had caused. Watching Charley's mouth drop open and old Joe shake his head, she continued, "An ah want seven fully trained and reliable crews, and six able-bodied marines."

Meanwhile, Ada began writing out the rag prices so Lizzie could have some basis for negotiation when the Scottish buyer came calling.

"Go get the handcart and somebody ta pull it, dumplin," the girl whispered to the Chinese boy, who was gone in an instant. "You'd better call and see Lumpy at Brown's Yard on yer way home, Charley."

Joe had finished his pipe and began to rise from his chair.

"Better go see Mick," he muttered.

"No you don't," Lizzie exclaimed, jumping out of her chair, slipping her arm across the old man's shoulders and helping him up.

Even though she was tired, Ada noticed Lizzie's concern for the older man and it struck her just how much Lizzie had grown in height recently. It won't be long and she will be as tall as me, she thought. She was no longer a little girl that was certain.

"You, my lad, are on yer way ta bed, an them is orders, not a request," Lizzie gently scolded Joe, all the time leading him toward his bedroom. Joe just nodded as he let himself be gratefully led away.

Quon Lee returned with Charley's transport and a strong young man to pull it. The man helped the disabled engineer climb aboard; then, with a wave, they were off at a fast trot along Slaughter Lane.

"That only leaves you now, Ada," Lizzie said.

"Oh, I'd better see to Willie, an catch a nap in a chair," Ada sighed tiredly.

"Oh no ya won't, yer off ta yer bed for awhile, too," Martha told her gently. "That bairn an me will be just fine on our own."

A sudden knock at the door brought a quick, "Come on in," from Lizzie and Mick, stepped inside.

"Sure, hoy be wunderin if there's anything you'd be wantin help with now?" he asked, wasting no time on niceties.

"Yes, there is," Ada muttered, quick to grab the offer of help. Shuffling through her book she stopped at the right page, propped the page open with a small ruler and looked up. "If you can get all this list delivered, it would really help a lot," she said in a tired voice.

Mick walked with long strides around the table and glanced at the book.

"Sure hoy'll be doin me level best, me darlin," he said quietly, laying his arm around Ada's shoulder. She wriggled away from him, beet-red with embarrassment and headed straight for her room.

"You romantic Irish dog, you," Lizzie laughed, as Mick's face now turned crimson and he headed for the door.

"Hey, Mick, I have some news," the girl called as the Irishman's hand reached for the latch. He stopped and slowly turned back to face the girl, a frown creasing his brow and anticipation in his eyes as he waited. "We go in five days," she whispered, as if it was a secret to the others.

"How many men?" Mick asked sharply. The news hadn't surprised him at all and he showed his ability to organize by wanting more details.

"Seven crews and six marines—about a hundred and all the equipment," Lizzie answered.

"Best we be talkin tonight—it would be a good thing ta have all the heads around the table at the same time," he suggested.

"At nine tonight, then," she answered confidently.

"I'll be here," Mick replied, and he was gone.

The partners looked at each other, reached out and clasped hands.

"We do it Wizzy, you see, damn," Quon said with conviction.

Another knock sounded on the door and Martha, who had been watching fascinated by the interaction between Lizzie and Quon, held up her hand for silence as she moved to answer it.

"Ach, am I noo at the rright place?" a very broad Scottish accent asked.

"Right place for what, luv?" Martha asked. "Yer av't told us what it is yer lookin for yet."

Both the youngsters giggled at the mixture of Yorkshire and Scottish accents in the open doorway.

"Ach, yerr rright, lassie," the voice said. "Patrick Sandilands, from Aberdeen, buyer of rraags forr my paperr mill."

Martha smiled, shuffled her large frame to one side, and invited the man in.

Stooping to get through the door, the Scot entered—all six feet six inches of him, with shoulders almost as wide as the doorframe itself. He was a red-haired man of about thirty years old. His gleaming white teeth smiled at them from a very pleasant face.

Quon Lee's hands went wild with gesticulations as he eased himself a little closer to the girl.

"No, no, he's not a giant, dumplin, he's just a big, big lump," Lizzie reassured the boy.

A bellow of laughter erupted from inside the huge frame, as the Scot realized what they were talking about.

"Ach, 'am only a man, son," Patrick said gently, kneeling on the floor in front of the boy. He reached out with a huge hand and patted the lad's knee in friendship. Raising his huge frame once more to a standing position, Patrick asked, "Would the man of the house be available to talk business?"

Lizzie's eyes turned to slits.

"Sit down, sir, you will be talkin business with me!" she snapped.

The big Scot sat down with an astonished look on his face.

"Ye be funnin me, lassie."

Shaking her head, Lizzie motioned toward the Chinese boy. Quon immediately picked up the papers Ada had left with them and turned to the Scot who reached out with his large hand to receive them.

"This is not quite what ah had expected," Patrick Sandilands muttered as he took the papers. He was looking a little perplexed and glanced at Martha for some assurance.

"By gum lad, tha'd better pay attention if tha wants ta buy rags," the older woman announced before she turned to go back to her work.

"But is yourr father not afraid ah would cheat yerr?" the Scot asked.

Lizzie smiled innocently. "Maybe you will have enough trouble watchin yer own purse, Mister Sandilands!"

Again, the Scot looked confused, but began the negotiations by asking for a sample of quality. The girl pointed at Quon Lee who hurriedly left the room. Patrick asked about the continuity of supply and Lizzie convinced him there would be a plentiful stock always on hand.

The Scot asked about their delivery methods and she informed him it was by ship into the port of Aberdeen and landed on the dockside.

Quon came running back in with an armful of rags and dumped them at Patrick's feet. The inspection was both thorough and brief.

"It's only a matterr of prrice now, lassie, and the contrract is yourrs."

Lizzie smiled sweetly. "We know you're buyin from the continent and it is our intention to save you money. So, it would make matters much simpler if you told me your cost for rags now."

Patrick Sandilands studied the girl for a long silent moment and let a smile creep across his face.

"Yourr the first perrson who has ever trried to make me into the buyer and the seller all in the same breath," he chuckled. "'Am not quite sure ye know what ah pay now, but ah dare not take that chance and lose the supply." He thumped the table and laughed out loud. "Here," he said, writing some numbers on a sheet of paper, "this is what I pay now—match it, and the contract is yours.

Lizzie studied the numbers, then reached for her own papers. Lifting the corner of the first sheet, she peeked at the blank space on the second page. Nudging Quon Lee, she pointed to the same blank space. He nodded and fell silent again.

"I think we have a deal, sir," the girl said, adding, "if you can produce and ship to me a skilled whisky maker."

"If that's your only condition; we have a deal, lassie," Patrick affirmed, sticking out his hand to shake on it. "Now tell me lassie, ye had my figures already written down there, didn't ye?"

Lizzie chuckled happily. "Mister Sandilands, sir," she laughed, "yer goin ta have ta wonder about that for ever more, cos 'am not about ta tell yer!"

Patrick Sandilands laughed heartily. He was a satisfied man and, taking his leave, promised to come back in the evening with a formal contract.

Chapter 6

Leaving the cottage, the youngsters decided to call at the building site, to check how Mick was coping with the huge amount of deliveries he had undertaken to complete. Shires pulling huge drays and smaller carts with light horses buzzing in between and around them, mixed with men shouting and dogs barking—this was a scene of complete bedlam or so it appeared.

Above the din, Quon heard a faint call. Searching the sea of activity, he finally located Mick, who was over at the far side of the site signalling for them to come over. Tugging on Lizzie's sleeve, Quon pointed to the Irishman and slowly they began to thread their way through the throng of activity.

When they got close enough, Mick yelled to them.

"Go down to the brewery and tell Angus McClain I need every man he can spare, right now!"

Realizing by the sound of his voice that this was an urgent request, they quickly turned back toward the door through which they had just come. Taking off at a run, they cut through the back paddock and easily jumped the stone wall into Drover's Lane. Running at full speed, they crossed Slaughter Lane beside Joe's cottage and carried on down Goat

Hill, to Corn Street and Bell's Yard, up the loading ramp and through the big doors, skidding to a halt in front of a startled Angus McClain.

"Are yer bein chased?" the brewery manager inquired, looking puzzled and staring through the open doorway behind them.

"It's Mick," Lizzie panted, trying to catch her breath, "he needs all the help you can give him and quick."

Angus McClain reacted instantly, orders cracked out with a startling air of authority—men ran for the gate or spilled into a nearby dray and were off before Lizzie could even catch her breath.

"Sorry lass, ah'll noo be able ta come misen," the manager apologized beckoning them to come in.

"Mister McClain," the girl said, as they walked toward his small office," you seem ta have the knack of being able to make quick, accurate decisions, every time you need to."

Angus smiled shyly and shuffled his feet uncomfortably.

"Ach, av noo always been a cider maker, lass," he explained. "My responsibility noo is ta ma bairns and tay yerself, an the past is dead an gone."

His curious statement aroused Lizzie's curiosity and she would have liked to question him more but there was no time for that right now.

Angus broke into her thoughts by handing her the tally sheet for the barrels delivered during the previous evening. Then he led her out to the storage area where she saw the long rows neatly sorted according to type, age and potency. They would soon be stacked away in another storage area or sold, except for the few that had been tapped and were in the process of being transferred into one-gallon stone bottles ready for sale.

The men who had been busy doing all this stacking and filling had obviously left in a hurry minutes before. Knowing Angus had work to do, they reminded him of the meeting at nine that evening at Joe's cottage and left the brewery.

Now having nothing particular to do for the rest of the day and knowing they would hear about the excitement at the slaughterhouse later, they headed in the direction of the docks and began to discuss the impending expedition.

"We're goin to need some strong team leaders."

"Mick, him stlong damn," Quon answered, flexing his tiny muscles.

"Aye, he's strong, but I mean strong in the head."

The Chinese boy looked puzzled.

"Is muscles in head, Wizzy? Me not know dat, damn."

The girl suddenly stopped in mid stride and turned to face the boy, exasperation clearly showing on her face.

"That had better be the end of that, my lad," she snapped, wagging her finger at him.

Quon looked stunned and confused.

"Me end of what, Wizzy damn?"

She threw up her hands in frustration.

"The end of the damn on the end of everything ya say—so never say it again, yer little bugger!"

Neither of them moved. The girl stared hard at the boy and he scratched his head and frowned.

Suddenly a very sad looking expression came over his face and he looked cautiously at his friend.

"Wizzy mad wi' dumplin?"

"No lad, yer me best friend," she assured him, slipping her arm around his shoulders. "Ye'll always be me dumplin, but don't say that word again—it sounds daft."

She pushed him playfully away, aiming a kick at his backside before she set off at a run toward the docks, leaving him standing alone in the roadway.

Quon felt deflated but realized he was only feeling sorry for himself. He knew Lizzie's disapproval was always short-lived and besides, she always knew the best things, so he quickly set off after her.

They were still a distance away when they noticed the crowd of men and carriages at the dock. Many were standing around in groups obviously waiting for something to happen.

"Wonder what's goin on," Lizzie quietly commented to her partner who had now caught up to her.

Slowly inching closer to the crowd, Quon noticed something strange and grasped Lizzie's arm.

"Ship, she gone difflent," he whispered urgently, pointing to the French ship Captain Davis had captured, now tied up second in line and being guarded by a small group of soldiers. On its deck they could see Captain Davis talking to a group of very official-looking gentlemen dressed in business suits and top hats.

Let's find a good place to watch," Lizzie suggested eagerly, looking around. "There," she said, indicating a great pile of lumber stacked to one side ready for loading aboard a vessel. Scrambling up the side and standing on top of the lumber, they had a great view of the proceedings.

First came an announcement from a man with a voice like a foghorn.

"Your attention, please gentlemen," his voice boomed out.

Men began to push forward, carriage doors flew open and their occupants spilled onto the dock. Among them, they were surprised to see Nathan Goldman, the tailor's cousin.

"We are conducting an auction of this wonderful vessel *Le Canard*, made in France and a prize of war—on behalf of the Crown," the announcer shouted so all could hear. He paused momentarily to get his breath. "All cargo on board is included in the sale, funds to be paid within 24 hours." Once again, he paused. This time he took a moment to look out at the crowd and up at Captain Davis, before drawing a deep breath and continuing.

"Can we proceed, gentlemen? Will someone open the bidding at 30,000 guineas?" Up shot a hand and the announcer continued, "Sir John bids 30,000. Do I hear 40, do I hear 40? I have 40 from *The East India Company*. Do I hear 50, do I hear 50? I have 50 from *James Langton and Son*. Do I hear 60, I hear 60. Sir John bids 60."

The voice pleaded for more bids but it was useless.

"Going once, going twice, sold to Sir John for the small sum of 60,000 guineas—thank you, gentlemen, that is all."

"Did you hear that?" Lizzie asked her partner excitedly, as they watched the crowd of businessmen and carriages quickly disperse.

Quon Lee nodded, his face showing no emotion.

"Sold too cheap damn . . . oops, solly."

The girl grinned at him. "But we intend to steal seven of them. That amounts to a fortune of 420,000 guineas," she gasped.

"Too cheap," was all she received in reply.

Captain Davis was waiting for them as they carefully descended the lumber pile. He was wearing a big grin on his face, highly unusual for this gruff seadog. From under his cap, laughing eyes scrutinized their serious faces.

"Comin ta see me are ye me hearties. Let's go aboard *Falcon* so we be in private," he suggested with a grunt, and began walking along the dock in the direction of his own vessel.

One-Eyed Jack and Ben Thorn were approaching from the other direction when they all met at the base of *Falcon*'s gangplank. Ben respectfully begged the Captain's pardon and requested he be allowed to buy caulking rope from the ship's chandlers.

"We be needin a few damp spots pluggin, sir."

"Then be off with you and get it done," Davis snapped. "We sail in five days, lad, even if it drowns the lot of us!"

Lizzie smiled at One-Eyed Jack and gently rubbed her jaw. The fierce-looking mariner turned his head slightly to allow her to see there was no swelling left in his previously grotesque cheek and they moved quickly off to do the Captain's bidding.

Walking up the gangplank onto a deck buzzing with activity, Davis threaded his way through the jumble to his cabin, holding the door open as the youngsters hurried in. Reaching for his drink and offering cider to his guests, he began to pour. Sliding the tankards across to them, he sat down at his desk and began to mutter. "Bloody robbers, two percent an we did all the work."

Lizzie thought for a moment, considering what the Captain had just said.

"Aye, two percent of 60 thousand, that's 1,200 guineas, not a bad pay day when yertake into account what ye'll get from us when it's all reckoned up," she snapped.

Captain Davis set his black eyes on Lizzie's face, staring at her from under bushy eyebrows.

"Hmph," he grunted doubtfully, as he began to let a smile creep through the lines on his mouth. "Them government dogs won't get a penny piece from the next trip, will they lass?"

"Not even a farthin, Mister Davis, sir!" Lizzie countered fiercely, drinking her cider down with a flourish. "What we came for is yer tally sheet, and to tell you to be at the cottage tonight at nine sharp," she concluded, rising from her seat.

Captain Davis burst out laughing and thumped the desk. This little woman never failed to amaze him. That's why he liked her so much.

"Here," he chuckled, pushing some papers toward her. "That's your copy, mine will stay wi' me."

Suddenly, a call came for the captain from somewhere out on deck, and the visit was over. Davis dismissed them and disappeared through the door.

Lizzie and Quon Lee left Davis' cabin and strolled outside. Squinting against the light, they stood for awhile to watch the activity from their good vantage point on the poop deck, then walking down the gangplank and back onto the dock. Their little dog was patiently waiting for them under the edge of the gangplank. Barking a greeting, he bounded after them and they headed toward home.

As she walked along the dock, thoughts of Nathan Goldman began to niggle at Lizzie's brain and she mentioned it to Quon. What was he doing at the auction? He never made a bid . . . all he did was watch. There had to be a simple explanation.

"Me hungly, need apple pie," Quon said, ignoring her. He slipped his hand under her armpit and tickled her.

She leapt forward giggling and half turned, swinging a punch at him and missing. The dog nipped at her heels thinking she was playing with him and she bent down to give him a loving scratch behind the ears.

Quon, meanwhile, found a stick, threw it a distance away and the dog joyfully took off after it's new toy. The youngsters began to run, following the dog, only slowing to a walk as they neared Mast Lane.

Suddenly, the Chinese boy tugged on Lizzie's sleeve to get her attention. He pointed his arm toward Abe Kratze's shop—in the doorway stood the tailor and his cousin, Nathan Goldman, talking intently.

Veering across the cobbled street, the girl headed straight for the tailor's shop. The two men saw her coming and a smile of pleasure lit up Nathan's face.

"Come in, come in, we talk a while," Nathan babbled, backing into the store with the youngsters following. "A drink for your guests, Abe," the little man said, sitting down at the table.

"You were at the auction," Lizzie said, getting right to the point even before taking a seat.

"Sit down, sonny," Nathan commanded Quon Lee.

"Leave him be, I like him there," the girl said sharply, feeling Quon's hand tighten on her shoulder. Not receiving a reaction to her earlier statement, she continued on a slightly different track. "Are you a ship owner, Mister Goldman, sir?" Lizzie asked bluntly.

The fat man smiled and shook his head negatively. "Insurer."

"In what?" the girl asked, with a puzzled expression.

The cousins exchanged glances, smiling.

"We were carrying the insurance for the Frenchmen and that means we shall lose a few guineas on this one," Nathan explained.

Lizzie gave the businessman a long, hard stare.

"Must be money in this insurance thing," she commented quietly.

Nathan Goldman quickly wiped the smile off his face.

"Have you money to invest, my dear?" he asked gently.

"Between us, we've a guinea," the girl chirped brightly, looking expectantly at the city broker who was once again beginning to smile.

"Not quite enough, my girl," he said, patting her hand.

Lizzie put on her innocent look and asked meekly, "What would be enough, kind sir?"

Nathan puffed himself up to his most important height.

"Ten thousand buys a goodly share, fifty thousand buys the company."

The girl flicked the golden guinea across the table and Nathan Goldman trapped it under his hand with a thud . . . as their eyes met.

"Better take this guinea, mister—on account—an ah'll start savin up."

Both Abe and his cousin's mouth dropped open as Lizzie and Quon got up and walked quickly to the door. Making a fast exit into the street, they were soon running hard for the Johnson bakery.

Back at the tailor's shop, Abe and Nathan were still speechless.

"What do you make of that, cousin?" Nathan finally asked.

Abe rubbed his chin thoughtfully. His answer was quiet and deliberate.

"I think she beat you again, cousin. Furthermore, it wouldn't surprise me one bit if you had just been tricked into puttin a price on the company."

"Come, come, now Abe, you're reading too much into a little silly conversation with a child." He didn't sound as confident now, however, and his cousin merely grinned, showing all of his blackened teeth.

"She's planning ta use you cousin, an you've just fallen into her trap," the old tailor mused. Alarm showed on his relative's face as he pushed his chair back and stood up.

"How?" he whispered, his face turning beet-red.

"Why, you accepted her deposit, didn't you?"

Nathan Goldman sat back down with a thump, moaned and held his head. Then, recovering some bravado, he pulled himself together, sitting up straighter.

"She doesn't have fifty thousand and she's only a child," he growled.

Abe chuckled again, rose from the table and began walking toward the shop front.

"Ye'd better be off cousin, I have work ta do," the old man announced, as he began to sing a few lines of an old Yiddish song.

No one had heard old Abe sing in forty years and the effect it had on Nathan at this moment was devastating. Scooping up his hat and cane, he ran for the door, whimpering a little, as if wounded.

Chapter 7

Dashing into Bill Johnson's yard, the youngsters almost bumped into Tom and Billy who were just leaving with their cart loaded high.

"Bit late boys," Lizzie snapped.

Tom halted beside her, sweat running down his face.

"It's the wheel on this goddamned cart," he swore fiercely. "This is the third time it's come adrift in two weeks, an it makes us awful late finishin when we av ter come back for a repair job," he grumbled.

Lizzie clapped her hands, pointed her finger at the bread cart and then in the general direction of the slaughterhouse commanded, "Go lad."

Without any more urging or discussion, Quon Lee raced out into Baker Lane and away.

With a look of astonishment on his face, Tom shook his head and looked questioningly at Lizzie.

"Come on, me lad, we'll look after it tamorra mornin. Now get going an move a bit faster; then yer won't be late," the girl snapped with authority.

The grateful lad threw his weight unceremoniously into the cart moving it forward with young Billy grinning and pushing his hardest from behind.

Bill Johnson, who had been doing the cart repairs and still held the hammer in his big hand, turned to Lizzie with a stem look on his face.

"Yer were a bit hard on 'em lass, they're a hard-workin pair, them two is," he said.

Lizzie laughed. "Aye, Bill," she said, smiling, "yer a great big lump of loveliness, but I don't want them two to start feelin sorry for themselves, an being mad at me will take their minds off it! Ther'll be a new cart for them in the mornin."

"Ee by gum, yer a deep thinker, lass, and yer good to yer workers, too," Bill said, walking through into his bake house. Reaching for half of a big apple pie, he promptly cut two big pieces from it, flopped them onto tin plates and slid them toward Lizzie.

"Want cream?" he asked, dipping his hand into a cut-off barrel full of cold water and drawing out a large tin can.

Lizzie nodded as she shovelled the first bite into her waiting mouth. Bill placed the can on the table, pulling the tight lid off and reaching for the ladle.

The rattle of light iron wheels on cobblestones alerted them to Quon's return with another cart. He came puffing into the bake house, and dropped onto a sack of flour, gasping for breath.

"Me need much big pie now damn . . . solly," Quon announced, pretending to faint as the baker chuckled at his antics.

"If he's fainted, give me his pie!" Lizzie shouted to Bill, causing an instant recovery to take place in her partner.

"No, no, Mister Bill, my pie, my pie," he said, scrambling to the table and digging in.

Lizzie cleared up the plates, rinsed them under the tap and prepared to leave. "Can you fix the new cart up with the barrel stays off the other one Bill, or do you want me ta send somebody down ta do it?"

"No, ah'll do it misen," he called from across the room, adding as an afterthought, "it's what ya had planned anyway, in't it? Yer crafty little bugger."

Lizzie laughed, thanking Bill for the pie and she and Quon left the bakery.

"It's early yet—why don't we pay a call on old Lumpy," she suggested, breaking into a trot.

Fifteen minutes later they arrived at Brown's Yard. Creeping up to the entrance and peeking in, they saw Charley Mason's cart complete with the old chair on top, standing in the yard. There was Charley and with him were Lumpy and the young man who took him home that very morning.

Slowly the pair crept forward, intending to eavesdrop on the conversation but what they heard changed their minds completely. It was Charley who was doing the talking.

"Them two scalawags think we haven't seen 'em creeping up behind us," he said, loud enough for them to hear.

"Must av nothin better ter do," Lumpy growled.

"So yer knew we were here. Why aren't you in bed, yer must be tired after last night?" Lizzie asked.

"Go away, woman, we've work ta do and not enough time ta do it," Charley yelled at the youngsters.

Quon tugged on the girl's sleeve.

"We go, damn . . . solly," he said, moving toward the lane.

"What did he say?" Charley asked.

The youngsters trotted off and Lizzie shouted over her shoulder.

"Mind yer own business, nosy bugger, there's a meetin at nine tonight . . . be there!"

Leaving Charley with no time to reply, they were gone.

Later that afternoon, they passed the alehouse called *The Swan* down on Cooper's Lane. All the locals called it *The Drake* after the great mariner from the 16th century, Sir Francis Drake. Sitting outside were half the *Falcon* crew along with One-Eyed Jack and a large group of sailors from other ships.

Jack yelled at the pair and waving for them to come over, quickly produced two seats.

"These two fine people are my friends," he announced in a loud, menacing voice. "So you'd better be on yer best behaviour, me hearties, or old One-Eyed Jack will be introducing yer ta me fang!"

Taking his knife from the safety of his high-topped boot, he stabbed it into the tabletop with a flourish, laughing crazily. Quon felt cold shivers go down his back and he eased a little closer to his partner. He watched the big knife still quivering on the table and shuddered.

"Two ciders," the big mariner called, "an look you lively, boy," he continued as the waiter scurried away. "I be tellin this ugly bunch, how we paid a visit to that dentist fella the other night."

A howl of laughter came from the next table, as Jack leapt to his feet and banged the table with his fist.

"You tell 'em, Lizzie," he growled fiercely, "how I sat there an never moved a muscle when he yanked my tooth out by the roots!"

With that Jack returned to his seat and waited for the now uncomfortable girl to continue the story.

Lizzie knew there was no way out of this predicament. Quickly, she considered her options. Climbing onto the seat of her chair, she surveyed the gathering of rough sailors. Each had a drink either in his hand or on the table in front of him. She gave them one of her nicest smiles before looking down at Jack, whose one good eye was pleading for her to say something nice about him.

A joker from the corner, shouted, "Go on, missy, tell us how he screamed!"

Another ripple of laughter went through the group and the girl felt Quon's hand on her ankle as she summoned the courage to face her audience.

"What we saw the other night at the dentist . . . ," she said, to the eagerly waiting men, "was nothin short of heroic." She paused as a hush settled over the gathering. "This man is a man amongst men," she announced, pointing to the old sailor. "He stood more pain without a whimper, than most of you feel in a lifetime." She paused again for effect. "I'm proud of him and so should you be, he's a real sailor."

Shouts of 'well done' filled the air as the girl stepped down, her back to the men. She winked at Jack, who sat there with his mouth open in amazement and gratitude at her convincing oration to his mates.

The youngsters drank up and were preparing to leave just as someone yelled, "Three cheers for Miss Lizzie an our Jack . . . hip, hip, hooray . . . hip, hip hooray . . ."

Exiting hurriedly up the lane, they could still hear the noisy throng cheering. Quon had to keep stopping, he was laughing so hard.

"Dem men don't know how big Yack yumped when tooth man pulled!" He stopped again, holding onto a gas lamp for support.

"I thought he had wings when he flew out of that chair," Lizzie gasped, staggering with laughter.

Rounding the corner, their mirth immediately stopped. Halfway down the lane Tom, Billy and their bread cart, were surrounded by a group of unsavoury looking footpads, well known in the area for their viciousness.

"Go get Jack . . . sharp now!" she whispered.

The Chinese boy tore off back the way they had just come, as the girl melted into a doorway. Tearing into the alehouse yard, Quon Lee quickly made the sailors aware of the situation—within minutes he was back at Lizzie's side, accompanied by ten strong looking sailors wanting to fight. As they spread out across the lane, another ten appeared at the other end. Panic quickly spread through the ranks of the would-be robbers as they searched for an escape route and found none.

Stepping out into the middle of the lane where Tom and Billy could see her, Lizzie called out loudly.

"Come on outa that bloody mess yer in, yer two."

A sigh of relief was heard, as the iron wheels rumbled on the cobbles and the cart came to the top of the lane. Young Billy looked anxiously at the girl as he passed.

"Keep goin . . . yer late, we'll deal with this now," she muttered fiercely.

One-Eyed Jack had walked forward beside the girl, a big piece of wood swinging from his hand ominously.

"What yer want done with this lot, yer ladyship?" he asked, loud enough for the rogues to hear.

"Teach 'em it's not nice ta stop crippled sailors and young lads around here," she answered coldly. "Then throw 'em in the river, an if they ever come back, kill 'em!" She said these last words loudly enough to make sure her threat, serious or not, was heard clearly.

A mournful wailing sound came from the group of robbers, which quickly turned to screams as the sailors set about their task with relish.

A long way up the road to Joe's cottage, they could still hear the screams; then all went quiet.

"Lesson number one," the girl snapped, "don't mess around with anything that belongs to TLS and Company, or we will get ya," she said, slipping her arm around the Chinese boy's shoulder and pulling him closer.

Quon Lee looked up at her, his face as white as a ghost, as he stammered, "M-m-me b-b-big glad you my flend, Wizzy!"

Chapter 8

Joe Todd heard the youngsters calling as he opened the garden gate. He waited, holding it open for them—they looked tired, but happy.

"Bet yer checked everybody, ain't yer, lass? It all went so smooth last night."

Lizzie moved forward to give the old man a squeeze and he patted her affectionately on the back.

"No need ta bother checkin that big Irishman," Joe mumbled, smiling. "Yon lad has everything running like clockwork up there," he chuckled, pointing in the general direction of the slaughterhouse. "And Ada's up there with him right now—hard workin girl that one is, too." As the old man walked along the garden path, he stopped to admire a pretty patch of flowers he had planted.

"Are they collecting the money as they deliver?" the girl asked pointedly, cocking her head to one side and holding the door so Joe could enter the cottage first.

"Aye, that they are," Joe answered, holding up the cloth bag he was carrying, "an Ada is keepin a tally. It's all workin well luv, yer don't have ter worry."

Joe dropped into his chair with a sigh, reached for his pipe and began to stuff it with tobacco. Martha, who was making dinner at the fire, turned to him with a long splinter of wood in her hand.

"Ready?" she softly asked the old man.

He nodded—she lit the splinter and handed it to him to light his pipe—then moved off into the corner to tend to the baby.

"Told 'em all ta come at nine, for a meetin," Lizzie announced casually.

The old man nodded again as Martha returned to the fire.

Stirring a large pot of stew, and without looking up, she suddenly asked, "Can yer build me a room on't back?"

Not sure if his ears were serving him correctly, Joe sat up in his chair and glanced at Lizzie.

"What did she say?" he asked, removing his pipe.

Lizzie grinned. "Wants a room buildin at the back, she said." Her expression indicating she was having trouble believing it too.

"That's wot ah said," Martha verified, turning to face them.

Joe blew out a great cloud of smoke, eyes narrowing in thought.

"Can't see why not," he said, looking directly at the youngsters, "Why you want ta do that?" Lizzie asked, mystified by the request.

"Well, 'am ere most a time, an when 'am not ere, ah worry about all of ya, an ah want ta be ere," she said emphatically, wiping her hands on her apron.

The old man's pipe drooped in his mouth and both Lizzie and Quon laughed at the way the cook expressed herself.

"She talk stlange language—best we say yes—find out later what she mean," Quon said, giggling.

"Well, that's nice comin from you, dumplin . . . nobody talks stranger than you do," Lizzie chuckled. "Martha luv, you just tell Mick what you want an how you want it done."

The cook beamed with anticipation and Joe returned to puffing on his pipe and the art of blowing clouds of blue smoke toward the blackened ceiling.

As dinner started, there were only the three of them sat at the table. They had already eaten their stew when the sound of iron wheels and the rattle of a cart being bounced and jolted over the rough cobbles, told them the engineer would very soon be on his way up the garden path.

A high-spirited Charley soon tapped on the door and entered the cottage. He had obviously been laughing and shouting instructions to the poor boy all the way to Joe's. Quickly washing his hands, he plunked himself down on a chair.

"Holy mackerel, am I hungry!" he chirped, as Martha loaded his plate with food.

By this time, the other three were enjoying apple pie and steaming hot custard. The meal kept them busy . . . and silent, until Joe dropped his spoon onto his empty plate.

"'Am full ta burstin Martha, that were a great meal, luv," he sighed.

Click, went the door latch, and in walked Ada, book under her arm and Mick right behind her carrying two heavy bags—both looking tired but happy. Ada disappeared into the back as the Irishman dropped the bags at Joe's feet and walked over to the sink, turned the tap and dowsed his face with the icy cold water.

"Moy, oh moy, I be a'needin that!" he said, catching the towel Martha threw at him.

"All gone?" the old man asked, quietly.

Mick winked at the old man. "Sure it's all gone an paid for—what else would yer be expecting when yer send a slave droyver ta be keepin an oye on me!"

Lizzie giggled, having noticed Ada listening from inside her doorway as she buttoned up her clean blouse. Quon Lee doubled his fists and placed them knuckle to knuckle. The girl nodded in agreement, sitting well back in her chair.

Ada walked across the room smiling sweetly and asked cook how the baby had been.

"Ee's bin na bother, lass," Martha assured her, as Ada moved across the room to her child.

Just as she was passing behind the Irishman, she spun around and belted him across the arm—hard. Mick feigned being hurt as Ada snapped, "That'll teach you to talk about me behind my back."

The Irishman groaned loudly to the amusement of everyone.

"Yer see, sir," he whined, addressing Joe, "she's still beatin on me."

The meal was a long drawn-out affair and quite noisy, everyone having started at different times, but it eventually ended around seven thirty.

"How do the numbers tally up. Ada?" Lizzie asked.

Ada lowered her mug of cider, raised an eyebrow, and whispered, "Too good to be true, lass. A little over eighteen thousand guineas and we haven't calculated the barrels of liquor in yet."

"Any trouble with collectin the cash, Mick?" the girl asked.

"None at all, the drivers were all treated well and the payments were in cash."

He waited for the next question, but none came. Charley, who had remained quiet, not understanding all they were talking about, began to relate the day's events at Brown's Yard. As he finished, he turned to Mick.

"That's a good lad who took me home this morning."

"Don't be thinkin another minute on it," the Irishman laughed. "Angus McClain bless im, sent me all his men. Ah 'twas a hair-raisin day though, if it hadn't ah been for the luvly colleen, hoy would be stark ravin mad by now," he chuckled, teasing Ada again.

"Why, thank you for the compliment, sir," she said, smiling at him. "To be really honest, I thought you were a marvel, too. Those men of ours may be Navy discards—gimpy, grumpy and many of them disfigured—but I think they are wonderful and loyal to a fault," she ended passionately.

A knock came at the door and Martha yelled, "Cum in."

Angus McClain stood there grinning, as the door swung open.

"Well, are yer ta be comin in, or are yer wantin ta be standin there all noyt, yer kilted heathen," Mick greeted him in mock anger.

"Ach, watch yer mooth, sonny," the Scot snapped back. Grinning, he held out his hand to shake the Irishman's.

"That were fair grand of ya ta send me yer men today," Mick said seriously. "It made the difference we needed, friend."

Ada added her thanks, too.

Angus looked around the room and his eyes came to rest on Lizzie.

"Ach, it were noo me, she said we wer a team, an by God we'd better be actin like one." And, with a smile, he pointed his finger at Lizzie, "An she be right. We can all be vouchin for that noo, can we not?"

"What was the final tally at your place, Angus?" Joe inquired, sliding the tin of pipe tobacco, with the lid off, onto the middle of the table.

This was an open invitation for the men to help themselves. Mick reached over, pulled the tobacco closer and began filling his pipe. Angus took some papers out of his pocket, straightened the wrinkles, laid them on the tabletop, and began to read them over silently. Ada opened her book, dipped the pen into her bottle of ink, and waited.

Finally ready, the Scot began his accounting, reading carefully from his papers.

"67 brandy, No. I Grade; 43 rum, Best Jamaica; 52 red wine, and 47 white wine. That makes 208 barrels in total—all big 45's."

"No estimate of cost and profit yet, I suppose?" Ada asked, glancing up from her book.

"Noo, but ah shall be attendin tae that today," Angus assured her.

Lizzie tapped the table with her fingers.

"Just calculate them roughly, Ada, at forty guineas for hard liquor and twenty for wine."

The bookkeeper began to write on a piece of paper, as Lizzie continued.

"That makes about 6,340 guineas or more, by my reckoning."

Ada went on scratching with the pen for a while, when she'd finished she looked up.

"That's exactly right love, but then I knew it would be," she complimented the girl, who smiled innocently back at her.

"This pirating business is mighty profitable," Lizzie mused, quickly adding, "half of that goes to the *Falcon* and Captain Davis."

The meeting was interrupted abruptly by a loud knock at the door and Lizzie motioned to Mick to answer it, as Martha was busy attending to little Willie.

Captain Davis stepped inside, nodded a greeting to everyone and gave Lizzie a wink. A seat was made available and a tankard of cider filled and placed in front of him. He sat down and came straight to the point.

"How well have we done?" he asked eagerly.

He carefully watched their faces, but no one answered. At last, Lizzie broke the silence.

"We have 9,000 in cash for you and there will be more when we sell the liquor."

Captain Davis' intake of air could be heard across the table. He sat back in his chair and turned to face Lizzie.

"Say it again lass . . . but slow this time," he said, almost in a whisper.

"Nine thousand," Lizzie said slowly, watching the captain's face.

A chuckle of laughter ran around the room as Davis shook his head in disbelief.

"An all because I listened to the craftiest little woman in London," he muttered, beaming at Lizzie.

Quon Lee shuffled his chair a little closer to his partner.

"Me an my shadow," Lizzie giggled.

Chapter 9

Another knock sounded at the door.

"Oh, that'll be another Scot . . . Patrick Sandilands, with a contract ta be signed for rags," Lizzie announced.

Someone answered the door, whilst chairs were being shuffled around to make room as the giant Scot moved toward the table. Quon instinctively drew even closer to the girl. Lizzie patted his arm and stood up to greet the newcomer. She shook his hand, introduced him to everyone, and then offered him a seat.

Ach 'am noo interruptin anythin important am'a?" Patrick Sandilands asked, bringing out a sheaf of papers and laying them on the table.

No, you are not," Ada answered. "It's just a bunch of pirates sharing up the spoils."

The joke was understood by all present, except Patrick Sandilands, who seemed quite surprised at the outburst of laughter.

"Ach, there must be a jest there somewhere, but fer the life of me, ah dinnae see it," he said, looking inquiringly at Lizzie.

That's because it's true," the girl said quietly.

Finally, the laughter diminished enough for the giant Scot to suggest that they complete their business. He proceeded to read the contract aloud to a now silent audience, each one trying to digest all the contractual obligations of each party.

"That sounds about right to me," Lizzie murmured, "just that bit about payment, needs altering to read 'at the dockside before unloading'.

"Ach, we know what we agreed tae. Ma uncle, John Hope, wrote it up last night," the Scot said, emphatically.

"Ah, and we'll be changin it, right now!" Lizzie answered, pointing to Ada Mason, who reached for the papers and began writing.

Charley eyed the Scottish papermaker carefully, before directing his observations at Mick.

"We sure could do with him to lift the big pulleys."

Patrick listened, but remained silent.

Captain Davis, deciding Charley might have a worthwhile idea, took up the conversation.

"Ever been ta sea, lad?" he asked, receiving a gentle nod and a smile from the Scot. Then the captain surprised everybody with his next question. "Like ta get yer first shipload delivered free, Mister Papermaker?"

An instant hush fell on the room as they awaited the reply.

"Och aye, it's a Scot's dream tae be gettin sumthin fer nothin," he laughed, "or so you English say!"

Not one person passed a comment at his sarcasm.

Ada returned with the contract ready for signing. Both Patrick and Lizzie read the alterations, signed their names, and one copy was passed to the bookkeeper. The Scot carefully folded his copy and deposited it in an inside pocket, patting his coat just to make sure it was there. Then to the surprise of everyone he suddenly burst into laughter for no apparent reason.

Lizzie chuckled to herself. She liked this big Scottish papermaker who had a touch of the genteel about him.

"Either tell us or go, the choice is yours," the girl snapped, stopping his laughter instantly although he doubted her seriousness.

Patrick and Lizzie eyed each other over, a tiny smile played around the corners of his mouth. The girl's eyes were mere slits, full of intensity as they stared hard back at him.

The giant Scot was the first to break the silence.

"Ma family has taken parrt in everry battle ever fought in Scotland and done it with distinction an valour. We keep our worrd in everything and trrust and supporrt our friends all the way." He paused for a breath, then continued. "Now if ye be havin a proposition for me, then spit it oot or 'am oot of here!" He sat back in his chair, folded his arms and waited.

"Sit still an not a sound outa yer," Lizzie said, pointing her finger menacingly at the Scot. "Who's for takin him along?" she asked.

Charley stuck his hand in the air first, quickly followed by Angus, Mick, Ada, Joe, and finally, Captain Davis.

"Well that's unanimous then, cos us two want him in as well," the girl snapped, thumping the table.

"Rright, so ye have voted me in, but av noo agreed tae a thing yet," Patrick teased. "Ach lassie, 'am a Scot, an adventure's in me blood," he continued, grinning at everyone.

Lizzie coughed and all the faces turned her way as she began her explanation of the task at hand.

"Ta put it in a nutshell lad, we are about ta execute the biggest act of piracy the world has ever seen, and all in the course of helping the war effort for merry old England."

All eyes were on the big papermaker now, awaiting his comments.

"How long will ye be away then?" he asked screwing up his eyes in deep thought.

"Three weeks at the most, if all goes well," the captain answered.

"Aye, an forever if it does na!" Angus chipped in.

The Scots eyes met and held each other's gaze for a moment.

"Would ye be partaken in this madness yersen, Angus?" Patrick asked quietly.

"That ah will, if 'am allowed," Angus replied, just as quietly.

"Then if like yer say, ah'll be gitt'n two deliveries of rags shipped free . . . 'am in."

Captain Davis nodded as Lizzie yelped.

"We said one delivery not two, yer damn pirate!" Lizzie's reaction brought a round of laughter from around the table. "But . . . if yer do yer part well, an ask for no more, yer can have two!"

Patrick smiled but he had a look of deep thought on his face.

"Are ye tryin tae tell me lassie, it's a wee bairn like ye that runs everythin arouwn here?" His fingers drummed the table impatiently in front of him as he waited for the answer.

It was Joe who provided it. Clutching his smouldering pipe in one hand and quickly rising from his chair, he leaned over the table and snarled fiercely into the face of the Scot.

"Aye she do, lad. Always has, an always will." He paused for a moment to catch his breath. "You ask 'em all in this room, She's smarter than a boxful a foxes. Best yer know now, what she says is law around here, an we all profit that way. If yer don't like it yer free ta go now."

The old man slowly sank down in his chair and both Quon Lee and the girl moved quickly to his aid. Soon he was again puffing contentedly on his pipe, soothed out of his flash of temper by the gentle hands of his loving youngsters.

Lizzie turned slowly toward Patrick, a look of pure innocence on her face.

"If yer ever upset that old man again by yer stupid jesting, ah'll kill yer. Mark my words well, Patrick Sandilands, or ye'll wake up dead one mornin!"

The room was absolutely silent as the girl returned to her chair. Seating herself and now smiling at the Scot, her eyes were little dancing balls of fire as she continued.

"Now, are yer stayin or goin, declare yerself, man?" Lizzie's voice was almost a whisper as she menacingly asked her question.

"Stayin," Patrick said, with a serious note in his voice. "An ah apologize fer actin the fool—it won't happen agin."

A noticeable sigh ran through the gathering relieved that any further unpleasantness had been avoided.

"Time ta get down ta the real business, gentlemen," the girl announced, making a sign at the Chinese boy.

Quon left the table immediately and returned quickly with the model. Sliding it onto the table, he scooted away again returning this time with a large chalkboard which he propped up in front of the fireplace so they could all see it.

Lizzie struck the table with her fist as she began to speak.

"Take a good look at the model—any questions will be answered by Mick," she announced loudly. Every pair of eyes was focused on the clay model.

"Ach, weer is that place?" Patrick inquired.

"Zarauz, just west of the French border in Spain," Mick cracked back, causing the Scot to look up frowning. "Sure, hoy lived there a while ago," Mick clarified the situation for the frowning Scot.

"What's that?" Angus muttered, pointing to a spot on the model.

"Beacon Rock, not used for years."

"Here are the seven vessels," the girl offered, placing seven pieces of wood shaped like ships onto the table. "Be obliged, captain, if yer'd put 'em in where yer last saw 'em."

Davis leaned over the table, scooping up the tiny ships and proceeded to carefully place them on the clay model, stroking his beard as he studied the placement.

"How in God's name are we going to move all 'em vessels outa there unnoticed?" the captain asked pointedly.

"Cos there won't be anybody in town ta see ya," Lizzie replied.

"An moving 'em is easy if we all work together," Charley interrupted, wriggling in his chair to ease his cramped legs.

"With what?" Captain Davis asked, doubt in his voice.

"With a quad-reduction pulley," Charley snapped.

"Never heard of one," Davis snapped back.

"That's because I only designed it last week!" the engineer returned with a chuckle.

Maybe it was because he had no idea what the engineer was talking about that made the captain go quiet, but it gave Mick the opportunity to ask a pertinent question.

"Did hoy not hear yer say, not a soul would be in town?" he asked quietly, looking directly at Lizzie for an explanation. "Then where in heaven's name will they all be?"

Lizzie and Quon Lee were grinning like two Cheshire cats in a milking parlour.

"Why luv, they'll all be at the fire," the girl chuckled.

"What fire?" the Irishman shot back, as the undivided attention of the group had now been attained.

"The fire in that big building in the little valley right there," she proclaimed, pointing to the model, "and set by me and my shadow, one hour before the operation begins."

A look of amazement suddenly appeared on many faces in the room. Captain Davis sat with his mouth open in sheer surprise and Charley Mason's eyes were bulging in disbelief at the simplicity of the answer.

"My gawd!" Patrick Sandilands muttered.

Only Joe and Ada were totally unmoved. The old man went on puffing his pipe, as Ada sat back and just shook her head.

"You see what we mean, Mister Sandilands, she's a smart one is our Lizzie, and it will work. I would bet on it," Ada stated emphatically, her admiration for the girl obvious.

"Aye, ye be damned right it will! Gawd, I wish she were a lad . . . such lethal innocence . . . and wasted on a girl!" Captain Davis exclaimed, with more than a little excitement in his voice, although the last comment had been barely a whisper.

"Ach, tis Scottish blood she must be havin in her veins," Patrick laughed.

Mick thumped the table a mighty whack, making tankards jump. When the laughter subsided, the Irishman raised his tankard toward Lizzie.

"A toast, fellow pirates," he shouted, lifting off his chair.

There was a scraping of chairs as they all rose to their feet, except Charley, and raised their tankards.

Then Mick shouted, "To our Lizzie!"

The whole gathering followed suit, repeating, "To our Lizzie!"

The noise grew louder in the room as they all now tried to talk at once but, if anyone had noticed, the two youngsters had snuggled even closer and were now sat cheek-to-cheek hugging each other quietly.

Then silently, they arose and moved slowly toward Joe's chair, sitting one on each arm and putting their young arms around his neck as he wiped away a flood of tears with a soiled rag.

"Gawd, 'am so proud of you two little scallywags," whispered the old man through his emotion.

Captain Davis called for order and the noise slowly subsided.

"Can we give yer new fangled pulley a try down at the docks, Mister Engineer?" he asked.

"Aye, just pick the time an we'll be there," Charley gruffly replied, as the youngsters too, slipped back into their chairs.

"Can ah be theer, too?" Angus requested of the girl, who quickly nodded her consent.

"And ah suppose you have the crews ready?" the captain asked, smiling.

"Tell 'em, Mick," Lizzie encouraged the Irishman.

"That we have, Admiral," the reply came with a jest. "All they need is your own wonderful heye castin over 'em, an sum of them luvly wisdom words yer famous for, shoutin into their thick heads."

Davis narrowed his eyes, not quite sure how to deal with this kind of joking, until Angus interrupted.

"Ach, pay him nay mind man, he's only a wee daft Irisher."

Seeing the brewery manager laugh at his own joke, a smile finally came to the captain's face.

Patrick cast his eyes around the room, resting on each participant in turn. "And do you have a special role in mind fer the likes of me?" he asked.

Before anyone else could speak, Charley shouted, "I have, he's just about big enough for the job of moving those pulley blocks . . . let him work with me." They all smiled at the eagerness of the young engineer.

"What say you, Mister Sandilands?" Lizzie asked.

The Scot studied the situation for a moment.

"Ach, t'wud be a grreat honour to be associated with an inventor of such magnitude," he said, seriously.

Charley's face went beet-red, as the rest of the group burst into laughter.

Quon made some signs to the girl.

"What's a magni . . . whatever yer called him?" she asked.

Patrick chuckled. "Aye lassie, it just means, a grreat perrson."

Joe rose from his chair and declared the meeting over, telling them all, except Ada, to be at the dock at ten in the morning in front of Captain Davis' vessel, *Falcon*. No objections were uttered from the group as chairs were slid back from the table.

"Patrick," Lizzie spoke sharply, "where are yer stayin, cos it's awful late, an yer can stay with one of us."

The Scot looked somewhat relieved at the offer.

"Ah'd noo be wantin tae put a body tae any trouble," he said, quietly.

"Sure, you'll just be stayin' wi me then, boyo," Mick quickly intervened. "Hoy be on me own, an two empty beds wi nobody in 'em. Sure, that's settled now."

A roar of laughter filled the room as Ada took a swipe at the genial Irishman.

"So you have two empty beds with nobody in them, have you," Ada giggled. "Sometimes I think you're as daft as a brush, you big wonderful lump," she said, smiling sweetly at him.

Everyone was just about to leave when Angus McClain spotted Charley still sitting at the table.

"Hey . . . hey there, hold it now. Who's tae be seein tae the laddie there, he canna be walkin."

Without a word, Patrick turned back from the doorway, picked up the engineer, and walked outside into the moonlight, shouting over his shoulder as he followed Mick.

"Ah reckon he's ma responsibility noo?" he said with a smile, swinging Charley around onto his back.

From the doorway Lizzie and Ada watched the visitors leave. Her soft eyes and gentle smile caused Ada to stop for a moment and realize just how young their Lizzie really was; and she felt suddenly maternal toward this motherless girl who seemed more like an adult than many who were much older in years. She slipped her arm around Lizzie's shoulders and gave her a little squeeze—the girl did not pull away.

"Sometimes men can be so kind and considerate to each other and other times they're proper horses' tails," Missus Mason whispered, steering the girl back inside and closing the door.

Chapter 10

Breakfast was eaten quickly as the morning sun came streaming in through the tiny windows. Martha was scurrying around trying to do her work.

"Cum on, fill yer gizzards and get outa here. Ah don't want you lot under me feet all morning!" she said bluntly, banging pans and throwing mats outside onto the grass.

Startled by the noise, the little dog took off at a run toward his favourite place—the bone heap, up at the slaughterhouse.

Quon and Lizzie walked up Drover's Lane to watch the gypsies as they brought in a herd of fat cattle and sheep and penned them expertly in the holding paddock. The dogs they used as helpers were a mixed bunch of hounds that were superbly trained to obey their masters' whistles and calls. Only half of the drovers were mounted, the others were young lads who ran along the side or in front of the cattle, blocking entrances and lanes and generally keeping the herd heading in the right direction.

The leader rode around to the front of the slaughterhouse and dismounted. As he talked with the butcher foreman, they walked through the building and out the back to the holding pens to count the delivered stock. Then, armed with his payment slip, he remounted and rode on down to the cottage to see Ada for his money.

The youngsters were still sitting on top of the wall when he returned up the lane at fall gallop. The other mounted drovers had each taken a boy up behind him, riding pillion. The leader slowed down as the last of the gypsy boys nimbly vaulted into position, then with a wave, they were gone.

"Now, that was a slick operation," Lizzie commented in admiration. "If we can perform anywhere near that good next week, we'll be long gone when they realize what's happened," she chuckled.

Quon nodded and jumping down from his perch asked, "Where go now, Wizzy?"

She landed beside him and whispered, "Ah saw the minister walkin across yonder." She pointed out onto the heath—that was the common land.

Quon Lee cocked his head and frowned, but it was his eyes that asked the question.

"He had somebody with im, an ah didn't recognize 'em so we'll go take a look."

Trotting off up the lane, they crossed the common land, but saw no one. The girl stopped holding her finger to her lips for silence and they strained to listen. Then, they heard a cough from behind a nearby wall. Quietly sneaking closer, they heard a voice, which had a rough, hard tone to it, certainly not the Holy Man. They listened intently, with their ears to the stones, and they soon heard the minister speaking.

"Catch them in mid-channel and sink the dogs, not a man must survive, you hear me?"

The youngsters looked at each other in surprise as the second voice continued the conversation.

"We be flyin the English flag—they won't suspect a thing until we open up on 'em," the rough voice said, with an evil chuckle as the sounds came clearly through the wall.

"Just make sure you don't mess it up," the minister snarled back.

Then, it sounded as though the owner of the nasty voice had jumped to his feet in anger.

"Pay yer damned money, an my *Golden Lady* will sink the *Falcon* to the bottom of the channel!" There was a clink of coins, some grunting then the sound of the Holy Man's voice again.

"Go now. I don't want to be seen with the likes of you! Be gone man, be gone!"

Lizzie and Quon looked at each other in silence, stunned by what they had just heard.

"Quick, see who it is," Lizzie whispered urgently, scrambling up the wall to cautiously peer over.

There, walking away were the minister and a man known only to the youngsters as Long John Stroud—a mean, hard mariner, feared and hated by all who knew him. It had been Lefty, Mick's one-armed messenger, who had warned them of him.

Fifteen minutes later they were at the docks, inquiring where the *Golden Lady* was tied. It took some time to locate, but finally they found her docked at the end of Tower Wharf and they began their visual inspection. It carried twenty-four cannon, arranged twelve a side on the second deck, and numerous smaller cannonade on the main deck. An old sailor, who happened to be passing and noticed their interest, stopped to talk.

"That's a bloody pirate ship if I've ever seen one!" the old mariner growled. "Ye keep well away from it," he warned them, in a concerned tone.

Turning, the youngsters ran all the way back to where the *Falcon* was docked, just in time to see Mick, Patrick and Charley arrive along with old Lumpy and the new-fangled pulley. A smiling Captain Davis came down the gangplank to meet them. As Lizzie and Quon ran toward them, the captain noticed another arrival.

"Mornin, Angus," he shouted good-naturedly, "good ter see yer brought some refreshments with yer."

All eyes turned to watch the brewery manager, striding along with a small hogshead of cider on his shoulder.

"Right, let's get on with it," Davis announced, taking charge. "There's nothin between *Falcon* and the end of the wharf—let me see yer move her quiet-like."

Lizzie and Quon were eager to talk to the men about their overheard conversation but realized it would now have to wait until after the test run.

Patrick picked up Charley and walked right to the end of the wharf, setting him down on a barrel next to the last capstan. Mick and Lumpy followed in the horse-drawn wagon.

A tiny longboat, along with two oars, was the first thing out of the wagon and they were quickly dumped into the water. Next, a great thick rope appeared over the side of the wagon. It was fed over the dock, into the water, and made secure to the longboat. Mick ran down the stone stairs to the water, jumped into the little boat, and began to row expertly for the other side of the dock. Corks on the rope stopped it from sinking as Patrick eased his end over the side of the wagon coming to rest on the ground below.

In no time at all, Mick had the end of the rope attached to the opposite capstan and was on his way back. A second rope was thrown to him as he arrived back at the dock, and he took off again, but this time he stopped halfway and waited. Leaning over the side of the wagon, Patrick gave a mighty groan as he lifted a huge pulley out onto the ground and quickly attached it to the main rope, giving it a push that sent it skidding down the line into the water.

At the same time, Mick, pulling hard on his oars, made for the far side, towing the now-floating pulley into the middle of the open water. Again, he tied his rope and came back. Patrick was now ready to hand him another rope. This time Mick rowed toward the *Falcon* and gently bumped her side with the longboat. Rope in his teeth, he scrambled up the side, ran to the forward lash link just behind the figurehead, and tied it on tight. Then over the side he went again, into the longboat and returned to the end of the wharf. Captain Davis, under orders from Charley, was already casting his docking lines as a group of twenty TLS sailors stood holding the tail rope.

"Now, we shall see," the young engineer said, eager with excitement.

Patrick, Mick and Angus heaved on the rope and, ever so slowly, the *Falcon* began to move. Silently and smoothly, it pulled away from the dock and headed toward the river.

"Enough," shouted Charley as the three brawny men stopped pulling.

"Hold her back there," yelled Captain Davis to the sailors holding onto the tail rope. "Pull her back in lads, look lively now," he screamed at his men, as they strained and groaned.

At least ten extra men were needed to rebirth the *Falcon.*

When it was all over, an elated Charley sat up and cheered from his perch on the barrel.

"Damn it, lad, ah never thought yer would do it, but it works like a dream," the captain complimented Charley, slapping him on the back.

It was much harder work recovering all their equipment, but finally the job was complete and Davis gave the order to stow it all on board.

"Amazing display," the captain muttered. "Amazing!"

The men were all shaking hands at the successful display when Lizzie saw her opportunity and stepped forward.

"We have a problem boys . . . better if we had a talk, either here, or at the building site after lunch."

The laughter suddenly stopped. Captain Davis looked at Lizzie's face and made a snap decision.

"Now!" he shouted, beckoning toward his ship and leading the way up the gangplank and into his cabin. Seated at his desk, the now-scowling captain muttered, "Squeeze in an shut the door."

Everybody managed to push inside, except old Lumpy, who stayed on the dock to take care of the horse and wagon.

"A problem yer say, girl?" Davis growled. "Then out with it."

Lizzie pushed to the front to face the captain.

"It's Long John Stroud and his ship the *Golden Lady*. They're goin ta meet yer in mid-channel all friendly-like, then blow you outa the water . . . not a man's ta be left alive."

"Who gave the order?" the captain asked, already having a suspicion.

"The minister at the local church," the girl hissed.

Davis nodded, understanding the why of it now.

"Ta hell with the black hearted pirate, we go as planned," the captain snapped fiercely.

"Now, just wait a minute," Lizzie said, urgently. "We should be able ta outwit that pig somehow."

Patrick coughed to draw their attention.

"This is just a thought, mind yerr," he said, grinning with devilment, "if we took him rright here in porrt, when he least expects it, then sailed his ship oot rright behind our own—we could leave it strranded and an easy catch for the Frrench or Spanish."

There was dead silence in the cabin as these words sunk in.

"I think that's a splendid idea," Lizzie said. "It's all we have time for now. You pick the crews after lunch captain, an Patrick can work on a plan."

"Send all the tackle an rope we're goin ta need, Charley," the captain said, rising from behind his desk, "I can give yer two men if yer need 'em. Take One-Eyed Jack an Ben Thorn . . . they're good men. Now, get outa here, I've work ta do."

Standing on the dock beside the wagon, the group contemplated their next move. Patrick had just deposited the young engineer in the wagon on the seat next to old Lumpy when the two sailors, Jack and Ben, came bounding down the gangplank.

"Yer needs us, the master says?" Ben asked, breathlessly.

Mick pointed to the wagon, and Ben and Jack climbed in.

"Let's go friend, back to yer yard," Charley ordered the old man, who shook the reins and clucked at the horses.

"Think ah'd be better back at ma own work," Angus muttered to himself and set off walking toward the brewery.

"Would yerr be knowin the berrth where the *Golden Lady* is sitting?" Patrick asked Lizzie, with a frown.

"Tower Wharf, last on the right. Wanna see?" she asked eagerly.

"Ach, that I do, tis the very vessel I be most interested in."

Patrick directed many questions at the youngsters as they walked along the cobblestone road from the dock. Some of them seemed quite foolish—like, did they know if Stroud had a lady friend, or had he a favourite drinking place. Lastly, he asked who made the pirate's clothes. This answer the youngsters knew, having seen Long John leave the tailor's shop back when they had the bread route.

Walking along Dock Street, they were almost at the entrance to Tower Wharf, when Lizzie spotted Captain Long John Stroud and two of his crewmen walking toward them and quickly informed Patrick.

"Move over, let 'em pass easy," Patrick ordered quietly, gently pushing the youngsters to one side, and coming to a halt. Stroud and his men passed by with nary a glance in their direction.

The Scot leaned over and whispered to the youngsters.

"Follow 'em, but keep well back. Go on now . . . and be careful!" he urged.

They walked for several blocks, keeping well back and out of sight. As the three mariners continued down Dock Street, Lizzie and Quon sauntered after them.

"Run through the alleyway an sit watchin 'em from opposite Abe's shop," the girl instructed her partner. She stopped to lean on the wall, watching the ships pass on the Thames with one eye, and following the progress of the three swaggering sailors with the other.

Quon raced ahead like the wind. Reaching his destination, he flopped down onto the edge of the kerb, completely out of breath. He watched as Stroud and his men approached the corner of Water Lane and turned north, but be couldn't see any sign of Lizzie. The mariners turned into *The Robin*, and disappeared inside.

Quon strained his eyes against the brightness of the midday sun to see down the street but there was still no Lizzie. His heart was beginning to pump madly, as he whispered desperately to himself. "Wizzy, where you be?"

A giggle at his elbow made him jump.

Spinning around in surprise, he yelped, "How you get dare?"

Lizzie laughed at Quon's reaction. "Came up on the back of that last coach, silly."

The youngsters picked a spot across the street where both the back alley and the front entrance of the coaching house were visible to them, and waited. They both agreed later, it was one of their most boring assignments.

At precisely two in the afternoon, the three re-emerged and staggered out the door of *The Robin*, arguing fiercely. The youngsters were on their feet and back on the job.

Down the road the men wobbled, pushing and shouting abuse at each other, until finally Captain Stroud fell headlong onto the sidewalk, with the other two falling on top of him.

"Quick!" Lizzie commanded, "let's get their purses and watches."

The two youngsters leapt into action. They wanted to appear as if they were helping the fallen men back onto their feet but as they rushed forward, Stroud took a swing at Quon. The blow, although without much sting, knocked the boy to the ground momentarily, but he quickly got to his feet and Lizzie grabbed him.

"Come on, let's go dumplin," she said urgently, pulling him along after her.

Chapter 11

Passing the tailor's shop, they decided to pay Abe a visit. He was delighted to see them and quickly poured three mugs of cider and sat them down at his table at the back of the store. The conversation was light and friendly as Lizzie slipped in her question.

"Do yer know Captain Stroud?" she asked innocently.

Abe's face turned white and he began to shake.

"He's a bad one, girl. Stay away from him!"

"Stop gettin upset, it's just that we saw him five minutes ago, drunk out of his mind, sprawled in Dock Street," she said, smiling.

Abe wiped his sweating brow.

"He's comin here Saturday morning for his new coat an britches, an I hope they fit good or he gets wild mad with me," the tailor whined.

"Oh you'll be just fine, yer worrying for nothin," Lizzie reassured him as they left his shop.

Calling at home for one of Martha's meat and pickle sandwiches, Lizzie asked if she knew where they could find Patrick. Ada informed them that he and Captain Davis were up at the building site with Mick. Cramming the food down their ravenous throats, the twosome quickly departed walking up Slaughter Lane onto the site of the new stable block. Patrick saw them immediately and made his way to their side.

"Tell it tae me slow an easy," he suggested, leading them off to one side to sit on a log.

"They went directly to *The Robin* on Dock Street, came out at exactly two, fallin down drunk," she said, innocently.

"Ach, will noo be learnin much from that now, will we?" the Scot grumbled, shaking his head.

"Hold out yer hands," Lizzie said, quietly.

Patrick frowned deeply but complied with the request and the girl dropped three watches and three small purses into his huge hands.

Whistling through his teeth, the Scot began to examine the loot.

"Ach, 'am afraid ter be askin how you acquired this lot," he mumbled, clicking open the back of a gold pocket watch. "Spanish," he said, moving to the next watch. "French," he confirmed opening the last one. His face suddenly grew dark as he read the inscription inside the case. "The bastard," he muttered, reading the inscription aloud, "To my dear father, Alex Douglas, 1803."

This was clearly upsetting to Patrick, so Lizzie took the watch out of his hand and read it herself.

"That's only a year or two ago," she mused, fastening an inquiring look on the Scot.

"Aye lass, and that were a Scottish ship too, an just so you know it all, that watch belonged tae ma Godfather, lost at sea, they said," Patrick spoke clearly and deliberately, then hung his head in sorrow.

Lizzie opened each purse looking for more telltale bits of information. She found gold coins from several different countries, but no incriminating evidence.

"Did yer look the vessel over?" the girl inquired, slipping the purses and two of the watches into her pockets and holding the third timepiece by its gold chain.

"Och aye, it would be nay bother sailing her," he said, not lifting his head.

"Then you keep this," Lizzie said, handing Patrick his Godfather's watch.

"Thank yer Lassie, but 'am thinking more on the lines of cutting somebody's throat," the big Scot snarled.

Just then, Captain Davis and Mick interrupted them.

"Did yer select all the men we need?" Lizzie asked.

"Oh ta be sure now. He shuffled 'em around a bit," Mick said, nodding at the captain.

Davis started to move off, then stopped and turned, grinning at his own thoughts.

"Bring all the men we picked, down to *Falcon* at first light, then we'll go down the Thames an do a little practical training."

Without waiting for an answer, he stalked off.

"How did he like yer men?" the girl wanted to know.

The Irishman could not contain his merriment as he began his explanation.

"Oh begora, yer should av seen the look on Captain Davis' face, when our bunch of crippled ex-sailors paraded out in front of him. But he had to admit, they have the experience—most of it under fire too, an they're all eager an willing ta follow orders. So, by thunder, he accepted 'em," Mick said, proudly. Then, as an afterthought, he continued. "Oh, by the way missy, hoy took them two young fellas on—the ones we wus watchin on the roof that day."

"For what job?" Lizzie asked, frowning.

"Ter be lookin after you two!"

Patrick looked a little shocked at the suggestion of Lizzie and Quon going on such a dangerous expedition.

"Oh, yer moy't as well get used ta it Scotty, me boyo, when the lady says she's goin, then she's goin," Mick mumbled, shrugging his shoulders.

Lizzie turned to Quon and they grinned broadly at each other.

"Wizzy got big job fol us," the boy spoke up with pride.

"What did he say?" Patrick asked, looking at Mick.

"Hoy'd be havin no hidea at all, at all," the Irishman replied, chuckling.

The Scot shook his head. "Och aye, mine's Scottish, yours is Irish, but what in the Lord's name does he speak?

"His own version of English, don't you dumplin?" Lizzie said with a giggle slipping her arm through Quon Lee's.

Patrick Sandilands stood up and eased his massive frame to its full height.

"How do we get all the men off the *Golden Lady* at the same time?" he asked.

Mick shook his head, having no answer to the problem.

"I think us two can probably make that happen," ventured Lizzie.

"How?" the Scot asked.

"First things first, lad," Lizzie snapped gently. "Captain Stroud and whoever is with him can be taken easy . . . just wait 'til they're drunk! But we have ta find out how many men are on board, an pick 'em off one or two at a time."

"Ach, yer noo telling us how tae get 'em off the vessel, lassie," Patrick urged in frustration.

"Just be listenin, and shut yer mouth, yer big daft bugger," Mick advised him, grinning.

"Oh we'll get 'em ta chase us up an alley, then you lot can get 'em," Lizzie explained with a laugh. "Maybe you should be checking up on Charley," she continued, pointing at the Scot. "And you get yer arse back ta work, ya lazy Irish lump," she snapped at Mick, leaping out of his reach and taking off at a run. Quon Lee followed.

With hardly any discussion between them, they made their way back to Tower Wharf. Making themselves comfortable on top of some bales of wool ready for loading onto one of the ships—they began their surveillance of the *Golden Lady*'s crew. They saw twenty-one men, not including the captain or the young lad who was about Quon's age. The poor lad always seemed to be getting shouted at by the men.

"Oh, dat boy velly un'appy," Quon Lee observed. "Plobly help us if he knew.

"Lizzie nodded in agreement as they continually heard his name being called out by the wretched sailors.

"That's a strange name he's got," the girl commented.

"Him's name Fish," said Quon Lee.

"Well, that's what he answers to, but it sure is a strange one," Lizzie whispered, as some sailors passed by their perch.

At that moment, one of the crewmen let fly with his hand—cuffing the boy hard about the ears and knocking the lad clean off his feet—sending him sprawling onto the deck.

Lizzie started to react, but Quon laid a warning hand on her arm. She made a silent promise then and there, to do what she could to help this lad before those evil sailors killed him.

Chapter 12

Six o'clock boomed out on the big clock over the Parliament Buildings, and instinctively everyone checked their watches. As the youngsters watched, a row blew up on the deck of the *Golden Lady*. This brought Captain Stroud dashing onto the scene with swinging fists and foul language, kicking one of his men hard enough to knock him down.

"Me tink Patlick make him scleam soon," the Chinese boy muttered to his partner. Sliding off the wool bales on the blind side of the *Golden Lady*, the youngsters made a quick exit from Tower Wharf, setting off at a steady trot for home. They rounded the corner into Water Lane and almost bumped into Nathan Goldman as he was saying goodbye to Abe at the tailor's shop.

"Hello, children," Nathan bubbled, good-naturedly slapping Quon Lee on the back. "I'm afraid I have no time for talk today," he said, turning away.

"Not so fast, my lad," Lizzie spoke, putting some authority in her voice.

The fat, little man stopped dead in his tracks, turning slowly to face the girl—his face growing quite red with anticipation.

"Ah have another guinea to put toward buying that business," she purred, flicking him a gold piece.

"But . . . but I was only jesting, my dear," Nathan whined, catching the gold coin before it fell to the ground.

"Look here, sir, the law is quite clear," she snapped, "you named your price, ah paid a deposit, which I might add, you accepted, and that makes it a deal by the law of this land. Also, I just made another payment, so please keep an account in order, sir, for I intend to pay you the full amount . . . and remember, it is illegal to adjust the price now. Good day, sir," Lizzie finished coyly. She turned her back on the stunned businessman and she and Quon Lee hurried up the street.

Abe, who had been listening to the conversation, stepped to one side, allowing them to enter.

As soon as they were inside, Lizzie let out a little giggle and then burst into laughter. She laughed so hard she was unable to stand up and staggered up the shop to a seat, tears rolling down her face.

"Yer don't really like that pompous little city gent, do yer?" she asked the old tailor.

"No, but he is my cousin, and he knows a lot of important people," Abe whimpered.

"Aye, an lords it over ya, like he's a rose an yer dog muck," Lizzie chuckled. "Well, 'am goin ta change all that for yer, old friend," she muttered, more to herself than anyone. "Now to our business," she said sharply. "You will not have Captain Stroud's coat and breeches ready until late Friday afternoon," she ordered.

Abe shrank away from her in fear.

"But ah daren't, he'll kill me," the old man whined.

"Ah ha, but would you dare for a golden guinea?" she asked, leaning over the table and watching his fingers twitch at the mention of money.

A wailing sound erupted from the tailor as he pondered his dilemma.

Lizzie waited, smiling innocently. She felt Quon Lee's signal through his fingers on her shoulder and she slid a shiny new gold coin onto the table. The wailing grew louder as the old man's hand crept out and clasped the coin.

"Good," she said, calmly rising from her chair. "Tell him two o'clock Friday . . . an thanks, old friend."

The youngsters happily ran up Water Lane toward home. It was now past seven and they were ravenous. When they arrived at the cottage, they found Mick, Patrick, and Charley along with Ada and Joe, talking of their impending adventure into the world of piracy. The men were all puffing on their pipes and Ada had her books out, as usual, trying her best to keep the accounts straight. Martha, in her normal motherly way, was soon laying heaping plates of hot, steaming pease pottage in front of the youngsters. It wasn't until after the apple pie and custard had all been disposed of, that anyone spoke.

"Ye learn anythin?" Patrick asked casually.

"Aye, lots," Lizzie declared firmly. "We saw twenty-one crew, but there could be more who were off in town, then Stroud, an there's a kid on board who's regular whipping boy for everybody," she said, tapping the table with her finger tips.

"Why so agitated?" Ada asked, looking up from her account books.

"It's that kid that bothers me," Lizzie answered, mumbling more to herself than Ada. "He hates it there so why does he stay?" Then she looked into the faces around the table waiting expectantly for more news and pushed all thoughts of the boy aside. "We found out that Captain Stroud is having some new clothes made and we bribed the tailor to have him in the shop at two o'clock on Friday."

"Why two o'clock?" Ada asked quietly, knowing there must be a good reason.

"Cos he'll be drunk by that time, an easy ta take . . . we might even get two or three more of 'em who might be with him," the girl suggested smiling, though her eyes were portraying her deeper thoughts.

"Ach, yer quite a schemer, lassie. Yer forever surprising me," Patrick muttered. "An shall we be having any trouble with the tailor?"

"No, old Abe Kratze is a good friend of ours."

The room grew quiet, each thinking their own private thoughts.

Ada broke the silence.

Turning to Patrick and speaking quietly, she said, "We told yer she was special, now yer getting a sample. How do yer like it?"

Patrick only shook his head in amazement as Charley and Mick grinned like Cheshire cats.

"Sure, hoy be thinkin yer a believer now Scotty, an if yer not, she'll be for surprisin yer many times more," the Irishman laughed, enjoying Patrick's puzzled look.

Charley broke the spell by giving them an account of his accomplishments during the day. By the next afternoon—that would be Thursday — he should have it all done. The ship's chandlers had looked at him a bit peculiar when he ordered the long heavy ropes and asked what he was going to do with it all.

"So what yer tell 'em?" Lizzie asked.

"Oh I just told 'em I wanted ta tie me dog up," he answered nonchalantly, causing a round of laughter to run through the room.

"Did yer fit Angus McClain into yer plans?" the girl asked Mick.

"Sure we did," the Irishman replied. "He's ta be bringin the first vessel back. He'll not be havin any trouble with that, hoy be thinkin," Mick stated unconcernedly. "Patrick will sail the *Golden Lady* over to Zarauz, an bring the last vessel out. That will be the most dangerous part."

Ada glanced up again with a concerned look on her face. Mick noticed her worried look and reached over to gently pat her hand.

"Now don't you be frettin over me, moy darlin, hoy'll just be keepin everythin movin smooth loyk," he assured her.

"Please be careful, yer big daft lump," Ada pleaded, lowering her reddening face back into her account books.

Lizzie had been doing some hard thinking all through this conversation, not paying any attention to Ada and Mick's little scene. Suddenly, her face brightened and a little smile crept across her lips.

"Now what's goin on in that head of yers?" Mick asked.

"It'll noo be good fer some poor devil," Patrick commented flippantly.

"I was wonderin what it was that I'd missed," the girl said seriously. "It was old Abe Kratze . . . and Long John Stroud coming for his clothes at two o'clock on Thursday, that's tamorra."

A bunch of blank faces looked back at her from around the table, not one of them understood her concern.

"Abe's goin ta put Stroud off for a day an there might be trouble," Lizzie explained.

Now they understood.

"But if we fill the shop with people, it might stop all that—bullies like Stroud don't like an audience."

Ada nodded, agreeing with Lizzie's philosophy.

"But if he gets angry, then what?" Ada asked in a concerned voice.

"Ach, that's noo trouble at all. One of the customers will be myself, just ta protect the old fella," Patrick assured them with some pleasure.

A wagging finger from Lizzie brought a look of innocence onto the Scot's face as he sheepishly protested.

Charley indicated he was tired, but asked if he might be allowed to partake in the adventure, since he had put so much effort into its success.

Lizzie looked at him sadly, her eyes full of anguish for the crippled ex-ship's engineer. She did not want to disappoint him, but . . .

Patrick's voice broke into her thoughts.

"Och aye, lad, that yer can, but only if yer agreeable ta comin back wi Angus McClain on the first ship out." He looked toward Lizzie for her approval . . . and even Charley noticed her slight nod.

Charley thanked Lizzie profusely and she sighed with relief at the practical suggestion from the Scot.

"Now it's home an bed for you, me lad," Patrick said, to the young engineer who had also moved into Mick's place for convenience.

Walking around the table, Patrick picked Charley up as easy as if he were a child. "We'll see yer at home, Mick," he called over his shoulder, as his big strides took them down the garden path and out into the lane.

Lizzie watched as Mick also slowly rose to leave and Ada quickly closed her book.

"I'll walk to the lane with yer Mick," she announced softly.

Thursday morning was uneventful for the youngsters who were again sat atop the wool bales keeping a close watch on the *Golden Lady*. They spotted the boy, Fish, just as one of the sailors gave him a shove sending him careening into a storage chest on the deck. Quon Lee looked sideways at Lizzie who had clenched her fists and had a strong look of hatred on her face.

Then they noticed the captain departing for the coaching house with a different pair of men than they had seen the day before.

Around noon, the youngsters returned home for lunch, and were met by the dog at the gate. The terrier had been spending a lot of time down at the Johnson's. He had developed quite an attachment to their little boy during his convalescence in Joe's garden. He seemed to desire the boy's company over Lizzie and Quon, as they were so busy.

They ate a leisurely lunch and suggested to Martha that they would like to meet her at the tailor's shop at two o'clock. Having heard all the conversation the night before, she readily agreed.

Next, they walked down to the bakery and received a royal welcome from Bill Johnson.

"Elow doy," he greeted them.

"Will yer do us a favour?" Lizzie asked, giggling, explaining the situation to the Yorkshireman.

Without hesitation, he replied, "At two tha' says. By gum lass, it would be a pleasure ta be of 'elp ta yer. Ah'll be there."

Next, it was around the corner and into the brewery yard.

After receiving some directions from one of the workmen, they found Angus testing the cider for strength in a distant corner. Looking up, he saw the pair watching him.

"Ageing some real good stuff," he muttered, as an explanation of what he was doing. "What is it ah can do for yer?"

"Be in Abe Kratze's tailor shop at two o'clock with three of yer men," Lizzie directed him. She went on to explain why, and he nodded.

Taking out his pocket watch, he realized they didn't have much time and he went to round up some men immediately.

Quon tugged on her sleeve to get her attention and made some signs with his hands. She nodded, yelled goodbye to Angus and they made their way toward the tailor's shop.

As they arrived, they realized it was almost two and waited across the street to see how their plan would unfold. In a few minutes, the big clock boomed out 'two' and a smile flitted across Lizzie's face as she saw how many people were now milling around inside the shop.

Then, with a huge stroke of luck, down the street came the carriage of the local minister. It stopped directly in front of Abe's shop. No sooner had the Holy Man disappeared inside when around the corner from the alehouse came a stumbling Captain Stroud and his two men.

"This should be good," Lizzie giggled, "better than we could ever have planned it!"

They waited until the sailors were going into the shop and quickly crossed the street so they didn't miss anything. They could still watch through the window, have a great view of the proceedings . . . and be safer, too.

Captain Stroud stumbled into the tailor's shop, almost knocking the minister down. Martha tittered with delight at the unfolding scene and played her part well. Deliberately walking into the two swaying sailors, who were really lucky that drunks feel no pain, she held her balance against the smaller men and they were soon crashing off the nearby wall. They finished sitting on the floor looking quite dazed and surprised.

The minister angrily spun around, screaming at the captain who wondered why his men were sitting on the floor.

"You're drunk, you fool. Leave immediately!"

Stroud tried to focus his booze-laden eyes on the person speaking and raised his fist as if to strike the Holy Man.

The minister shrank back in fear.

"Throw him out, throw him out!" he shouted.

Bill Johnson was only too happy to oblige. First, the captain came flying into the street, followed quickly by his two men, who were unceremoniously hurled after him.

"Thank you, sir. I shall pray for you on Sunday," the minister mournfully droned in the same tone of voice he always used at Sunday service. "May I be attended to first, I really don't feel well," he whined loudly, pushing to the front and getting the attention of the tailor.

Old Abe held a parcel out to him. Coins clinked into his outstretched hand; the minister grabbed the parcel and rushed out of the door. The carriage door banged shut. The driver whipped the team of horses into a lunging start, and they galloped away as fast as they could go.

Waiting until Stroud and his men had run off, Lizzie and Quon walked into the tailor's shop. She held up her arms for silence.

"Thank you, one and all, the fun's over for today," she laughed, as the tailor sat down looking mystified. "Angus, you an Patrick stay back with us, just in case there is any trouble," the girl ordered, as the rest filed out onto the sidewalk.

"Don't look at me like that, Scotty, I never planned on the minister turning up here," Lizzie snickered, walking over to Abe who was leaning on the counter still ghostly white and shaking. "It's all right, me dear," she said, slipping an arm around his shoulders, "yer didn't think I'd leave you ta face that animal on yer own, did ya? Well, these two fine gentlemen will be here ta protect you again tamorra. This one is Angus and that big lump is Patrick," she said, pointing to each one of them respectively.

"We'd better go an let the old lad recover," Lizzie proposed, after ten minutes had passed with no one coming into the shop. She urged Quon Lee toward the door. "You comin to the docks with us, Patrick?" she asked, moving off.

"Aye, ah reckon ah will," the Scot said, following them outside.

The girl suddenly stopped and turned to Patrick, pointing up the hill.

"Yer might as well get yer bearings while we're here," she suggested. "First lane up that way is Mast, turn right, an Bill Johnson's bakery is at the corner of Baker Lane. Next lane is Corn, turn right, an the cider brewery is in Bell's Yard, up a-ways on the left." Lizzie thought she had done a good job of explaining it for the Scotsman and they now continued on their way toward the dock.

Drawing closer, they could see the empty berth where the *Falcon* usually tied up.

"Not back yet," the Scot observed.

"Just wait here 'till we take a look," the girl said, scampering off with Quon Lee close behind.

Running all the way, they were soon in the yard behind the tailor's shop and climbing the rickety stairs to the roof of the carpenter's workshop. A quick look back told them no one had noticed. They moved carefully around to the front, then climbed onto the adjoining roof to sit astride one of the dormer roofs.

Quon Lee extracted the spyglass from inside his clothes, handing it to the girl who pointed it down river. Steadying the instrument, she watched silently for a moment.

"There they are! " she cried out excitedly, "coming in under half-sail and looking good."

Lowering the glass, she handed it to the Chinese boy, who took a long look himself.

"Dem quick come. We go," he said urgently.

Carefully they descended from their perch, high on the dormer. Creeping around the building to the backstairs, they peeked over the edge to check the yard below. All was clear and the youngsters made their exit down the stairs, walking casually until they entered the lane, then running like hell for the docks.

"See her?" Patrick asked, as they arrived panting at his side.

"Be here soon," Lizzie gasped.

As the *Falcon* came into view, Quon Lee's elbow made contact with his partner's ribs. Instantly she turned, scowling at him. He nodded at a stack of barrels farther along the wharf, looking hard at the barrels and the sailor sat cross-legged on top of them.

"What?" she whispered, still keeping her eyes glued on the sailor.

"Him flom Stloud, him is," the Chinese boy said, urgently.

"You sure?" she whispered back,

"Me velly sure," Quon Lee growled.

Lizzie tugged on Patrick's shirt to get his immediate attention and as he turned, she said quietly, "Follow us, an no questions."

The tone of her voice warned him there was something wrong. The three of them moved back down the dock, away from the berth of the *Falcon* and well out of earshot of the sailor on the barrels.

Turning, she looked back and motioned with her head.

"See that sailor sat on them barrels?" Lizzie asked.

"Och aye," the Scot replied.

"He's a spy from the *Golden Lady*."

Patrick cocked his head to one side and that familiar wicked little smile appeared.

"Well, lassie, he ain't goin home to his mummy tonight. Ach, ah think ah should invite him ta stay with us," the Scot decided, giving the youngsters a wink.

At that moment the *Falcon*, rounded the corner and sailed smoothly toward her berth. The sailor sitting on the barrels was so intent upon watching the ship arrive, he was totally unaware of Patrick coming up behind him.

The Scot slowly reached out, clasped one iron hand around the man's neck, and yanked him clean off his perch. Then, holding him about a foot off the floor, Patrick squeezed hard and the sailor's legs kicked out violently.

"Put him down, yer daft lump. He's gone all blue!" Lizzie hissed.

The Scot simply opened his hand and the sailor flopped unconscious onto the cobbles in a heap.

Ben Thorn had watched the whole scene from the deck of the *Falcon* and now quickly jumped ashore and ran over to the little group.

"What we got here, Lizzie?" he asked, peering down at the unconscious man. "Why it's one of Stroud's men, the one they call, Weasel."

"Ah asked him ta stay with us for a few days," Patrick said, grinning.

"That were right friendly of yer lad," Ben chuckled. "Looks like he accepted yer invitation."

The mariner shouted for some help to load the man into the hold. Two of the *Falcon*'s crew quickly carried the prisoner away.

"In irons, bosun?" one of them shouted, giving Ben his seagoing title.

"What the hell's going on?" Captain Davis demanded, as he stormed across the wharf. "That was one of Stroud's trusted men!"

"Calm down," Lizzie cried. "Weasel were here ta spy on yer, so we took him a day early. We'll get 'em all tamorra, including Long John Stroud," she predicted confidently.

"Aye lass . . . but quietly," Captain Davis muttered, letting a grin slip back onto his face.

They questioned the captain about the men he had been trying out and received a glowing report of their suitability.

"Hope the weather stays good," Davis commented as an afterthought, casting his eyes toward the heavens as he returned to his vessel.

Mick had all the men lined up on the dock in true military fashion.

"I want the slowest men in the front ranks," yelled Mick, and some of the lame sailors changed places, moving into the front.

The Irishman walked to the front of the group and acting like a general began yelling loudly.

"You all know the song, as ye march back to barracks, I want to hear it!"

A murmur ran through the ranks.

"Are you ready with that tin whistle, John?" Mick asked one of the younger lads . . . a couple notes on the tin flute told him he was. "Then take 'em home, boy," he ordered.

Off moved the small column to the sounds of the whistle. A mish-mash of men's voices began to sing loudly . . . albeit not in tune.

We are the boys, the boys of the TLS
If yer don't want a beatin, with us you never mess.
We are short of a limb and we got a lump or two,
But we're more than a match, for any ten of you.

Lizzie's mouth dropped open in surprise and through her smile, a tear splashed down her cheek. Quon Lee moved closer and took her hand.

Mick walked over to them and said very quietly, "Sure, tis the words that gets to a man." Then they all held their breath listening intently, trying to catch the next verse.

We're all for the company
Our fame will make you dizzy;
And we swear by a single name,
And that name is . . . our Lizzie!

Hearing these last words almost overwhelmed the girl.

"Did yer hear what they were singin?" she asked, incredulously.

Mick grinned. "It's just their way of sayin, they love ya, an have every confidence in yer," the Irishman said, quietly and sincerely.

A voice suddenly boomed out from the deck of the *Falcon* breaking the seriousness of the moment.

"Go home girl . . . I've seen enough of yer for one day, yer little witch!" It was Captain Davis and he followed it up with great guffaws of laughter as he retreated to his cabin.

A pleasant supper and a quiet evening fit the mood in the cottage that evening, each one of them wrapped in their own thoughts. It was going to be a big day on Friday and the great adventure was about to begin.

Chapter 13

Unable to sleep, the youngsters were out on the street before dawn. They helped Tom and Billy load the bread cart and visited with Bill Johnson, happily sampling some of his freshly baked cakes. They walked around the corner and watched the first of the cider brewery drays being loaded for the first delivery of the day and then wandered into Water Lane and down to the Thames riverbank.

The sun was quickly rising, giving a magical sparkle to the old river, dancing off every ripple as daylight began to illuminate the whole dockland scene. Ships moved out as they caught the early morning tide—their creaking and groaning combining with the many voices that filtered through the morning air.

"It's a grand place, this London," Lizzie sighed.

Quon just looked up at her with a look that told her he agreed with everything she said.

Moving at a steady trot, they were soon back at the cottage and able to hear Martha's giant frypan crackling with the sounds of breakfast bacon cooking on the fire. Joe stood in the open doorway puffing on his first pipe of the day.

"A perfect day for a kidnappin," he chuckled, as the youngsters pushed past him.

"Just av't eggs ter do luvy, then it'll be ready," Martha said, glancing up from the fireplace. "Is Mister Charles an Patrick comin fer breakfast?" she asked.

Just then, they heard Joe greeting Patrick and his pillion passenger.

"Ah reckon they are, cos they're here now," Lizzie answered.

As Patrick and Charles entered, they were greeted with a mixture of friendliness and camaraderie. Soon plates were clinking and chairs scraped the floor as the eager group drew up to the table.

"What, noo oatmeal," Patrick pretended to complain.

"Martha turned slowly, placed her hands on her ample hips, and let loose a barrage of words.

"Tha'll not be gettin any a that slop here," she advised him, causing the Scot to laugh with his mouth full, almost choking him.

After the meal, Lizzie began questioning him.

"Have you an Mick got the tailor's shop covered this afternoon?" she inquired. Then, watching his reaction, she added, "He might have two or three men with him."

"Och aye, they'll be nae bother at all," he chuckled. "But where are we going ta hold 'em until we get the lot?"

The girl's eyes narrowed.

"That's goin ta need some thought," she muttered.

All of a sudden, Quon jumped off his chair and began his miming. They all watched in amusement as he finished by grabbing his empty plate and pretended to nail it to the table.

Ada, who had been watching every detail of this act, had a puzzled frown on her face.

"That lot has me beat. Tell us, Lizzie, what did he say?"

The girl burst out laughing. She jumped out of her chair, pulled the boy into her arms and hugged him.

"Dumplin, yer a genius," she giggled.

"Are ye noo goin ta tell us then?" Patrick asked in frustration.

The girl nodded her head, regaining her composure as she returned to her chair.

"He said it's easy, just nail 'em into barrels like little prison cells, an deliver 'em to the ship by dray—nobody will take any notice of barrels being loaded on board."

"He never said all that," Charley piped up, a look of disbelief on his face.

"Oh, I bet he did," Ada said, laughing. "And a great idea it is, too. What do you think, Patrick?"

The big Scot was grinning from ear to ear.

"Perfect," was his only comment.

Joe blew out his smoke and cleared his throat.

"About twenty-four barrels we're goin ta need, an two drays ta load 'em onta." The old man rose, knocked his pipe out on the fire-grate and prepared to leave, "Ah'll have two drays and all the barrels in Water Lane at two," the old man said, as he opened the door and disappeared.

Quon Lee made another set of signs and turned to look up at Lizzie.

"Need big sleep, how make?"

Lizzie nodded vigorously and translated for the group.

"He has a point. How do we keep 'em quiet in them barrels until we load 'em aboard the ship?"

"Anybody any ideas?" the accountant asked, turning to the men.

"Easy," Charley replied with a barely contained smirk. "Same way we did it on board fighting line ships, for a prank."

Patrick looked at him with a puzzled expression.

"Ach, are you noo goin tae tell us, lad?" the Scot chided the engineer.

Charley smiled, taking his time, as he remembered the long-ago incident.

"Course I am," he replied, drawing himself up straighter in the chair. "We simply poured a couple of gallons of rum in each barrel. The fumes kept 'em asleep and drunk for as long as we wanted. Mind you, our barrels didn't have lids on!" he mused, with a grin.

Quon Lee's hands gripped Lizzie's arm with excitement and he giggled as he heard Charley's solution.

"Gland headache ta wake to," Quon said, a pleased look glowing on his face.

"Come on, dumplin," the girl addressed her partner, "let's go tell Joe how ta prepare them barrels." She jumped off her chair and walked toward the door.

"Can you find him?" Charley asked, frowning.

"He's at the brewery with Angus McClain," Lizzie stated emphatically. Just before she closed the door, the girl poked her head back in and spoke to the Scot. "Better be at Abe's at one o'clock, just in case Stroud comes early."

"Och aye, lassie, ah'll be there," Patrick confirmed.

As the youngsters walked into the brewery yard, two huge drays were being loaded with empty topless barrels. The brewery cooper was adjusting the top iron bands on the barrels so that the tops could easily be put back on and made secure. Children were always fascinated with the art of barrel making and this day was no exception.

Angus and Joe were supervising the whole operation, whilst the teams of huge Shire horses stood waiting in the corner of the yard. Lizzie and Quon Lee hurried away from the cooper, skirted the busy scene and attracted Angus' attention. He, in turn, tapped Joe on the shoulder and pointed to their visitors. All four of them moved out of earshot of the nearby workers.

While Lizzie told them about Charley and his rum barrel story, Joe and Angus took the opportunity to light their pipes.

Joe had just put the light to his, when he snatched the pipe from his mouth and cried, "Damn it, why didn't I think of that! We did it when I served on the Man of War's, too. Bloody nearly killed a gunner once with that trick," the old man chortled.

"Ach it sounds tae be a waste of good liquor, tae me," Angus commented dourly. "A good rap o'er the heed wi a stout stick would just serve as weel," he mused, grinning.

"Bloody heathen," Joe snapped at the brewery manager and Angus gave a sly little wink at the youngsters.

Lizzie told the old man about Patrick going to the tailor's shop at one o'clock. He thought that was a good idea and asked who was going with him.

"I have no idea," the girl answered, "maybe Martha!" she giggled.

"Yer a cheeky little devil," he muttered, with a chuckle.

Running out of the brewery yard and waving to the men as they went, Quon Lee suggested, "Go watch Stroud, maybe see Fish."

The girl agreed and they set off down Water Lane toward the Thames, catching a glimpse of Billy and Tom delivering bread way up Dock Street.

Slowing to a walk to better observe the activity around them; they took special note of the traffic and how it all seemed to go where it wanted and usually without incident. Captain Davis had once described it as organized chaos.

The corner of Tower Wharf was a solid mass of horses and drays trying to move on or off the cobblestone docking area. There, in the middle of the whole jumble, was their own meat delivery wagon, with its big white letters on the side, TLS and Company. The driver was fighting to keep his Shires moving forward.

"Is no suplise we have accidents in dat mess," Quon Lee commented.

Every ship on the dock must have been getting their provisions delivered at the same time. There were people milling about everywhere and the noise level was deafening.

Slowly they made their way toward Long John Stroud's *Golden Lady*. Mixing with the crowd, they were soon within sight of the infamous ship and had a perfect view of its tyrant captain.

At that very moment, Stroud could be seen holding Fish by the scruff of the neck and shaking him.

"Ah'll do fer im, the bastard," Lizzie spat out. She was dangerously close to losing her temper and Quon Lee's hand gripped her elbow to calm her down, lest she draw attention to them.

"Quiet Wizzy, we kill im yeselday."

The girl could not help but smile at her protector.

"No dumplin, yer mean tamorra."

"Tomollow just as good," Quon said, with a serious expression.

Stroud marched down the gangplank, still holding a firm grip on the boy's neck. Following close behind were two of his mean-looking men.

"Now!" Lizzie hissed, picking up a rock and throwing it. The men stepped aside as the captain reached the bottom of the gangplank.

The stone whistled through the air, catching Stroud full on the temple, his eyes glazing as he staggered backwards, falling over the men who were close behind. His grip on the boy loosened.

Lizzie grabbed the boy's arm, pulling him away from Stroud's grip, and the young threesome escaped into the crowd amidst the confusion. Behind them, they could hear the terrible cursing of Captain Stroud.

"Come on, quick," the girl panted breathlessly, clambering over the edge of the dock and dropping into the first longboat she came upon. Fortunately, her sharp eyes had noticed that this one had a tarp covering. She and Quon helped Fish under the tarp and they lay very still, trying not to breathe.

Slowly the noise of the search drifted away.

"Av a look," Lizzie ordered in a whisper, and Quon peeked out from under the tarp.

"Wait," he whispered, climbing slowly back up onto the dock.

People were everywhere, but neither Stroud nor his men were in sight. Returning to the boat, Quon flipped the tarp off to reveal Lizzie and a very sad-looking little boy.

"Clear, Wizzy, we go qlick."

Fish spoke for the first time.

"I must go back," he said, a tear finding its way down his dirty cheek.

"Oh no, you don't, my lad," Lizzie snapped.

"But ah must, he'll kill me mother, if ah don't," the boy's terrified voice sobbed.

"Wait till we get outa here kid, then tell us, but that bastard ain't goin ta kill nobody, I promise you."

She firmly urged the boy forward, pushing him onto the dock in front of her. A quick glance around, as the big clock boomed out 'eleven', and with Fish between them, they each took one of his little hands and ran like the wind—only slowing briefly to catch their breath. In and out of alleyways and back lanes they ran. When they reached home safely, they were totally out of breath.

"Na then, who's chasin you?" Martha inquired, moving to guard the door.

The girl shook her head and gasped, "Nobody. Ah reckon, we're clear of 'em now."

The cook relaxed a bit and laid her hand on Lizzie's shoulder.

"Clear of who, lass?"

Lizzie, having caught her breath now, looked up at Martha and smiled, "Oh, just that Stroud fella from *Golden Lady*."

Martha took a step backwards in surprise.

She reached over her cooking pots and raised the huge iron frypan, muttering, "By gum ah'll kill im if he cums here!"

The youngsters laughed at Martha's fighting spirit and then she noticed Fish hiding behind Quon Lee.

"Na, who have we here, then?" she asked.

"We want yer ta feed Mister Fish, our new friend. He was the cabin boy aboard *Golden Lady*"

"Fish ain't me name," the boy said, shyly.

"Then wor is it, lad?" Martha asked, placing a heaping plate of meat pie in front of each of them.

"It's Walter Drake," he said, looking totally unhappy.

The door opened, and in walked Joe, puffing on his pipe and grinning contentedly.

"Na, who's this 'ere rascal?" he inquired, noticing the stranger sitting at his table wolfing down food.

"This," Lizzie said, stopping the spoon on its way to her mouth, "is Walter Drake, ex-cabin boy off the *Golden Lady*."

The old man sucked on his pipe for a moment, deep in thought.

"Wouldn't be any relation ta Bessie Drake who's cook at *The Robin* would yer lad?"

The boy burst into tears, his head falling onto the table.

"That's me, mother," he cried, fear sounding in his voice.

"What's he crying fer?" Joe asked.

"Oh, he thinks Stroud's goin ta kill her if he don't go back to the ship," Lizzie answered putting her arm around the boy.

"Well, yer two can fix that . . . go get her, right now," the old man ordered.

The youngsters were almost at the door when a knock sounded. Opening it revealed the gypsy drover with a paper in his hand, authorizing payment for cattle delivered to the slaughterhouse earlier that day.

"Come in, friend," Joe smiled. "Go on you two, do what ah told yer ta do," he said, pushing them out of the door.

He called Martha and gave Walter Drake a little pat on his shoulder as he passed.

"How about fixin some apple pie for the drovers, while they wait for Ada?" Joe suggested, grinning at the gypsy.

"Ee, aye it wud gimee great pleasure ta do that. Bring 'em down inta't garden lad," Martha tittered, as she hustled around the kitchen getting freshly baked pie for the men.

Smiling broadly, the gypsy gripped his flatcap tightly and backed out of the door, just as the clock boomed 'twelve' in the distance. Joe stuck his still-smoking pipe into his waistcoat pocket, pulled out his watch and checked the timepiece.

"Gained a minute again," he muttered in disgust.

Mick soon arrived for lunch, followed closely by Patrick.

"Where's Charley?" asked Martha, serving plates of steaming food around the table.

"Left him in the garden talking to them gypsies," the Scot said, nonchalantly. Just before he refilled his mouth with meat pie, he continued, "Ach, leave him, he'll eat out there."

"Would ya be ready now for this day's work ta be startin?" Mick addressed Joe, who nodded in the affirmative.

"Are you?" the old man retorted.

"Hoy av all moy men placed around the streets, from one o'clock 'til Lefty calls 'em in," Mick informed Joe, who wrinkled his brow, a puzzled look on his face.

The Irishman laughed. "That little witch will need some quick help before this day's done. We av ta tek twenty-two men with us, an she's goin ta be movin fast an dangerous."

Patrick interrupted. "Ach eat, an stop yer blathering—we need tae be going in fifteen minutes."

Mick laughed and dug into his meat pie. He liked the Scot and knew, as a fighting man, Patrick would never let anyone down. Sounds of running feet came up the garden path. Patrick sprang to the door like an enormous cat, and opened it to allow Lizzie, Quon and a young woman to quickly enter the room.

Walter Drake leapt into the woman's arms.

"Mum, oh mum!" he cried, happily.

Ada returned just in time to witness the touching scene.

"Sorry I'm late Joe, what's happened?" she inquired, watching Walter and his mother hugging and crying.

"Tell yer later. Get the gypsies their money, I left the account there by yer plate," Joe said, hurriedly. Then turning to Missus Drake and gripping her by the shoulder, he continued, "Do yer want ter stay in London or go away somewhere?"

The lady looked at him in amazement, considering his statement.

"To York, sir, mi sister's there, but I ain't got no money."

Joe turned to Lizzie.

"Arrange it with them gypsies outside. We have ta go now."

The three men left quickly.

Ada walked back into the room, jingling a bag of gold coins and sat down at the table. Martha brought two more plates of food and, as the women ate, Ada began to question Walter's mother.

"What's your name, my dear?" she asked.

"Bessie Drake, ma'rm," came back the instant reply.

"And do you have some belongings at your lodging?" Ada continued, between mouthfuls of food.

"Yes ma'rm but ah darsn't go back for 'em," Bessie said timidly, her fork in mid-air.

"Call the gypsy in, Quon lad," Missus Mason requested.

Within seconds, the gypsy leader arrived, cap in hand.

"Here's your money," Ada said holding out the bag of gold coins. As the gypsy moved forward, she hesitated, withdrawing the bag. "We have need of a favour from you."

The dark-skinned man stopped, his eyes soft and gentle.

"For Joe Todd, we'll do anything."

The gypsy listened carefully while Bessie Drake explained where her room was and what she needed.

"You come with me, lady, we get. My name is Jeb Dark . . . no one will hurt you now," the gypsy said in a confident tone.

He opened the door and disappeared outside. From inside the cottage, they could hear Jeb shouting to his men in Romany. Soon they heard two horses riding away.

"Come lady," Jeb called as he appeared in the open doorway, motioning to Missus Drake.

Lizzie nodded encouragingly at the woman. "Go with him, Missus Drake, you'll be safe now."

Quon Lee was making some signs with his hands.

"Yes, he's right, Lizzie, it's time you went into battle too," Ada said.

The girl looked surprised.

"Yer knew what he said?"

Ada winked at her. "Go on with yer, I can handle this lot."

Saying their goodbyes to Walter Drake felt a little strange, for although they had only known him a few hours, they had been concerned about him long enough to consider him a friend. The boy gave them a tearful hug and told them he had something he wanted to tell them.

It seems Walter had discovered two very interesting pieces of information during his stay on the *Golden Lady*. The first, was that Long John Stroud kept his treasure in the false bottom of his sea chest in his cabin . . . and the second, was that the old cook on board never came up on deck—always stayed below. It was almost like he was afraid of being seen, but he always came into the galley when he heard the words, "Casting off!"

Lizzie wasn't sure how they could use the second piece of information, but she certainly liked the first bit. She thanked Walter and he and his mother left with the waiting gypsies.

Chapter 14

It was well after one o'clock when the youngsters passed the corset shop, nearly halfway down Water Lane. Ahead, they could see the brewery drays loaded with barrels. Joe Todd sat up beside the driver of the first dray, puffing on his pipe as though he didn't have a care in the world. Farther down the lane and closer to the tailor's shop, two men leaned against the wall chatting—it was Angus McClain and one of his men.

Lizzie and Quon crossed the street to sit on the stone windowsill of the hatter's shop. They looked at the beaver skin top hats and the shorter Johnny hats, made of cheaper fabric and worn by merchants and not-so-well-off city men. Down on the corner of Dock Street, they could see Lefty, Mick's one-armed messenger, patiently waiting for the action to begin.

Fifteen minutes passed before Lefty suddenly began walking up the street toward them. Angus and his man came to attention, watching the corner intently. Captain Stroud staggered from the bar at the coaching house, swearing and cursing at his three companions as they stumbled into Water Lane, heading for the tailor's shop.

Lefty was opposite the youngsters by now, walking slowly he grinned broadly, displaying an almost toothless mouth, as he passed.

"Stay here," Lizzie hissed, keeping her voice low as she hopped off the windowsill. "Tell Mick there are four more coming, real soon." Then she noticed Angus and his man following Stroud up the sidewalk.

Quon was already moving down toward Dock Street.

"We gotta wun Wizzy, we gotta wun," he warned her.

Lizzie caught him up at the corner and they were off at a fast pace. Tearing along Tower Wharf, they slowed as they came alongside *Golden Lady*. A sailor looked over the side of the ship.

"Captain Stroud sent us," she gasped loudly. "He needs four of yer at the tailor's shop in Water Lane, urgent like."

The youngsters turned and set off again, running back along the dock. At the corner of Water Lane, they noticed Lefty watching as they arrived with the four Stroud men close behind. Lefty disappeared and Lizzie hoped he had gone to warn Mick and Patrick. She and Quon slowed to allow the sailors to run past.

"Me lest, me pooped out," the Chinese boy gasped, sagging onto the sidewalk.

"Yer damned right, dumplin," the girl coughed, as she tried to get her breath back.

Looking up the lane, they saw old Joe standing on the first dray, a wooden mallet in his hand, hammering the barrel tops back on and grinning as if he were enjoying himself.

"Look at that old bugger," Lizzie commented wryly, "he's really enjoyin himself."

Within ten minutes, there were another four barrels with the tops on—when out of Abe's shop sauntered Mick, Patrick, Angus and his man, followed by Bill Johnson.

Lizzie must have looked surprised at the sight of the baker.

"Ach, we invited the Yorky lad to join us," Patrick explained with a chuckle. "We sorta took a likin tae him when he threw Stroud out of Abe's shop on Thursday! He's a damn good man is wee Billy, an strong as a bull."

"Mother 'o Murphy, he's daft as a brush, ses he loyks a bit a fun," Mick added, pretending to be outraged.

Bill sheepishly looked at the girl.

"Ee ah just wanted ta 'elp yer, luv," he stammered apologetically.

Lizzie walked over to the big man, stretched her arms out wide and hugged him, even though her arms only went partway around him.

"Bill Johnson," she exclaimed, jumping up to kiss him on the cheek. "Yer bloody luvey!"

"Steady on, now lass," Bill, now a little embarrassed, chided her as a titter ran through the watching men.

"Lefty," Lizzie shouted for the messenger. "Call all the men in, an tell 'em ta go ta the brewery."

Lefty gave the girl a mock salute to let her know he had heard her, and scurried off on his mission.

"You go an take charge with Angus, Bill . . . an we'll send the rest of the *Lady's* crew to ya, two at a time."

"An just what little job would ya be havin in moynd for us two lads then, missy," Mick asked, cocking an eyebrow in anticipation.

"Oh you two can come with me for a little walk," she giggled turning away.

"Ah suppose we can feed the lads a flagon a cider," Joe shouted after her.

Lizzie spun around, not saying a word but wagging her finger at the old man, who let out a blast of laughter.

Settling Mick and Patrick in a position where they could keep watch, the youngsters proceeded to the *Golden Lady*.

Shouting to a sailor, they explained that a drinking party was on at the brewery and Stroud suggested they all get their share of free cider, but only two at a time so as not to cause any suspicion. The lure of free drinks washed all mistrust from the minds of the men, as they eagerly awaited their turn to leave.

Lizzie suggested that they leave at ten-minute intervals. This would give Angus and Bill time to do their work. When the last two sailors had disappeared out of sight up the road, Mick and Patrick sauntered up to the side of the *Golden Lady*.

"It's all over noo, an done wi the ease of a real general," the Scot complimented Lizzie.

"Not just yet," she said with a frown.

After explaining about the cook and telling them what to shout to make him appear in the galley, they had no trouble capturing the last man on the *Golden Lady*.

"Now, it's all yers," the girl said. "I just want to visit the captain's cabin for a minute."

The two men were checking the supplies on board and familiarizing themselves with the vessel while Lizzie and Quon visited Stroud's cabin. The sea trunk, that Walter Drake had forewarned them about, wasn't hard to spot sitting under the captain's desk. It's huge padlock provided a momentary problem, however.

"We need to find a hammer, Quon," Lizzie ordered.

The boy was quickly back with the necessary tools and the lock gave way after a series of mighty blows. The noise brought the men running. Scooping out the personal belongings of the captain, Lizzie let Quon search the bottom of the trunk. The men watched with puzzled expressions on their faces.

"Gor it," gasped Quon, as he lifted out the false bottom, revealing a wondrous array of jewels and gold pieces.

"How in heaven's name did yer come ta know that was there?" Mick gasped, peering closer at the hoard.

"Ach man, no time to check it out noo . . . just bag it up. Yer can do the sortin later at Joe's," Patrick snapped. Two small Hessian bags were filled and tied before the Scot spoke again. "Now, you three, go. Take this bag with yer, Mick. 'Am stayin here until my crew arrives, then ah'll bring the other bag tae the cottage."

Mick nodded his agreement, took the bag in hand, and he and the youngsters set off for the cottage. At the end of Tower Wharf, they met up with the new crew and stopped to exchange words.

Suddenly, the leader announced, "Sorry miss, but we gotta go." He pointed up Dock Street as the dray filled with barrels, moved slowly toward them.

"Bejaybers, that were quick!" Mick exclaimed.

"Like sheep ta slaughter, never knew what hit em," a black-bearded, ex-naval gunner with one leg, chuckled.

As the laughing group moved away, Lizzie called after them, "What about the other dray?"

A young man with a hook for a hand, answered, "Gone ta't *Falcon*, Miss."

The girl nodded. Patrick had informed her that the plan for the disposal of their prisoners had been slightly changed and they were now loading them into two ships. They would drop the barrels, with the prisoners inside, onto the docks at Zarauz. In the confusion, they would be well out to sea before the prisoners were even found.

By suppertime, the ships were ready to move out on a few minutes' notice. The equipment was stowed away and the prisoners loaded below deck in their rum-sloshing barrels. It was a perfect evening and they only had the tide to wait for now . . . as the team sat down to eat at Joe's cottage.

"The Drake family get away all right?" Joe asked between puffs on his pipe.

"That wer a grand thing tha did for them, master," Martha said in her broad Yorkshire, looking up from her cooking.

Conversations flowed back and forth across the table, making their last meal together a noisy affair. When Martha's apple pie and fresh cream was served, the room went quiet as everyone savoured each mouthful. It would be a while before they ate like this again. Then the meal was over and the men took the liberty of lighting their pipes.

Captain Davis was the first to broach the subject.

"We leave at ten tonight," he said, matter-of-factly. "Puts us in the channel at midnight—tides and weather in our favour, we'll be stood off Zarauz about a week hence." He stopped, looked around at the waiting faces and added with some hesitation. "I have something else ta tell yer though . . . the wind, in that part of Spain, always blows off the land from midnight to six in the morning."

He looked straight at Lizzie whose eyes were beginning to show a little devilment in them.

"Then yer going ta have ta drop me off early . . . or ya won't get in, will you?" she asked, without a sign of fear.

Davis nodded slowly, his eyes riveted on the girl's face.

"We'll have ta torch that building in daylight or yer goin ta be stranded outside the harbour."

Again, Davis nodded in agreement.

Lizzie's forehead furrowed as she pondered the problem.

"Well then," she began slowly, "let's use the disadvantage to our benefit."

The group remained silent hanging on every word and watching with great interest as their leaders made plans for the coming adventure.

"How?" Davis whispered, his eyes unwavering from Lizzie's face.

"By dropping all the men with me, so they're ready ta spring into action the minute the confusion starts. You'll be able ta come right in flyin no flag, cos nobody will have time ta notice," Lizzie said enthusiastically, waiting for a reaction from the group.

Davis thought hard for a moment, rubbing his chin . . . his eyes were now mere slits as he considered the girl's suggestion.

"Could be just bold enough ta work," the captain muttered, rubbing his chin in thought.

"Ach, nuthin ventured, nuthin gained," Patrick commented.

"An hoy meself would follow the little witch ta hell an back," Mick stated with some passion, thumping the table.

"Then let's do it, boys!" Lizzie exclaimed, with an excited voice.

A cheer rolled around the group—now the die was cast. The wicked grin on Captain Davis' face showed he was happy with it, too.

"We got one more little job ta do," the girl informed them. "So sit up an pay attention . . . and no damned touchin," Lizzie said, with a serious note in her voice. She motioned to Mick to retrieve the little bags from the corner of the room. The others watched curiously, wondering what was coming next.

"Empty them bags on the table, Mick," she said quietly, tapping the wooden surface gently.

The Hessian bags dropped on the table with a clink, bringing the group to immediate attention. They stared at the table in disbelief . . . watching with fascination as Mick spilled the contents out onto the tabletop.

Ada Mason gasped, blinking at the sight of the precious metals and jewellery. A gold coin rolled slowly across the table to land in front of her.

"My gawd, it's a King's ransom," she spluttered.

"Patrick, my friend, you look it over first," Lizzie invited the Scot.

His eyes raked the mound for anything familiar. Leaning over, he pushed the pieces around so he could see them all . . . carefully picking out a ring and a gold chain with a crucifix attached.

"'Am done, lassie, an ma grateful thanks fer yer consideration," the Scot said sadly, his voice barely audible.

"Now, the rest of yer, that's yer bonus. Every man on this adventure will get an equal share . . . but not till later. Take a good look, cos it's gone in two minutes," Lizzie informed the gasping, boggle-eyed watchers. Approximately two minutes later, she stood up.

"Now get it put away, Dad," she said to Joe who seemed quite unmoved by all the excitement and was still puffing away on his blackened pipe. But it was an order and Joe nodded and left the room. He returned quickly with a metal container that easily held all the valuables. The contents on the table were soon put out of sight again.

"Carry that damn thing for me, Mick lad," he said, leading the way into the back.

As the Irishman left the room, Charley looked up at Patrick.

"Is there a story to the pieces you took, Scotty?"

Patrick kept his eyes on the table, rolling the ring and chain in his hand.

Ada looked sternly at her brother-in-law.

"Charley, mind yer own damned business," she snapped.

Lizzie intervened before any more could be said.

"Time we all left for the docks an got settled in," she said, as Mick and Joe returned.

When the room emptied, Joe stood with his back to the fire, watching his two young charges make their final preparations. Two small bags constituted their travelling supplies. They dropped them at the door and slowly made their way across the room to stand in front of the old man who meant so much to them.

"Time for hugs, Dad, but no tears now," Lizzie said, as she and Quon Lee wrapped their arms around him.

"Just be careful," Joe mumbled, his voice breaking with emotion.

"You two take care of him for us," Lizzie said to the women, receiving a hug from each of them. Then the youngsters stepped out onto the garden path and the door closed behind them.

Chapter 15

It was a pleasant walk down to the docks and onto the deck of the *Falcon.* Lizzie and Quon eagerly stowed their bags and watched the crew making their last minute preparations for Zarauz, expectation glowed on their faces. They found Lefty at his post on the upturned barrel, quietly keeping his vigil. The regular crew moved with slick efficiency to make their sailing adjustments, and time passed quickly as last-minute discussions took place.

It was almost ten o'clock when Captain Davis came to the rail.

"Ten minutes, Lefty."

The one-armed messenger jumped off his seat and scuttled away down the dock. Soon afterwards, Lizzie and Quon heard the order to cast off and felt the *Falcon* begin to move away from her mooring. A puff of wind caught the sails as the vessel got underway and moved into the main channel of the great river.

Passing Tower Wharf, they saw the *Golden Lady* was just beginning to slide out into the river behind them and Davis was heard to murmur. "Well done, Scotty, keep her close now."

Lights lit up the shore as the ships silently made their way toward the open sea. Two hours later they had passed the last of the twinkling shore lights, and were heading directly for the lighthouse visible in the moon's glow.

There was a flurry of activity as sailors scrambled into the rigging, sails dropped, masts creaked and the vessel lurched forward as the wind picked up. They steered a little to the north of the lighthouse and soon were in the fast-running English Channel bearing south, the ship heeled well over as they made the turn.

"Give her all the sail we have," Ben Thorn yelled above the wind to the sailors high in the rigging.

"Right, now it's time for sleep, you two," Davis growled at the excited but tired twosome. "Use my bunk," his voice grated again as he pointed to the corner of his cabin.

The rattle of tin plates woke them at first light, around five o'clock, with the wind rattling the sails as it forced the ship forward at a fast pace.

Breakfast at sea was a new experience for Lizzie and Quon, not being used to the way the plates occasionally skidded across the table.

"Should a brought hammer and nail, keep plate still then, maybe!" Quon Lee commented, trying to hold onto his plate and eat at the same time.

Out on deck, the seaspray felt cold even in the warm sunshine of a perfect English day. The constant heaving of the vessel in the choppy water made standing and walking very difficult as the inexperienced youngsters gained their sea legs. All the men from below were now visible on deck and obviously enjoying being at sea again.

Off to starboard slightly and not too far behind, the *Golden Lady* was keeping pace as they rounded the White Cliffs of Dover and headed down into the English Channel toward their destination.

During the voyage, Captain Davis had time to point out many landmarks to the young visitors and explain the goings on aboard a sailing ship. He also taught them how to use the compass and find the North Star at night . . . to use the rising sun to set a guide due east . . . and to read the great ocean charts always available in his cabin.

The weather was perfect for sailing and the crew was kept very busy. Having extra hands available there was time for fun, however, and some of the men delighted in demonstrating to the visitors how they often entertained themselves during times of calm seas. Those were the periods of no wind and ship travel could be boring indeed.

They often saw vessels off in the distance, but were being cautious and acted to avoid any chance of recognition or contact. These manoeuvres added a bit more time to the journey but finally on the ninth day, they sailed into the Bay of Biscay and anchored close to shore.

Patrick brought *Golden Lady* skilfully alongside and hands tied the vessels together securely. All sails were furled, the sea flat and calm, as cook prepared a huge supper—no one would have time to eat a proper meal for many days.

After supper, Captain Davis showed off the new guns that he had acquired—two Sakers, complete with wheeled carriage, and a goodly supply of nine-pound balls.

"Ah hope we don't need 'em though," he commented wryly.

Lizzie asked if this was the landing site where they would leave the ship. Davis nodded nonchalantly but she noticed the serious expression on his face. The sailors gathered around their leaders and the girl took this opportunity to move onto the steps of the upper deck so she could address them all.

"Listen lads," she shouted. "Each crew has a job to do and you know what it is. Follow the instructions of your leader, stay together and for gawd sake keep outa sight, if yer meet anybody, take 'em prisoner—tie 'em up and leave 'em, they'll be good company for our barrel prisoners!" she said with a grin, breaking the serious mood.

When the men's laughter subsided, she continued, "And don't hurt anybody unless ya have ta." She waited to see if anyone wanted to speak, but all was quiet. "Patrick is the overall leader, do what he tells yer an no damned questions. Once outa the dock, we'll make speed north by north-west, just like we discussed." Finishing, she stepped down off the stairs.

Then, it was Captain Davis' turn.

"The men goin with Miss Lizzie had better be prepared, cos if anything happens to them two," he pointed at the youngsters, "ah'll hang yer from me yardarm!"

Boats were soon being filled with men, lowered, and rowed to shore. Each crew disappeared quickly into the heavily wooded timberline setting out on foot for the harbour. Finally, Lizzie's men along with Patrick departed the *Falcon* and rowed to the shore. Jumping out of the longboat, they raced for the trees. Once inside the treeline, they stopped, breathing heavily.

"Got yer compass, lassie?" Patrick inquired.

She nodded affirmatively.

"Then go," he urged, "it's a fair stretch of the legs ta yon building yer goin ta torch."

Lizzie, Quon, and the two young men, who were there to watch over them, waved to Patrick and his men and set off, moving inland at a steady jog. Lizzie sent one of the men on ahead to double-check their directions and scout the way, whilst the second one kept to the rear keeping an eye on their back trail—she wanted no surprises on this little venture. Four miles later, they stopped to rest, huddled together under a large bush.

"What's yer names, lads?" Lizzie inquired softly.

Grinning at each other, one of them gave her an unexpected answer.

"Wer twins, didn't yer know?"

The girl smiled, but repeated her question.

"But what's yer names?"

Again, the two grinned at each other.

"Don't laugh now," one of them mumbled, as Quon Lee and the girl waited. "He's Grey, an I'm Green."

Lizzie stifled a snicker. "Gawd, yer mother had a weird sense of humour, ah think," she commented, as Quon repeated their names.

"Glay an Gleen, sound stlaing ta me!"

They all giggled quietly, cautiously watching for people but they saw no one.

A few minutes later, Lizzie checked the compass and they set off again with Green in the lead. It was not long before they were climbing a small hill from which they had a clear view of their target.

They soon realized there was going to be trouble—too many people were in the area, constantly going in and out of the wide open doors of the building.

"Tink quick Wizzy, we no time to wait," Quon urged his partner.

"Green," she whispered, "sneak down an see what's goin on."

The lad moved off silently. Then they heard the gentle tinkle of a cowbell . . . then another . . . and another.

Green returned, breathing hard.

"Half of 'em are stacking some kind of fruit, the others are getting in hay, or that's what it looks like."

"Locate them blasted cows we just heard, Grey," she ordered, "while your brother gets his wind back."

The second brother dashed off in the direction of the cowbells.

"What's yer plan, Lizzie?" Green asked, but Grey quickly returned to their side interrupting their discussion.

"There, just behind that hedge, about fifty of 'em—great big things," Grey reported.

The girl moved instantly toward the cows. In the fast-fading light, she could still make out the gate at the bottom of the pasture.

"Listen," she whispered, "I'm goin ta open that gate down there." She pointed down the track. "You three drive the cattle through as fast as yer can, then shut the gate so they can't go back."

"It'll cause a lot of confusion around that building when them cattle get there," Grey observed.

"That's the general idea," answered the girl, wryly.

Everything proceeded according to plan. As the cattle began to run for the gate and poured through into the lane, they picked up speed, being urged on from the back by Quon Lee and the Grim brothers. By the time they entered the barn area, they were moving at a full gallop, bursting onto the scene and causing wild, panic-stricken shouts from the workers.

Lizzie, running behind the herd, shouted, "Follow me!"

The intruders kept behind the cattle until near the end of the building and then they broke away dashing behind it and out of sight of the workers.

"Hurry, get yer fires lit against that wall," the girl's urgent voice called over the clamour. She pointed out some dry branches nearby and they all quickly grabbed an armload and threw them against the wall—four matches flared almost simultaneously. With the help of the added dry material, the fire quickly roared up the tinder-dry wooden planking.

"Come on, an keep close," the girl ordered, dashing through the brush and up onto a knoll behind the barn.

A light breeze fanned the flames, and in no time at all the fire had transformed the building into a thundering, crackling inferno. Both cattle and people dashed for safety, bellowing and screaming all mixed together as they made their desperate escape. Suddenly, the whole sky lit up as the roof caught fire with a deafening 'whoosh'.

"Let's go, we've done our job," Lizzie cried urgently, "but stay close together. If this works, the whole town will be heading this way and it is going to be hard to see them once we get away from the fire."

They were travelling more slowly now, carefully picking their way as the night grew blacker and they neared the sea. Suddenly, a crashing body came out of the bushes heading almost straight for them. Dropping to the ground and lying motionless in the dark, they could just make out the silhouette of a huge cow as it ran past them, heading away from the fire in a terrified charge.

Staying off the main track that led to town, Lizzie and the boys made haste in the same direction as the animal and as they expected, many ghostly horsemen were soon galloping past heading for the fire.

Halfway to town, they could hear the crowd coming, even before the light from their swinging lanterns warned the invaders of their nearness.

It worked, thought Lizzie happily, and from their hiding place in the shadows, they watched the townspeople stream by using all manner of transportation.

As soon as the crowd passed, they were off on their way again and were soon in sight of the seafront town. They took a minute to rest and catch their breath before they were off again.

"Look like nobody there," Quon observed.

"Should look like that, dumplin, they're all at the fire," the girl answered.

However, as they drew closer to the dock area, they saw two horse-drawn drays filling with the last of the local workmen who spilled from the ships and warehouses nearby. As they loaded, there was panicked shouting and pointing toward the fire.

Lizzie's group was no more than fifty feet away when the full drays were set into motion by the sounds of wild yelling, and went careering out of town.

Keeping to the shadows, the four slipped silently onto the dock watching for their own men. They soon spotted Patrick and Mick walking up the gangplank to the third Spanish vessel, returning quickly to do the same routine on the next bark. By that time, the shapes of *Golden Lady* and *Falcon* could be seen moving slowly toward them.

A flurry of action brought their attention back to the first vessel where willing hands were now loading barrels, bales, and everything else imaginable, onto its deck. Almost immediately, the same action also began on the second bark.

At the other end of the wharf, *Golden Lady* docked and in the shadows they could make out the figure of Angus McClain as he jumped over the side of the ship running the length of the dock and leaping aboard the first bark, just as it cast off.

"I don't think Angus has moved this fast in years!" Lizzie giggled, talking to no one in particular.

The second and third vessels were also preparing to leave. Sails were quickly unfurled putting a strain on the tall masts, and except for the creaking of timber, barely a sound could be heard until the breeze caught the canvas.

The *Falcon* had now tied up to the three Spanish vessels at the other side of the dock.

As Lizzie and her team appeared on the wharf, they heard the voice of Mick in the crowd, only a few yards away.

"Over here, missy!" he called, urgently.

He quickly detailed the twins to a longboat joining others patiently waiting. At a barked command, in unison they pulled on their oars and were immediately moving across the harbour toward the *Falcon*.

"Get on board, me darlins," Mick ordered, his grinning white teeth gleaming brightly in the half-light. He pointed into the shadows below to another longboat already full of men.

Immediately they were aboard, the crew were pulling hard on the oars and soon it was on its way toward the *Golden Lady*.

"An for the luv 'o God, stay there!" he shouted at them.

Angus had the first bark clear of the harbour now and was piling sail on at a tremendous rate—the second and third vessels were not too far behind, their small crews working hard at getting them out to sea in record time.

The *Falcon* was now moving slowly across the harbour. Reaching the other side, Captain Davis brought the great custom ship alongside the *Golden Lady*. The twenty-three barrels were off-loaded and rolled onto the dock, just as a longboat arrived carrying Patrick, Mick and the Grim Brothers. Frantic activity followed.

The Grim boys went first, continuing upward into the high rigging of the *Lady*. Lizzie and Quon loved to watch these boys as they nimbly jumped from sail to sail.

Finally, as Patrick and Mick climbed up the side, the great ropes were pulled back aboard the two ships, more sails were unfurled and the vessels began to separate.

From the deck of the *Falcon*, those close by could hear Captain Davis yell encouraging words at Patrick and his small crew aboard the *Golden Lady*.

"Go, damn yer, go!" he roared . . . even the wind seemed to answer as it filled the sails and began pushing the vessel silently away from the dock.

The Grim boys were now flying through the rigging like monkeys, doing the work of six men as the vessel dropped her sails into a freshening breeze. There was an almighty jerk, almost stopping the ship for an instant and then she sprung back to life, moving forward again.

However, the jerk on the towline was enough to pull the Spanish brig away from the far side of the harbour and it now moved into the main channel behind the others. The boys dropped more sail and soon had it moving nicely in the strengthening breeze.

Suddenly, a lantern waved vigorously from the stern of the brig.

"Cast her off," came the sharp command from Patrick, followed by the splash of the towline as it hit the water.

Mick jumped onto the rail, slid down a rope and dropped into the empty longboat still tied alongside, casting himself off.

Lizzie, standing beside Patrick, saw Mick was alone and pulling hard on his oars . . . going back up the harbour in the direction of the *Falcon.*

"Where's he goin?" she asked, feeling the urgency of the moment.

"He's goin ta brring the last one oot, lass. Ach, yon Irisher is all man, an daft as a heeland haggis," Patrick chuckled. Then calling to the men for all the sail they could give him, he added happily, "We're on our way home, me girl!"

Captain Davis had no trouble moving the last bark out with Mick aboard. Once out of the harbour, Mick waved to Davis as he held back at the tideline. He knew the captain would guard his rear as long as possible, giving the whole fleet the chance to make good their escape.

Chapter 16

As dawn broke over the open sea, Angus McClain, aboard the first Spanish bark, surveyed the horizon to get his bearings and see how their mission was progressing. There were five other vessels in plain sight off his stern . . . only three remained to be accounted for.

Leaving orders for the crow's nest to watch for them, the brewery manager began attending to the duties of a captain at sea. With the assistance of his experienced crew, they set course in a favourable wind, leading the way back to the safety of England.

Six days of uninterrupted sailing followed, aided by a strong north-west wind bringing the lead vessel within sight of the British Isles . . . and home. The trailing ships had almost closed the gap and were now a visible line strung out across the sea. Patrick and *Golden Lady* were bringing up the rear. Davis was sailing well north, running a protective shield from enemy ships that might be lurking in the Channel waters.

The next morning, a thick fog hung over the sea obliterating ships and ocean from view. At first light, *Golden Lady's* lookout climbed to his post high in the crow's nest, searching for trouble. Shortly after sunrise, with the fog still thick on the water, the sharp-eyed lookout spotted the high masts of the two Spanish war ships as they appeared momentarily above the mist. During the night, and then under cover of the early morning fog, they had nearly overtaken the English vessels and now appeared to be on a collision course with the *Falcon.*

Due to the fog bank, which was finally dissipating under a westerly breeze, it was impossible to see exactly what was happening. They suspected the much larger Spanish vessels were gaining on Davis' ship and due to the fog the captain was still unaware of the danger.

The warning was sounded and all hands clambered onto the decks of the *Golden Lady*. Patrick cracked out the orders and the helmsman veered the *Lady* on a north-easterly course, which could intercept the Spaniards before they were in gun range of the *Falcon.*

"Go below . . . check for armaments and report back to me, quickly man!" he screamed into the wind at his first mate.

With only a crew of nine, the Scot knew if it came to a fight, he was at a terrible disadvantage. However, the lookout now screamed out his good news. The *Falcon* had obviously seen the problem and was making her turn as the last remnants of fog dissipated in the growing wind.

The first mate returned from below decks and gave his report.

"We got 6-eighteen pounders . . . three each side, 6-nine pound Sakers, that can be moved anywhere we want 'em, and 2-rail mounted Lombards," he shouted to Patrick above the noise.

"Plenty powder an shot?" the Scot yelled back.

"Aye, captain," the ex-navy man answered, "an we also got this," he said grinning, holding up a French flag.

Patrick smiled broadly, giving his answer loudly enough so all his hardworking crew could hear.

Then run 'er up lad, that's the advantage we need!"

In a few minutes, the French Tricolour was fluttering aloft from the highest mast.

"Whoever knows about guns . . . go get 'em ready . . . all to be firing on starboard side," the captain shouted, enthusiastically urging his men into action. "Lizzie . . . Quon," he bellowed, above the noise, "take the helm . . . head straight at their noses!"

Taking their positions, Quon hung on one side of the helm wheel and the girl on the other, and somehow their combined effort managed to keep the ship on course.

Grey Grim swung down through the rigging, landing light as a cat on the deck in front of Patrick.

"Ther runnin up all manner of flags, sir," he announced with a puzzled frown.

The Scot grinned, wickedly.

"Then run up an answer. Leave it two minutes an run it down again; change it slightly an do it all again, an keep on doin it. If that don't confuse 'em, nothin will!" Patrick cried over the noise of the whipping sails.

In the distance, the *Falcon* was speeding to aid *Golden Lady*, but their turn had lost precious time and the winds were not in their favour.

Captain Davis' pipe was gripped tightly in his teeth and his hands were turning blue as he gripped the handrail and glowered across the ocean at the enemy.

One-Eyed Jack screamed orders to the crew high in the rigging—altering sail in an effort to render aid to Patrick. Tossing wildly in the now wind-swept seas, *Falcon* tore through the pounding waves as their captain ranted and raved in frustration, knowing he was losing the race.

The approaching Spanish warships were now sitting close together, awaiting the arrival of the unknown, yet apparently friendly vessel, flying the French flag. Even at this distance, Lizzie noticed that their decks were lined with inquisitive sailors still unaware of the danger. *Golden Lady,* however, was moving quickly toward them and almost within firing range.

The gap was also closing between *Golden Lady* and *Falcon,* but was it closing fast enough . . . would help arrive in time?

"Get ready ta fire everything we've got," Patrick screamed, as he took the helm from the wide-eyed youngsters. "Go hide, you two!" he commanded, flinging his order to the wind, eyes still glued on the approaching enemy ship.

Up the ladder to the foc's'le deck the twosome quickly scrambled. Not yet sure whether to be excited or frightened, Quon's hand gripped her arm as he glanced hurriedly across the waves searching for the *Falcon* as it stormed toward them.

Suddenly the realization of impending disaster struck fear into their hearts when they noticed that the only man on deck was Patrick . . .

others were manning the guns while the remaining three were tending the sails. They quickly decided to do what he had suggested and immediately found a safe place behind some of the Zarauz cargo.

Now that they were getting a first-hand view of their own sea battle, Lizzie realized why Captain Davis had not wanted them along. However, it was too late for second chances as they hurtled toward the approaching ships.

Peering out cautiously from their hiding place, they were shocked to see the closeness of the enemy. They could now see the alarmed expressions on the faces of the crew . . . many of them not much older than themselves. They must have realized by now that no one was aloft to shorten the sails on the ship flying the French flag . . . and it was still careening toward them.

Patrick was screaming some unrecognizable Scottish words at the Spaniards as the enemy captain heeled the first huge gunboat over in a last minute effort to avoid the *Golden Lady*. Coming on broadside, Patrick was ready. Long red hair blowing in the wind, the Scot's deep voice screamed above the noise.

"Fire . . . Fire!"

All three of the eighteen-pound cannon boomed with violent veracity . . . blasting great holes along the waterline of the Spanish ship. The vessel began to tilt precariously, exposing the Plimsoll line and beyond. Straining timber cracked and groaned and the screams of Spanish sailors hung in the wind as confusion and terror filled the decks.

The Sakers with their deadly hail of mixed shot, crashed through the woodwork, felling the main mast and shredding the canvas of the once glorious Spanish warship.

Before the smoke from the guns cleared, the wildly racing *Golden Lady* crashed into the bow quarter of the second Spanish vessel, smashing a large hole in its timbers.

Lizzie and Quon tried desperately to see what was happening but when the impact caused the *Golden Lady* to lurch violently, they were taken by surprise and propelled head over heels across the deck. Desperately grabbing for each other or anything to hold onto, the return movement of the ship now sent them careening back into some bales near their original hiding place. Battered and bruised but unhurt, they dove under cover, breathing heavily and hugging each other with fright and relief.

Meanwhile, the wind was rising, filling the sails of the *Golden Lady.* It drove the vessel forward and away from the floundering, sinking gunboats, many of their crew having been dumped unceremoniously into the sea, without firing a single shot.

The nine members of the *Golden Lady*'s crew cheered wildly as they pulled away in a wide arc, waving to the oncoming *Falcon* to indicate they were all right.

They straightened their course and Patrick pointed the bow in the direction of their line mates, at last visible, but mere specks on the horizon. They would be close to the English shore and possibly unaware of the sea battle being carried on behind them.

Striking their French flag and raising the Union Jack in its place, all hands were now needed to coax the *Golden Lady* on a fast pace homeward.

"Wer's that little witch they call Lizzie?" Patrick shouted above the wind.

"'Am ere, yer damned crazy Scot!" the girl yelled, flinging herself into his arms with relief and pride.

Meanwhile, Quon Lee was hugging tightly to Patrick's leg and muttering, "You gland . . . and clazy, too! You, my flend!"

Captain Davis waved to Patrick and his crew as the *Falcon* completed their turning manoeuvre. He had never felt more helpless as he watched the drama that had just unfolded in front of him. Worrying about civilians had never been a priority to the experienced mariner, but these younguns had become very special to him.

It was almost unbelievable what that wild Scot had done. Both the great Spanish gunboats were now listing badly off their starboard side and they had struck their colours in surrender.

Slowing the *Falcon* almost to a stop, Ben Thorn called out to the stricken ships.

"Do yer need extra longboats?"

The answer was almost immediate from one of the Spanish officers.

"No sank you, mon capitain . . . but who vos dat madman?"

The crew of the *Falcon* burst out in peels of boisterous laughter.

"That was the new secret weapon of the English fleet. He was a Lizzie man," Ben shouted back, as the *Falcon* got under way again.

"Damn it!" Captain Davis mumbled, watching the scene from the poop deck. Watching the scene and hearing the banter caused him to again shake his head in disbelief . . . feeling quite miserable with his helplessness. "In all my years at sea, I ain't never seen anything like that before. That bloody, crazy Scot is a man to be avoided when he's mad!"

Epilogue

Two days later, at about 4 o'clock in the afternoon, Angus McClain dropped anchor in the bay off Southend at the entrance to the river Thames.

By midnight, under a beautiful moon, the fleet was gathered in the bay, that is, except for Davis and the *Falcon*. As the first light of dawn struck the darkness in the east, they could easily see the shadowy shape of the *Falcon* coming around the headland. Lookouts called the news and sailors on all eight ships lined the decks to cheer her arrival, allowing her to take her rightful place in the lead.

Anchors were raised and flags flying, the happy little fleet sailed up that mighty river in style, causing many heads on shore to turn and wonder what was happening. Up they sailed in single file, turning into the wharf at the bottom of Water Lane. Sailors high in the ships' rigging quickly furled their sails stowing them neatly away.

Captain Davis was surprised and pleased to find a great expanse of empty dock ahead of him—not a single vessel impeded the last remaining phase of their journey. *Falcon* eased slowly into her regular berth. Angus was next in, followed quickly by the other six Spanish vessels.

Lastly, the *Golden Lady* arrived to a mighty roar of cheering from the other crews, who by now had heard in great detail of the battle at sea. On deck, a beaming Patrick stood flanked by a proud Lizzie on one side and a grinning Quon on the other. Eager hands were quick to catch the *Lady*'s lines as she slipped into her place at the TLS wharf.

A small crowd had assembled on the dock to greet them. Lizzie and Quon easily spotted Joe, with little Willie on his shoulders. They saw the concerned look on his face as he searched for a sign of his children. He surveyed the damage to the *Golden Lady*'s bow, saw them waving happily beside Patrick, and they noticed the flood of relief wash over his face as he joyfully waved to them.

Joe took the baby off his shoulders, waving the lad's tiny arm in a greeting, while Ada and Martha wiped away tears of joy and relief.

The Johnsons were there along with their little boy—Lizzie's dog lying contentedly at his feet; and even old Abe Kratze was in the crowd, waving happily.

Someone unveiled a freshly painted sign, which read,

HOME OF THE TLS FLEET

Mick came running down the wharf and Ada ran to greet him. Unashamedly they hugged and kissed each other, as tears streamed down Ada's face.

When Joe saw his business partners hurrying toward him, he handed Willie back to the safe arms of Martha. Lizzie and Quon soon had the old man between them, hugging him tenderly. Then, with one on each arm to lend him support, they stood and gazed in wonderment at the magnificent sight before them.

Joe wiped the mist from his eyes with the sleeve of his coat and muttered, "Ah reckon y'ev won the big one, this time, lass."

The girl looked up at him as a big tear rolled down her cheek.

"No Dad, ah won the big one when I found you and dumplin."

This is only the beginning . . .

Read the continuing story of Lizzie and Quon Lee . . .

Book Two

Book Three

Lizzie's Legacy - Book Four

To be released late in 2004

More titles by J. Robert Whittle

Victoria Chronicles Series

Set in the Pacific Northwest in early 20th Century.

(see next page)

Leprechaun Magic

A Chapter Book for ages 4-9

by J. Robert Whittle and Joyce Sandilands

Visit the author's website:

www.jrobertwhittle.com